TWISTED KARMA

AN EASTERN SHORE MYSTERY

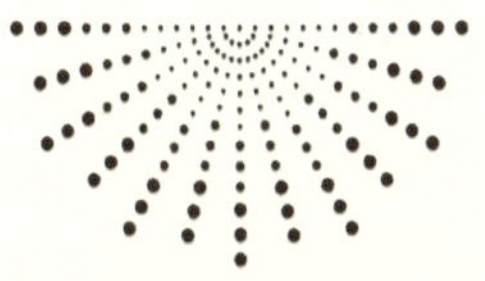

CHERIL THOMAS

TWISTED KARMA

On Monday, Grace Reagan meets a teenager who says he is her son. Two days later, her world is unrecognizable and there's a dead woman on her doorstep. Karma has arrived in Mallard Bay and murder is right behind it.

She's been ignoring the warning signs for weeks. Something bad is coming, but until it's right in front of her, Grace refuses to see it. When three seemingly unrelated disasters hit, her life flies out of control. In the center of the chaos is the stranger who believes she is his mother.

Small-town gossips say Peter Carlton is a murderer, but Grace believes he's telling the truth about *almost* everything. As a new client of Reagan and Mosley, Attorneys at Law, Peter complicates her life in ways she never could have imagined. Karma has come calling in the form of a boy with a bad attitude.

Did Peter kill a stranger in a drug deal gone bad, or is he the innocent, hard-luck kid he claims to be? And who is his mother? Grace needs answers, fast, as she searches for a murderer who is dangerously close to the people she loves.

TWISTED KARMA
Copyright © 2022
Cheril Thomas
All rights reserved.

This book is a work of fiction. The characters, events, and dialogue are a product of the author's imagination and are not real. Any resemblance to actual events or persons, living or dead, is fictionalized or coincidental.

Thomas, Cheril, Twisted Karma, (An Eastern Shore Mystery) 2022.
ISBN: 978-1-7334121-9-3 (Paperback version).
TRED AVON PRESS
Easton, Maryland, USA

Book cover created by MiblArt.

For Patrick and Kate

What is past is prologue.

William Shakespeare
The Tempest

CHAPTER ONE

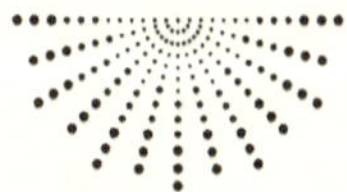

Grace Reagan raised her head to glare at the phone that was vibrating, beeping, and flashing a mini–strobe light into her weary eyes. Remembering that her electronic lifeline wasn't paid off, she resisted the urge to throw it across the room and settled for blocking the robocall that had awakened her. The nap at her office desk fell far short of the rest she needed, but it had been better than nothing.

"Work," she said, her voice raspy and loud in the empty office. "Your baby is with a sitter so you can *work*."

She'd been determined to keep her five-month-old daughter at the office when she opened her new practice, but Fiona's erratic sleep schedule made that dream impossible. In one short week, the new firm of Mosley and Reagan, Attorneys at Law, would be in business, and the Reagan half wasn't even close to being ready. The original plan of operations for her practice had been laughably naive. It was time to implement plan B.

"And exactly what does that look like?" she asked herself as she made a fresh pot of coffee.

Her spacious new office on the floor above Cyrus Mosley's

current law firm was filled with boxes and unassembled furniture. In her original plan, an office manager/secretary and a paralegal occupied the largest room and supervised the installation of all the electronic upgrades and renovations needed to turn the elegant Victorian-era rooms into a modern work space. She'd tried to hire a staff, but the few qualified applicants who'd expressed interest wanted to work from home and required salaries far beyond her budget. She'd insisted on carrying her own expenses in the partnership, but hadn't foreseen the tight job market that would make finding employees next to impossible. After three months of searching, she was desperate.

Plan B was pitiful, but it beat the alternative. She'd called a temp agency that morning, only to be told there was a minimum wait of three weeks for a legal secretary.

Plan C didn't bear thinking about until all other options crumbled into the dust, leaving her no choice but to join her octogenarian partner and his fiercely territorial secretary on the first floor.

She pushed all three scenarios aside and thought about the one positive thing she wanted to accomplish before the day was over. The special evening she had planned had nothing to do with work, but everything to do with the rest of her life. If she were successful tonight, everything else would surely work out, too.

Her phone went off again. She had no staff and no internet, but spam phone calls she had in abundance. Only this call wasn't spam—it was worse. Darth Vader's image filled the screen.

"I'm at your house, Grace," David yelled through the phone. "Why aren't you here with our child? We had an appointment."

"Fiona is with her nanny, and I fell asleep."

"What?"

"Okay, I forgot, then I fell asleep. I'm sorry." She had a few seconds to pull herself together while her ex-fiancé ran through his usual complaints about her inconsiderate behavior. "I said I was sorry," she repeated when he wound down. "Unless you drove over from DC just for this, can we talk later?"

To her surprise, in a very un-David-like move, he dialed back the attitude. "I'm at the river house for a few days. We got in late last night, and I'm tired. I'm sorry I yelled."

We? She straightened up, suddenly uneasy. Had he hired another baby nurse in an attempt to get joint custody?

"Grace, we have to talk, and it's important. If you could come home for a few minutes, I'd appreciate it. I don't want to have this conversation at your office."

The polite request surprised her so much, she agreed immediately. Something was definitely wrong. He always wanted to meet at his vacation home so she could be reminded of the waterfront estate she'd still own if she hadn't broken their engagement. She told him to give her twenty minutes and hurried to wrap up the work she'd been doing when she fell asleep.

Between calls and emails, she tried to guess what he was up to. With David, there was no telling. He'd pulled off so many outlandish stunts in their years together, he might be about to break any kind of news. She was certain of only one thing—she wouldn't like it.

It was as if the man had radar set to search for any possible happiness on her personal horizon. She didn't want this particular day to be ruined by him, but she grabbed up her tote and hunted for her keys. The faster she dealt with whatever was brewing, the faster she could get back to not working.

A tentative knock came on the outer office door just as she was ready to leave. "Now what?" she muttered.

A tall young man stood in the small hallway. "Can I help you?" She wasn't able to keep the irritation out of her voice and was embarrassed when he took a step back. Trying to sound more welcoming, she added, "I'm Grace Reagan," and held out her hand.

His fingers barely touched hers, but his cheeks flushed. "Peter Carlton," he said. He watched her with a hopeful expression and seemed disappointed when she didn't react to his name. "Can I talk to you? I don't have an appointment, but it's important. Please."

He was tall, and Grace had to look up to meet his gaze. He was handsome with side-swept, longish brown hair and darker eyes. She thought he looked familiar, but couldn't place him. "I'm not seeing clients until next week—"

"Please. It's, uh, personal, and I've already waited a long time."

Grace thought of David, who was probably working himself into a lather as he paced around her front yard. Whatever he had to say wouldn't age well, but this boy was compelling. "I'm on my way out to a meeting. Walk downstairs with me, and we'll talk on the way."

He didn't look happy about her offer, but stood aside for her to step out into the hall.

"Should I know you?" she asked as she locked the door behind her. "Have we met?"

"Yes." He was blushing furiously. "But it was years ago. You might remember my adoptive mother. Bethany Carlton?"

The name wasn't familiar to her. "No. Sorry."

"You really don't know me? Wow." He shook his head, then abruptly turned and trotted down the stairs.

When he showed no signs of stopping as he neared the bottom, she said, "Wait!" and hurried after him. "Just give me a minute. I meet a lot of people in my line of work."

He paused at the door. "This is a mistake."

"Okay." She stopped at the foot of the staircase, suddenly unwilling to get closer. "First, tell me how we know each other."

Whatever had been holding him back seemed to break, and his

eyes glistened. "We weren't together long, but you met me eighteen years ago."

"When I was in college?" she asked, confused. "Was your mother a friend of mine?"

"*You* are my mother. I'm the baby you gave away."

Looking back at that chaotic morning, Grace would think that her only stroke of luck was that the connecting door from the hallway to Cyrus Mosley's office was shut. Having witnesses to Peter Carlton's announcement would have been one drama over the line. As it was, it seemed to take a very long time for his words to make sense.

She stared at him, open-mouthed, until he said, "It doesn't happen like this on TV."

"I need to sit down. Come with me." She led him out and around the building to a small landscaped yard that bordered the parking area behind the office. Bright yellow forsythia bushes and redbud trees in full flower gave the area the feel of a fairy garden, but Grace had held more than one uncomfortable conversation here.

They sat on the old wrought-iron bench and she tried to think of something to say, but was too shocked to think clearly. Peter looked scared and said nothing. For a few moments in the warm spring sunshine, time was suspended as each of them waited to take the next step.

"Tell me why you think I'm your mother."

His face crumpled. "Oh, God. I was so afraid this would happen. That you wouldn't know me." He dropped his head into his hands. Grace reached out to touch his shoulder, but he jerked away.

"I've given birth only once," she said, gently. "And that was to my daughter. But maybe I can help you find the woman you're looking for."

"Why don't you call your husband?" he said, his distress turning to anger. "He'll be thrilled, too, I'm sure."

"My husband?" She shook her head. Could this situation get any stranger?

"Yeah. David Farquar." He stumbled over the last name.

And suddenly, she knew who he was.

"Even if I'm not your son"—Peter's tone said the issue was still up for debate—"that jerk is my father."

CHAPTER TWO

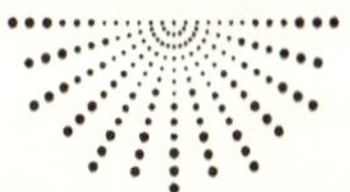

I t was hard to say who was more shocked, Peter when he learned Grace wasn't married to David, or Grace when Peter said he'd been looking for her since Christmas.

"I researched both of you and found this from last year." He handed her a copy of an engagement announcement from the *Washington Post*. "It said you were getting married last summer. That's when I decided it was time to see you. Bethany said he dumped you, too, and that's why you gave me up for adoption."

Her heart was racing with conflicting emotions. He might be on the verge of adulthood, but now that she knew who he was, all she could see was the child that David must have been. Peter had the vulnerability she rarely saw in David, except when he held their baby.

Fiona. Her daughter had a half brother. Now she knew why David wanted to see her. He thought they were going to have a rip-roaring fight when he told her about his son.

"This is hard. Way harder than I thought it would be." Peter's Adam's apple bobbed with the words, and he clenched and unclenched his hands in a way Grace had seen David do a thousand times.

"Does your mother—" She got a sharp look and rephrased her question. "Do the people who raised you know you're here?"

"No. I'm eighteen and I'm responsible for myself, so leave Bethany out of it."

"What about—"

"My father? He's a big-shot DC attorney who threatened to sue my adoptive mother when she contacted him. I was sick when I was a baby and she tried to get help from him, but he told her to get lost. She raised me by herself, and it was hard for both of us."

"I'm so sorry." Grace felt a rush of emotion for this boy. She'd given up trying to find David's moral compass a long time ago, but this was bad, even by his standards.

Peter shrugged. "I'm in a boarding school in Centreville for another month. I want to get all this straight now, before I graduate. I want to put my old life behind me with things settled in my mind."

"I can understand that," she said. "I don't know who my father is, and I'm still hurt about that. But for me, it wasn't a big deal until my mother died."

His eyes reddened again, and she got the full effect of David's genes in the searching look he gave her. It was unsettling. Then, he looked away and said, "Bethany always said there aren't any coincidences, just stuff we don't understand. She died three months ago."

"I'm sorry for your loss." She wished she had something more to offer in the way of comfort. "Let me call David and maybe we can get some answers for you, okay?"

He stood abruptly, picked up his backpack, then put it back down. "I'm not sure. I mean, it's what I thought I wanted, but it could be a mistake. You know he was with Bethany before you, right? He dumped her for you. Then, when you got pregnant, he called her and asked if she'd take me. I mean, what kind of guy does that? He'd lied to her for years, said he'd marry her, then wouldn't, and even tried to get her to believe he was sterile. Then he calls one day and wants her to take his child. When she did, he refused to admit he was my father and wouldn't pay child support. The judge sided with him, though, because they were friends."

Grace didn't know which of the issues to rebut first. The timing was all wrong for most of his story to be true, but one detail kept Grace from completely shutting his claims down. Until last year, David had thought he was sterile. Only Fiona's appearance had driven him to be retested with the surprising result of a low, but viable, sperm count.

It wasn't her story to tell, and what if this boy who looked so much like David wasn't his son? There were three Farquar brothers. One of the other two could be the father. Or a random collection of genes could have produced a doppelgänger. None of which could explain the lie this Bethany person had told him about Grace.

"I don't want to hurt you, but I can't let you go on believing that I'm your mother. I can go into more detail later, and I'll have a DNA test done if you still don't believe me. But surely your birth certificate doesn't name me? Who does it say your parents are?" For a moment she thought he would leave without another word.

"Farquar got a new birth certificate issued. One without his name or yours, just Bethany's. Now you're gonna say Farquar isn't my father, aren't you?" There was no heat in his voice, only resignation.

Sidestepping the question, she said, "Just give me a minute," then took out her phone and walked a few steps away. Tapping Darth Vader's helmet, she double-checked that the call wasn't on speaker.

David bypassed a greeting, demanded to know where she was, and bellowed, "I told you this is important!"

She hesitated, searching for a response that wouldn't alert Peter to the tantrum. "I'm on my way, but something's come up. Peter Carlton is here with me, and he'd like to meet you."

"Grace, focus. We have a situation we have to handle now. Whoever this Peter guy is, get rid of him and get over here. I need your undivided attention."

She disconnected and turned around, only to find Peter sliding his backpack straps over his shoulders. "I'm sorry," she said. "He was in the middle of something and—"

"And my name didn't mean anything to him, did it?"

"I don't think so, but you have to understand something." She took a breath and decided violating David's privacy was a small price to pay to ease this boy's pain. "He had mumps when he was about twenty-four. Do you know what that means?"

Peter looked confused. "No. What is it?"

"A childhood illness that kids have been vaccinated against for generations. David wasn't. His parents . . ." she stopped, realizing she was drifting into the weeds with the elder Farquars' rigid religious beliefs about medicine and vaccinations. "Mumps can cause a lot of problems, but one of the most serious can occur in adult males. Sometimes, it can cause sterility. That's what happened to him, or rather, that was the diagnosis he was given. Obviously, his condition wasn't as dire as he was originally told." She tried to smile. "He learned that with Fiona."

Peter paused, then shook his head. "He lied to Bethany and broke her heart, but it made her see she needed to get out of their destructive relationship. Isn't that why you didn't marry him?"

The abrupt change of subjects took her aback. This time, he sounded too much like David. "Look, I just met you. I don't want to be unkind, but that's very personal."

"Yeah. Right." He spit the words out. "Sorry I held you up."

She watched him leave and wondered how she would explain it all to his father.

The small, midcentury brick house Grace and her new baby had moved into in January usually felt cozy, if plain and sparsely furnished. Today, with David pacing around the living room, the walls seemed to close in. She let him blow off steam as she got water and a beer from the fridge.

His eyes narrowed when she handed a Corona to him. "You never offer me anything."

"Not true. I always offer to let you change Fiona's diapers."

He looked at her for a moment, freezing when his gaze fell on her left hand. "That looks like a new development."

The ring. She'd forgotten about the ring.

"My birthday was last Thursday." He had never remembered any personal dates without a prompt from his secretary, and his expression said nothing had changed.

"Is it from Mac?" he asked.

She nodded. The ruby in the gold filagree setting was lovely, but about as far as it could be from the huge diamond solitaire she'd returned to David. She waited for the inevitable comparison.

"Engagement?"

She almost said yes. If the evening went as she hoped, it would be true. But confiding in anyone, especially David, would be sure to jinx her plans. It had taken a long time to realize that Lee McNamara was the man she wanted to spend the rest of her life with, and she wasn't going to take any chances.

"Just a birthday gift. Look, let's not do this." Her words seemed to appease him.

"I wanted this conversation to go differently, but you still make me crazy." He took the only seat in the room, perching on the edge of the love seat like a man poised to run. Or jump. She got a chair from the kitchen. No way was she going to squeeze into the space beside him. He'd make a pass, she'd have to kill him, and then she'd never learn how he'd kept a child hidden from her for eighteen years.

Once again, he surprised her.

"I love you." He didn't look at her, but at his clasped hands. He'd said it before, many times, and for many reasons, most having nothing to do with romance. This time, though, he sounded sincere.

She didn't know what to do, but sensed the right answer was to wait.

"You were the one, Grace. I think the years with you were the best I'll have, but they're behind us now and life goes on." He stopped and cleared his throat.

This wasn't going the way she'd imagined. Maybe he was sick. He looked tired and older, and there was a slight tremor in his right hand. She didn't want him in her life, but for Fiona's sake, she wanted him to be healthy and happy. Or as happy as he ever got. His declarations of love were usually a prelude to a demand, but she heard regret in his voice.

"Well, here's the thing." He slapped his hands on his knees and straightened up. "A lot has changed for me recently. It's been hard to work everything out, but now that I have, I need to tell you what's happened. There's no easy way to say this. I have another child."

He waited for her to respond, frowning as the seconds ticked by. When he looked ready to explode, she said, "How long have you known?"

"A few months. I couldn't think of any way to tell you, so I didn't."

He wasn't being his usual cocky self, and she didn't enjoy

watching him squirm. He also seemed stuck again, so she gave him a little nudge. "I'm sure this is hard. And I'm so sorry you've missed his childhood, but you can start over now."

"What? He? Whose childhood?"

"Peter's. That's what I tried to tell you today when I called you earlier. He showed up at my office this morning. For some reason, he thought I was his mother."

"What are you talking about?" he said. "Who the hell is Peter?"

"Peter Carlton. He said his adoptive mother is—"

"Oh, my God!" The blood drained from David's face. *"Bethany."*

CHAPTER THREE

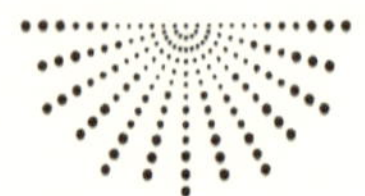

They both needed answers and talked over each other as the aftershocks kept coming. Grace didn't know enough about Peter to satisfy David, but he had more news than she could process. When he finally fell silent, she tried to absorb the revelation that her daughter's father had three children with three different mothers, the youngest of whom had wrangled him to the altar. David was married.

Her shocked congratulations sounded like a question. He nodded, unsmiling, and abruptly asked for more details about Peter. It was a brief conversation, but she promised to call him if the boy reached out again. Then he was on the phone to his assistant, issuing instructions for background searches on Bethany Carlton and her son. After a brief hesitation when he turned back to look at her, he was out the door, still barking orders into his phone.

She sat alone in the too-quiet house, thinking about his last words. He'd referred to Peter as Bethany's son. Was he? Had she lied to Peter about the adoption? All of it felt surreal.

Wait until Mac hears this, she thought as she left the house.

She wanted to share every bizarre detail of her morning with someone who would understand exactly how she felt, but she couldn't burst into the police station with this "you'll never guess what" story. And there was someone else she needed to see first.

A month earlier, just as her parents were approaching DEFCON 1 in their battle over what constituted appropriate childcare for Fiona, a former client of Grace's returned to Mallard Bay and offered a temporary solution. As the oldest girl in a family of eleven children, Hallie Overton had helped raise her younger siblings. From her first day with Grace and Fiona, it was clear that Hallie was a Baby Whisperer. David was apoplectic at the idea of a seventeen-year-old nanny, and Grace had to fight hormone-driven bouts of jealousy, but Fiona was in love.

There were complications, of course. First, David's opposition to Hallie was fueled by the fact that her guardian was Grace's best friend, Avril Oxley. His kindest reference to Avril was "that old witch," but he always checked to make sure the elderly fireball wasn't within earshot when he said it. Avril's razor-sharp tongue was matched only by her determination to right all wrongs. She loathed David, and it was mutual.

None of this was lost on Hallie, who delighted in making sure Fiona's father always got a good look at her latest tattoo. No one bothered to tell him that the art wasn't permanent. Each design was replaced after a few days, usually with something brighter and more outrageous. The last one he'd seen had been an intricate design of roses and thorns that Hallie told him was her gang initiation. She and Avril laughed at his strangled outrage, but Grace still lived with the fallout.

Despite the challenges it presented, she didn't hesitate to grab the lifeline Hallie presented. Avril had turned a suite of rooms in her home into a mini-apartment with a nursery designed for Fiona. The original intent had been to offer Grace and her baby a guest suite—or home. Now it provided an ideal space for Hallie and day-care space for Fiona. When Grace kept waffling between a schedule with baby drama at the office and one with occasional periods of productive work, Avril said, "That child has a nanny and a granny to watch her little fanny," and declared the matter settled.

Granny wasn't home when Grace arrived, but she found Hallie and Fiona in the sunroom watching Sesame Street. She picked up her daughter and her nerves settled as Fiona drew her back into their world. No matter how their lives might change, this was bedrock.

"I'm never having children," Hallie announced as she handed Grace a tumbler of iced coffee. "Drink this, it's half-cuff and mostly milk, so it should give you some energy without winding you up too much." In addition to her baby skills, Hallie had seen her two mothers through eight pregnancies and knew a thing or two about pre- and postpartum women.

Grace wanted to say if she were wound any tighter, she would snap, but then she'd have to explain what had happened that morning. She grabbed the low-hanging fruit, instead, saying, "I give. Why no kids? You're great with them."

"I love babies, my job's easy-peasy. You're the one who's on night duty. You look awful. Are you getting any sleep at all? Or is it work that isn't going well? I could help you at the office, you know. As soon as Avril gets home, I'll change and come help you get things set up."

The idea had a certain appeal, which was good, because Hallie was running with it. Grace was saved from an onslaught of decorating suggestions only by an unfamiliar ringtone from her phone. It was the first forwarded call she'd had since her office landline had been installed the day before.

"Your one o'clock is here," a sharp voice said while she was trying to keep the phone out of Fiona's grasp. A dial tone clicked in before she could answer.

"I don't have any appointments." She frantically pulled up her calendar, praying that what she'd just said was true. Monday, April 8, was reassuringly blank, so who was waiting for her? She wasn't seeing clients until next week, but this was the second surprise arrival of the day, and she hadn't even had lunch.

The phone rang again. "Are you coming?" Marjorie Battsley said, her voice sharp and loud. Known as The Bat to everyone she annoyed, which was everyone except her employer, the irritable secretary had worked for Cyrus Mosley for longer than Grace had been alive and wasn't dealing well with the new partnership.

"No. I'm not in the office. I don't have any clients today."

"Maybe not, but Mr. Mosley does, and he wants you to join them."

"Who—"

Again, she was dismissed with the click. She wasn't dressed to see clients, but there was no time to go home and change. If Cyrus was going to throw meetings at her without notice, her jeans and cotton sweater would have to do. Fortunately, she was wearing sandals instead of her usual running shoes.

Hallie took the baby from her, said, "Wait a sec," and disappeared. By the time Grace had wiped baby drool off her neck and tucked loose strands of hair into her French braid, Hallie was back with one of Avril's silk scarves. "She never wears this, but it's perfect with that sweater."

Grace tried not to act as annoyed as she felt. The scarf was perfect with the sweater, but she wasn't ready for Hallie to take over her entire life. With a firm "Thanks, but no," she was on her way to the office, hoping that this interruption to her day wouldn't be as shocking as the first one had been.

"You rang?" she said as she entered the elegant reception room of Cyrus Mosley and Associates.

"I guess you'll try to change it next week, but right now, we have a dress code," Marjorie said, looking her up and down. "I told him not to include you in this one, so don't blame me when you get in there."

The Bat rarely gave warnings, and Grace felt uneasy. "Who's the client?"

Loud voices interrupted them, then a woman screamed, "You'll kill her!"

Before Grace could react, Marjorie had covered the short distance to the conference room and burst through the door, squawking, "Who's hurt?"

Close on her heels, Grace jerked to a stop in the doorway and reversed course. She retreated to the staff kitchen, but she could still hear Cyrus reassuring Marjorie. The Bat was red-faced and breathing hard when she came in a few moments later.

"Are you okay?" Grace asked, trying to look innocent.

"Don't you dare pretend that didn't scare you. And you should see the mess in there! Papers everywhere. The boss will throw his back out getting them up."

Grace murmured sympathetically. They both knew who would pick up every piece of paper and read it all while she did it.

"Why did you run off? You saw who was in there, didn't you?" Marjorie said. "Well, don't worry, they don't need you after all. I told him that earlier, but does he listen to anything I say? No."

Grace knew exactly why her help would never be needed for these particular clients, especially the woman who'd been crying and wringing her hands. Without thinking of the consequences, she asked, "Do you think they saw me?"

"Yep." Marjorie's face lit up. "Maybe you'd better spruce up that wardrobe, huh?"

Disgusted with herself for looking for sympathy from the enemy, Grace went up to her empty office. The reasonable voice in her head said sleep deprivation and stress were causing her overly emotional reactions, but her eager inner critic insisted she do better. Avoiding uncomfortable situations wasn't the answer to anything, and hiding from people she didn't want to see was ridiculous. What was wrong with her?

This time her reasonable voice was silent, apparently out of helpful platitudes. She hadn't just skittered away from one of Cyrus's clients, she'd been avoiding Mac's old girlfriend.

She had to pull herself together. She had to do better.

CHAPTER FOUR

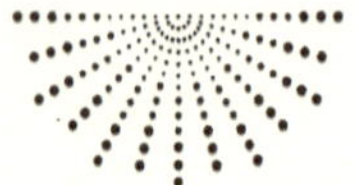

Ashley Greenburgh had been a thorn in Grace's side since their first meeting. Elegant and petite, she'd been hanging on to Mac's arm, and he'd looked much too happy. Grace had disliked her on sight, but it had taken a while to understand her feelings were rooted in jealousy. This was especially problematic since she was still wearing David's boulder-sized diamond. Ashley was popular and well respected as a compassionate veterinarian. Everyone seemed to love her. Everyone but Grace. The passage of time and realignment of Mac's affections had done nothing to endear either woman to the other. Seeing a sobbing Ashley in Cy's office had been unsettling. Her partner would eventually tell her what was going on, but until then, it was none of her business.

Reasoning that the bizarre day couldn't get much stranger, she tried to concentrate on work, but her mind kept wandering to the evening. This time when a knock on the outer office door interrupted her, she welcomed it—until she found Ashley and another woman standing in the hallway.

"Marjorie told me you weren't working right now, but I

thought you might make an exception for me. Us." Without waiting for an invitation, Ashley brushed past Grace, stopping a few feet into the office to look around. "Oh! I didn't realize this was a storeroom. Are you cleaning up for Mr. Mosley?" The tears and hand-wringing were gone.

With an insincere smile, Grace said, "No, but I am busy. If you'll stop by Marjorie's desk on your way out, she'll make an appointment for you."

Ashley's face darkened, but before she could respond, her companion came forward and stretched out her hand. "I'm Simone Lancer. I'm Ashley's sister. I'm afraid I arrived late for my meeting with Mr. Mosley, and now he's unavailable. Ashley tried to step in and handle the meeting for me, but it didn't go well. From what she's told me, I think you can help us with our problem."

Her voice was familiar with its distinct Baltimore accent, and after a second, her name clicked in. Late-night cable channels ran Lancer's ads between reruns of Seinfeld. The personal-injury lawyer usually wore a fierce expression while vowing to fight for her clients, but in person she looked nervous. No, not nervous, Grace decided. Worried.

"I keep telling you, she won't help us," Ashley said, interrupting. "But if you want to stay and waste your time, go right ahead. I'll see you at home." She left after a final glare at Grace.

Simone Lancer sighed, then said, "I shouldn't have insisted she come with me. If you could forget that she's my sister and spare a moment to hear me out? I've driven over from Baltimore and, frankly, I'm at my wit's end."

Grace decided there'd been enough conflict for one day. Plus, she appreciated the eye roll Simone had given her departing sister. "I'm in the middle of moving in, but ignore the mess and come through to my office."

Simone took the chair across from Grace's desk, but only after running a hand across the seat. "Moving shop is a chore, isn't it?" she said.

Grace saw the family resemblance in Simone's pained expression and noted with satisfaction that there was a streak of dust on the right arm of the lawyer's expensive black jacket. "What can I do for you?" she asked, and managed a smile.

"I'd like to hire you to handle a personal matter for me. My daughter's husband has filed for divorce, and if he's successful, her life will be at risk. I realize how dramatic that sounds, but it's true. Her husband's very angry, even though—and I know how this sounds, too—their split is all his fault."

Lancer's speech was as slick as her commercials, but with her next words, she had Grace's full attention. "I'm here, because you know the truth about what happened to them, and I think you're the one person my son-in-law might pay attention to."

It was difficult to listen to a stranger describe the traumatic first months Grace had spent in Mallard Bay, but she did it without comment or interruption. She'd always known the unresolved issues from that time would come back around.

It had been two years since Henry Cutter and his cousin Bryce had helped Grace renovate her mother's family home. The project had brought her to the Eastern Shore, but when she'd stumbled onto the drug ring Bryce Cutter was running, she'd almost died. She'd thought it was all behind her, but the uneasiness that grew as Simone Lancer talked said otherwise. Just a few hours ago, a boy she didn't know had claimed she was his mother, then David had turned up married and with children. Now she was being yanked back to one of the worst experiences of her life. Anger overtook fear and every other emotion she'd felt at the mention of the Cutters. She'd hear Simone Lancer out, then show her out. And then she'd lock up this office and go home to her baby.

"I know you and my daughter never met," Simone was saying, "but Mona is grateful to you. She'd never have gotten away from Henry's awful cousin if you hadn't testified against him. She's spent months in rehab trying to reverse the damage he did, but she's a long way from healthy."

"I'm sorry, but—"

"Mona is a victim, just like you were," Simone interrupted. "The difference is, she's never been able to move past what happened. Bryce preyed on her. She got addicted to the cocaine he gave her and let him take advantage of her. When he was arrested and everything came out, Henry dumped her on me and forgot about her."

Grace tried to absorb the idea that Ashley Greenburgh's niece was Henry Cutter's wife. How had she not known that? Irrelevant, she told herself. She knew it now, and would end this disaster in the making.

"Ms. Lancer, I'm sorry for you and your daughter. I really am. It was an awful situation, I agree, but Henry isn't a friend of mine, and I can't help you."

Simone ignored her and talked on, describing what the past two years had been like. As she did, Grace could understand why the woman referred to her daughter as collateral damage to Bryce Cutter's drug enterprise. He'd gotten his cousin's wife hooked, and despite three separate residential rehab programs in a year and a half, Mona hadn't stayed clean for longer than two weeks.

Grace tried again. "Nothing I could say would sway Henry." She didn't add that she knew from experience Henry would refuse to listen to her. "If you want to help your daughter through the divorce, I'm sure you know your best bet is arbitration."

Simone clinched her fists in her lap. "You're not listening to me! Mona is Henry's responsibility. Not mine, and not Ashley's.

We've paid out all the money we can to care for her. If he insists on a divorce, then he needs to pay for a private health insurance policy for her, in addition to the alimony, and her share of their house. Plus, he owes her half his retirement. She isn't capable of making a rational decision, so if he can't be reasonable, I'll have to have her declared incompetent, which isn't a quick or cheap process. There's no time for all that. All you have to do is leverage the influence you have over him to buy me some time to save my daughter."

"I'm sorry," Grace repeated. "I don't have any connection to Henry. I can't help you."

Simone didn't go quietly, and after the door closed behind Ashley's sister, the silence in the office felt unnatural. When Mac called to say he'd been asked to attend the business association's dinner meeting and would be late coming home, she felt more relieved than disappointed. Her plans for the evening would have to wait, but it was just as well. If she handled a marriage proposal with as much success as she'd managed everything else today, she'd be single forever.

CHAPTER FIVE

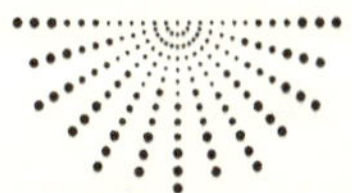

Lee McNamara hung up the phone slowly and looked around the two-room police station for something, anything, to keep him busy. Being chief of police in a small tourist town usually kept him hopping, but today, his work failed him. He had plenty of time to consider his monumental screwup.

Grace hadn't seemed bothered at all about his last-minute change of their evening plans, but as soon he told her, he remembered there was supposed to be a surprise menu for dinner. Her "Don't worry, it'll keep" sounded genuine enough, which only gave him more to worry about. The guilt that had been poking around the edges of his conscience for the past hour suddenly reared up and slapped him, hard.

For the past two weeks, he'd been living with Grace and Fiona in the little brick rancher she'd rented a few months earlier. It was a temporary situation while his cottage was undergoing renovations, and it felt as if they were kids playing house. Things were better between them than they ever had been—until now. He'd used a casual invitation to a business dinner as an excuse to avoid seeing Grace tonight. He'd wanted time to think, to make things easier when they finally talked, but he'd only added to the list of apologies he owed her.

He looked at his image in the security mirror mounted in the far corner of the police station's main room and thought he looked as bad as he felt. A combination of self-recrimination and right-eous indignation was playing havoc with his normally placid demeanor. He couldn't think of any way to get out of the mess he was in, and absolutely none of it was his fault. Mostly.

Women. It was always women.

A half-dozen tiny, but needle sharp, teeth pricked his ankle.

"Rocky!" He hauled a chunky black-and-white spaniel out from under the desk and held her up as she wiggled, snapping and licking, as if she couldn't decide whether to attack him or kiss him to death.

"Listen, girl. This biting has got to stop." He held the puppy at eye level and got a wet slurp across the nose for his trouble. "You know I asked for a male, right? A male golden retriever? Do you think you're anything close to what I wanted?"

Rocky seemed to consider the question, then lunged at his ear.

He distracted her with a chew toy, then settled her in the crate beside his desk. In a case of incredibly bad timing, he'd agreed to foster the twelve-week-old rescue, who was aptly named Rocket. He'd wanted a dog for a long time, and had been searching for a clone of his last retriever, a big-boned, shaggy golden who'd gone everywhere with him. Agreeing to take a hyperactive female spaniel had been a mistake, but Rocky had found him, and when the foster week was up, she stayed. It wasn't much different from the way he'd drifted into dating his friend, Ashley Greenburgh, now that he thought of it.

After ten years of bachelorhood following the death of his wife, he'd eased into a cautious social life and promptly found himself in a relationship that still embarrassed him. While he'd enjoyed most of the time he'd spent with Ashley, he'd also been falling in love with someone else. Someone who, to his amazement, was in love with him. His connection with Grace was wonderful, even though it had its consequences. They had a sweet, crazy life together, but Ashley wasn't giving up.

For months, he'd been oblivious to the increasing attention from his former girlfriend. He'd ignored her overly friendly greetings and pretended not to hear her suggestive comments. Today, she'd gone over the line, though, shocking him with her aggressiveness. When she'd shown up at the station in tears and thrown herself into his arms, he'd frozen as she sobbed about a sick niece, her brokenhearted sister, and Grace being cruel to all of them. He'd patted her back until she calmed down, and somehow, she'd ended up kissing him. On the lips. Right in the police station where anyone could have been passing by and seen her. Seen *them*, and told Grace. Grace, who hadn't cared that he canceled her special dinner.

He was an idiot.

He looked down at his phone and saw he had unanswered texts, emails, and calls. None of them was from Grace. It was ridiculous that he was doing this at his age.

"I'm a dead man, Rocky," he said, watching the puppy chew on the corner of her metal crate. He came to the slow, painful conclusion that the best course of action was to skip the rubber-chicken dinner, man up, and tell Grace what had happened.

"Hope you like sleeping in a construction zone," he told the dog. "I think we're gonna be evicted."

He hated salad-for-dinner nights, but since he hadn't thought he and Rocky would be in Grace's kitchen at this point, he was trying to look happy. It would have been easier to pull off if he hadn't seen the steak in the freezer and baking potatoes in the pantry's vegetable bin. The cheesecake in the refrigerator looked promising, but he didn't think he was getting dessert tonight.

"I don't want to argue—" he said, then stopped when she set her fork down and crossed her arms.

"Don't you mean continue arguing? I get it, Mac. Ashley's in a bad spot right now and she ran to you, and if you had it to do over again, you wouldn't let her get the wrong idea and take advantage of you." This last bit was accompanied by a look that said he'd better not contradict her.

He didn't. But if he had it to do over again, he'd go fishing and not see anyone, including Grace.

"I'm not upset," she repeated, then shrugged. "Strike that. Yes, I'm upset and jealous as all get-out, but I understand how it happened, so let's just drop it. I need to change the subject."

This was not good. Whatever was going to trump the scene with Ashley should be interesting. Then he saw the worry in her eyes and reached for her hand, but she pulled away.

"I have some news. Something's happened, and I don't want you to think I'm upset about it because I care what David does, but this changes Fiona's life and ours, and . . . Oh, God, I'm blathering."

Ashley and the salad forgotten, Mac leaned back and crossed his arms. "What's he done, now?" Once again, Grace's ex-fiancé had center stage in their lives.

"So many things," she said. "He's done so many things, it's hard to know where to start."

"Try the beginning," he said, gently.

"He called me this morning and said we needed to talk. I agreed and was getting ready to leave when a boy showed up at the office. A teenager." She stopped, suddenly weary to the bone, the day's multiple blows overwhelming her.

"Grace?"

He was reaching for her again when she said, "His name is Peter. He said he's David's son."

Mac stared at her, wondering if it would always be this way—them sitting around the dinner table either coming to terms with, or dealing with the fallout from, something David Farquar had done. He had to admit, though, this one was a whopper. "Why did he come to you?"

"For some reason I don't fully understand, he thinks I'm his mother."

He froze, wineglass halfway to his lips. She'd taken his confession about the kiss without killing him, so he pretended he could handle the announcement of yet another child he had no part in making. Trying to sound casual, he asked, "Are you?"

Her mouth twitched with a smile. She wasn't insulted by his question, and she wasn't buying his nonchalant act, so he relaxed a bit.

"When he was born, I was a senior in college. I didn't meet David for another four years."

He considered this, then said, "Are you sure he's David's son?"

"I'm not sure of anything, but he looks the part. His adoptive mother told him she and David were together, but he'd dumped her for me. She said when I got pregnant, David dumped me, too, and made me give the baby away. Then, in some soap opera way I don't understand, he talked her into adopting my child. And no, it won't make more sense if you keep thinking about it. Anyway, she died recently, and Peter—that's the boy's name, Peter Carlton —decided to look for David and me. He found that stupid wedding announcement in the *Post* and thought his real parents had finally gotten married."

Hopelessly lost in the convoluted story, Mac only nodded. He'd ask for a replay of the details when she was calmer and he had a scotch in his hand. He could think of only one safe question. "Have you told David?"

She looked nervous again.

"Come on, honey. It's a huge shock, of course, but surely you both had to realize he could have fathered more children. He got lucky, Grace. Much luckier than he deserves. He's got a daughter *and* a son." Early on in their relationship, he'd told her about his late wife's miscarriages and their stillborn daughter. He knew it was unreasonable, but the thought that a man so completely unworthy as David Farquar could be handed two children made him furious.

She leaned across the table and kissed him, then ruined the tender moment by saying, "There's more."

Of course there was. He sighed and said, "How does he top that?"

"He got married." Her expression said that wasn't the end of the story.

"I thought this Peter's mother was dead?"

"She is. I told David everything this morning and had the pleasure of breaking the news that he has a grown son. That's when he told me he'd just married a woman from New Orleans who's the mother of his one-year-old daughter."

"You're killing me, Grace. I have a bad heart."

"No, you don't."

"I do now. God Almighty, woman, are you making this up?"

"Nope. It seems a while back, David decided if he had one child, there could be others, so he had private investigators check out all the possibilities. Apparently, it took some time, but they found one."

Somewhere in the telling, her story of David hunting down past girlfriends and one-night stands floated from the sublime to the ridiculous, and Mac started laughing. This made her laugh, and both of them ended up holding their sides with laughter that woke Fiona and Rocky. Mac said maybe Fiona's father would like to come over and rock her back to sleep. Grace said David was much too busy to go anywhere, and they looked at each other in surprise as her words sank in.

"This could be good," Grace said, and smiled as the baby lifted her head from Mac's shoulder and yawned widely.

"He will certainly be distracted. Maybe I should check official records and see I can find more of his offspring."

Grace walked the puppy while Mac put Fiona down, and when it was all calm again, he and Rocky were still in residence. It was midnight before all three of his girls were asleep and he could settle his own thoughts. He rarely tried to analyze his own universe, and that night, he was reminded of why that was. If there were a celestial plan, he'd never understand it, but he understood karma.

And tonight, karma was good.

CHAPTER SIX

Tuesday started very early with a crying baby and didn't improve as the morning wore on. Mac said Fiona was so advanced for her age that she'd started teething early. Grace argued that it wasn't possible because the child still had occasional bouts of colic. They both knew he was right, and his announcement of a sudden emergency at his cottage was met with immediate suspicion.

"What kind of emergency?" Grace asked, knowing he wouldn't give her details.

His house was undergoing its first structural renovation in more than a hundred years, and he would tell her only that the final plans were a surprise. It was a sore spot between them, but since the project meant he and Rocky were living with Grace and Fiona on a mostly successful basis, they usually avoided the subject of, as Grace put it, his pigheadedness.

"Termites," he said as he scooped Rocky up and made his escape.

This, she decided, was just as well. Not the termites, but the distraction. She thought he was becoming obsessed with the renovations to the home he and his late wife had spent two decades in, but anything that wiped away reminders of the sainted Meri McNamara was a positive in Grace's book. She knew the renovations were for her, for their future, but she hoped whatever he was paying so much money for would enhance the resale value of the outdated little house. It was the last place she wanted to live.

Can I do anything about this? she asked herself as she watched him drive away. "Nope," she said out loud.

It was her new mantra, and so far, it was serving her well. For years, she'd counted her blessings when she needed to calm her mind, and she still did, but these last few months had required additional coping skills. She prioritized her troubles with those six words and took the first answer that popped into her mind.

Avril had overheard her one day and said Grace should buy a magic eight ball instead of talking to herself. She said the odds of a reasonable answer were better.

"Or should I just turn everything over to you?" Grace had asked.

Avril had never met a problem she didn't try to solve, and one of those solutions sailed through Grace's front door at eight o'clock sharp.

"You aren't dressed," Hallie said as she picked Fiona up. "You'll be late. Aidan will be at the office in a half hour."

Grace had set the appointment up herself, then promptly forgotten it. She made it to work just in time to meet Aidan Banks on his way up from the parking lot. He was pushing a handcart loaded with boxes and broke into a rare smile when he saw her.

The former police corporal had a fledgling IT business, and the expansion of data services in the Victorian building that housed the law firm was his biggest job to date. For the past two weeks he'd been at war with Marjorie over the installation of upgraded computers and a security system. To the relief of all involved, he was ready to move upstairs to Grace's suite of offices.

Normally dour and sarcastic, Aidan came bearing two breakfast specials from Three Pigs Deli, along with a twenty-seven-inch iMac Pro for Grace's office. It was as close as she had ever come to kissing her cranky friend.

The next hour was spent with Grace setting up her long-awaited dream computer and Aidan drilling holes in the old plaster walls to run cables and other mysterious wires. They were deep into their own universes when the first phone call of the day broke the silence.

"I owe you an apology, m'dear," Mosley said. "Marjorie explained the history you have with Dr. Greenburgh. I was unaware of the intricacies of your relationship when I asked you to attend the meeting with her yesterday. I was also under the mistaken impression that you were working upstairs. Now that I realize I was wrong about all of it, I see my actions must have appeared quite churlish. I hope you'll forgive me. And forgive me a second time because I must ask a favor."

Grace resisted the urge to say, you mean another favor? There was little she wouldn't do for him, and vice versa.

"We have a bottleneck of work down here," Mosley went on. "I'm hoping you'll agree to speed things up with the partnership by a few days. Can you be operational tomorrow?"

Grace thought the bottleneck probably involved a golf tournament, but she kept that to herself. After all, wasn't that why he'd offered her a full partnership with no buy-in? After a long career of wrangling justice and terrorizing courtrooms, Cyrus Mosley refused to retire, but had no intention of working unless he had to.

She looked around at her office and said, "We're not ready for clients up here, and I don't have any staff, but I can see clients down in Jake's old office if you'd like." She was surprised at the silence that met her offer. "Are you okay?" she asked when he sighed.

"It's my day for apologies to you," he said, his earlier smooth banter gone. "I've never admitted that you were right to warn me about going overboard in hiring him."

He hadn't, and she'd never expected it. Not even when Jake Briard reconciled with his estranged wife and took his family to join her in California. Mosley's decision to employ his friend and pay Jake's way through his final year of law school was based on his utter faith in the young man he'd mentored for so long. Unfortunately, it had cost him another employee he'd been equally attached to, Lily Travers. But Mosley's reason for living was to help the people he loved, whether or not they wanted him to. Now and then, his meddling went in the wrong direction. In Grace's opinion, Jake's hiring and losing Lily were prime examples.

"I know you thought I made a rash decision in selecting Jake and letting Lily go," he said. "But he will make a fine lawyer, and he'll repay me when he can. And as for Lily, she's doing well, but I don't think she'll ever forgive me."

It wasn't a subject that would improve with discussion, so instead, she repeated her offer of help and accepted several tedious tasks to lighten his load.

"Thank you, m'dear," Mosley said. "As soon as we're running smoothly, we'll talk about bringing another attorney in. I know you'll do the lion's share of work, but we also want the firm to grow. I'll continue to handle the fellows at the club, of course, but my other clients require attention, too."

"The fellows" meant all his cronies, male and female, who frequented the Mallard Bay Golf and Country Club. Grace had been astounded to learn how much money flowed into the firm from Cyrus's golf-cart consultations.

She heard Marjorie talking in the background, and then

Mosley said, "No more divorce work for me once I get the Cutters taken care of. I'm putting you in charge of stopping me, Grace."

Because she loved the old coot and knew how bad this case was, she didn't point out that he would take the next divorce that came along and neither she nor Marjorie would be able to wrench it away from him. He'd handle it from his golf cart, too.

She filled him in on her visit from Simone Lancer and waited while he sputtered and vowed to straighten Marjorie out on her lack of customer service. Then, knowing that she shouldn't put it off any longer, she told him about David's children and Peter's misconception that she was his mother.

"I wanted to be the one who told you," she said. "I think everything's straightened out now, but since David's in town with his new wife and baby, you'll hear some interesting gossip."

He was silent while she talked, but now he gave an un-Cyrus-like snort. "This may be a first. Usually, Marjorie announces the salacious gossip. I must admit, being in this position conveys a certain feeling of power."

"Knock yourself out, Cy. Just be sure your version identifies Peter as David's son, not mine."

"But surely there's a label for a woman who's the mother of one's half sibling? How will little Fiona explain things?"

"I plan to wait for her to tell me," Grace said dryly. "There's only so much room in this brain of mine, and I need to keep it on business."

"Good! Now, I have to hurry, or Marjorie will hear your news from someone else. I'm going to enjoy this."

She disconnected and, smiling about the scene that would take place downstairs, walked out to the main office. "Know any good admin people looking for work?" she asked the feet that stuck out from under the desk of the secretary she didn't have. As irritating as Marjorie was, Cyrus had a loyal, hardworking assistant.

"I'll think about it." Aidan scooted out of the knee well and stood up. "But at least you have cable and internet. All done."

"Great," she said, trying to sound sincere. The truth was, now that he was wrapping up his projects in the building, she didn't want him to leave. It had been nice to have an ally, even a cantankerous one. She told herself to get over it and listened to his instructions for troubleshooting the various systems and the security cameras. They knew that anything invented after 1990 would fall to Grace to troubleshoot.

"About the staff you don't have," he said when they'd finished. "Are you looking for your own fire-breathing dragon or some serious help?"

"Ideally, both. But right now, I'd settle for a warm body who's willing to dress and come into the office regularly."

"Tall order. Nobody jumps to mind, but I'll ask around. Meantime, you never told me why you decided to have a security system installed," Aidan said. The IT tech vanished, and the former cop emerged. "But if you want my advice, I'd recommend a few more locations for cameras. Starting out there." He pointed to the hallway outside. "You could keep the door locked and open it only after you check to see who's out there. You need to replace that frosted-glass window in the door, too. You can't see details through it, but you can make out movement, and it wouldn't take much to break through."

"Once a cop, always a cop," she said, and smiled at him. "For your information, it was Cyrus who wanted the cameras. I think he's worried that my clientele will include some actual criminals."

"Like he hasn't had any in his office? I seem to recall a few."

"That's true, but most of them were there because of me."

Aidan made a show of reconsidering, then said, "I'm gonna order a couple of more cameras."

It wasn't long before Grace wished he'd had that idea earlier.

CHAPTER SEVEN

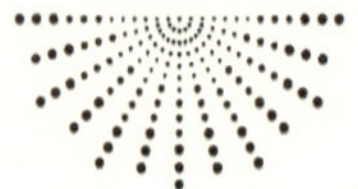

Not long after Aidan left, Ashley appeared at the top of the stairs.

"There you are," she said as she set a cardboard box on the reception desk and fanned her face. "I can't believe you're still up here. I thought you were working as an attorney, not a sherpa. Why are you stuck up here, anyway? Doesn't it just kill your feet to do those stairs in heels?"

"Not really," Grace said. It took everything she had to make herself smile, but she suspected she looked more like a dog ready to bite. "What can I do for you?"

"Oh, dear. I guess I've offended you. Again. Really, Grace, why can't we be friends? I'm over Lee, you know. I'm very happy for the two of you." She backed up a step when Grace tried the smile thing again. "Uh, in fact, I'm here to ask for a favor, but maybe it's a bad time."

"What can I do for you?" Grace repeated. She was still standing, arms crossed, wondering if all of Henry's soon-to-be ex-in-laws were going to pile in on her.

"Well, I hate to do it on the heels of the scene my sister made yesterday. I told her not to bother you, but she's so stubborn."

"I can't talk to Henry for you."

"Oh, I know. Believe me, if talking could have changed his mind, we wouldn't have a problem. But this isn't about any of that embarrassing mess. Can we just forget it? I know it's silly, but I'm going through a rough time emotionally, and I just can't deal with this." She gave the box a little push with a pale pink, perfectly oval nail. "Nothing to do with my sister and niece, I just need a favor from you. Pretty please?"

The girlish lilt and mannerisms set Grace's teeth on edge, but she said nothing, waiting for Ashley to get on with it.

"Oh, all right. If you won't be a sport, I'll just ask you. Look, it would help me out a lot if you could give this box to Lee. It's just a few things he left at my house, you know, on the nights he stayed over."

Grace's Hannibal Lecter smile froze, but she managed to say, "He must not have left anything important if he hasn't missed it in, how long has it been again? A year? Longer?"

"Please don't be mean to me."

Ashley didn't look as if she was enjoying herself. In fact, she looked ready to cry, but Grace thought that was a go-to move for her. "Why are you doing this?" she asked.

"I came back here even after you humiliated me yesterday. I know my sister told you everything, so you know all my embarrassing secrets. Can't you be a friend and help me out?"

A friend? The "mean" comment stung, so she bit back a retort.

"Okay," Ashley continued as if Grace had agreed with her, "I hoped that maybe you and I could, I don't know, just get past this unpleasantness, and I wanted to start by returning this through you so there would be no misunderstanding."

"No," Grace said slowly. "A misunderstanding occurs when

one person is mistaken about another person's motives. I am not mistaken about yours."

"Great!" Ashley said. "We'll have dinner soon. My place, and I'll make my special fried chicken. It's Lee's favorite. Now don't forget to give this to him." She picked up the box and held it out.

Grace wanted to let it drop on one of Ashley's tiny pink, spike-heeled demi boots. Instead, she said, "I have tape if you'd like to seal this." The box's flaps were folded closed, but would come open easily.

"No, Lee and I don't have any secrets. But that's thoughtful." Ashley pulled a small mirror from her purse and applied fresh lipstick.

Grace wondered if the woman binged on Doris Day movies, then decided she didn't care. "Are we done?" she asked, this time not masking her irritation.

Ashley pouted and said, "I can see this makes you uncomfortable. I'm sorry. Only, it's too awkward for me to give it to him. I was sure we'd make it, you know? He and I were so good together. But I know it's over—it's just hard for me, especially with everything going on with my family. Oh dear, I get so emotional these days."

Ignoring Grace's obvious impatience, Ashley again poked through the contents of her large designer purse, this time selecting a linen handkerchief. Dabbing at the corners of her eyes, she said, "Ladies' room?" in a way that implied gusher tears were imminent.

Grace pointed her in the right direction, wondering if there was time to peek in the box before the drama resumed. She really, really needed a secretary to handle interruptions such as Ashley. Or maybe an armed guard to throw them out.

She was leaning toward the guard when the phone rang. Mac wanted to know if she was free for lunch.

There was nothing she'd rather do than see him, give him

Ashley's box, and let him explain it all away. A quiet, romantic lunch would be the perfect setting for the conversation she'd wanted to have last night at the special dinner that didn't happen. But what she wanted to do and real life didn't mesh. "I'd love to, but Avril is coming over and bringing some furniture for the office. Why don't you come, too? That way, if she brings anything too retro, you can be on my side."

"What a tempting invitation," he said with a chuckle. "But how about I work through lunch instead and take off early? Meet you about four?"

"My place or yours?" she teased.

"You're still banned from mine. Don't want to ruin the surprise."

She knew better than to ask for details, or to argue about being left out of the project. She could make the delayed dinner tonight and finally carry out her plans. But first, she had to get through the afternoon. "Well, speaking of surprises, you'll never guess which pest is in my restroom."

"Gotta run," he said, his tone changing. She heard noises in the background. The low and calm voice of Deputy Tremaine Harper was competing with a woman's nasally words. Then Mac was gone.

"Love you, too," she said, stabbing at the End button and thinking that at least she knew the whiner wasn't Ashley. Not this time, anyway.

The outer office door to the hallway closed with a bang. As if this morning wasn't ridiculous enough, Ashley must have overheard her last comment. "I'll be hearing from Marjorie by noon," she thought, then revised her estimate. The rumor train ran faster than that.

CHAPTER EIGHT

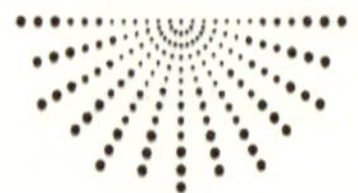

She needed to calm down before Avril arrived, and working on a motion for appeal in a zoning case wouldn't cut it. Even though she'd worn dress slacks and a silk overblouse hoping to reverse her mom-jeans image, she reorganized the scattered supplies that had been delivered over the past week. Several pieces of furniture had also been brought in from her storage unit, and she shoved them around until she was satisfied with the results.

A rectangular dining room table and chairs that hadn't seen daylight since she'd moved it over from DC fit the conference room. Her own office had a perfect spot for a small sofa and matching chairs. By the time she had broken down packing material and ripped tape strips, she was sweating, but the storeroom look was gone. Unfortunately, several wide-open spaces were left. Before she could decide what to do, she heard the next round of visitors on the steps, then Avril Oxley burst into the office, followed by Hallie carrying Fiona.

Hands on her hips, Avril surveyed the office. "I knew you needed my help."

"What took you so long?" Grace asked dryly.

"Well, for one thing, I was unaware that you were raiding churches for furniture."

The antique church pew that was the object of her disapproving look was Grace's one new purchase. Although elegant, it was amazingly uncomfortable.

Avril took Fiona from Hallie and said, "I have other work besides managing your life, so get moving, girls. The car's parked out front. Bring everything in, and we'll have a little decorating party."

Arguing was pointless, so Grace followed Hallie downstairs to find the trunk of Avril's ancient Mercury Marquis packed with chairs. The back seat was loaded with fabric, rugs, and shopping bags.

"Hope you like her taste," Hallie said. "Because if you don't, you're stuck with it, anyway. At least the food came from Three Pigs, not out of her zombie pantry."

Grace stopped in the middle of surveying her new furnishings to ask, "Zombie pantry? Do I really want to know?"

"Yeah! I'm proud of her for expanding her taste in books to postapocalyptic horror, but she got the idea that we need to plan for the survivors who may need to raid our houses for supplies after the meteor or whatever hits us. I thought at first she was just saying stuff like that to creep me out, then I found out it's a real thing. People actually do this, plan for the apocalypse, I mean. And Miss Avril's all over it. If anything happens, we'll have enough chicken noodle soup to carry us—or someone—until the Rapture."

Grace said the first thing that popped into her head. "Who else knows about this?"

Hallie laughed and said, "Your face! Honestly, you can be so gullible. I mean, she has a zombie pantry, but it's sort of a joke. Sometimes Miss Avril's more like one of my brothers than so-called adult supervision. Look what she gave me." Her left forearm now had a Mardi Gras–stylized skull that replaced the lizard she'd had the day before. "How many people her age know where to order such awesome artwork? She's the best."

Grace smiled, thinking of the stories Hallie would carry through life about her days with Avril Oxley.

Turning back to the unpacking, she was relieved to see that Avril had abandoned her own taste for 1960s mod decor and instead had raided her collection of family antiques. The car's trunk yielded two sedate armchairs and a Senneh rug in muted shades of red. She guessed the rug was older than Avril herself and in excellent condition. If the drapes in the back seat were as valuable, what would happen when the inevitable child- or dog-related accident befell them? "Let's wait on the rug and drapes. They're beautiful, but way too much for my office."

"Miss Avril said whatever happens to this stuff, at least it won't rot in a storage unit," Hallie said with a laugh.

Grace examined the rug and shook her head. "I don't think so. This should be in a museum."

"It was. She'll tell you all about it when we get it up there."

An hour later, they ate, picnic style, in Grace's newly furnished office. Avril and Hallie sat on the rug. Grace sat on a chair and tried not to wince as chips and crumbs landed on the Senneh. She was stunned by the transformation of the outer office and the fact that not a single gifted item was plastic, rubber, or had ever been labeled "Tupperware."

Avril's house was divided into two distinct sections: the front rooms she used and in which she enjoyed her mid-twentieth-century treasures, and the others, which were full of heirloom antiques and never saw the light of day. Apparently, there were also storage units. Not for the first time, Grace regretted agreeing to be the executor of her friend's estate.

She tried one more time to give the Senneh back.

"Too late," Avril said. "It wants to be here. Can't you tell? And you should thank Hallie, too. She took all the measurements and then helped me go through the storage rooms and the attic. I still think the Peter Max print rug would go well in your office, but she nixed that idea."

Grace said she'd love to see a real Peter Max, then caught the subtle shake of Hallie's head. "But I have some things in storage I want to use in there."

"Too bad. I'm pretty sure the stains could be removed. Although that one corner would have to go under your desk. Nothing really gets blood out, does it?"

Grace wondered why she was surprised. "I'm afraid to ask, but does the blood have anything to do with zombies?"

Avril and Hallie rolled their eyes at each other.

"Duh-uh, no. Zombies are, like, dead?" Hallie flicked her hair for good measure, and Avril's bottle of iced tea came seriously close to tipping over.

Grace thought she might have a heart attack if they didn't get off the rug soon.

"I'm writing my memoirs," Avril said. "All the details will be in there. Now, let's talk about things I want to know. What happened yesterday?"

Grace put down the chicken leg she'd been eating. She should have been prepared for this. "Regarding what?"

"That bad, huh?" Avril asked.

Fiona fussed, giving her mother an excuse not to answer for a moment. When the baby was settled again with a teething toy, Grace gave them both a mock glare and said, "Why don't you just tell me what you heard at the deli this morning, and I'll correct the inaccuracies."

"Buzzkill," Avril snapped. "Okay. I know all about Mona

Cutter's mother. She's a Baltimore scoop-and-sue lawyer who's trying to take Henry to the cleaners, and she's making her sister's life miserable. Poor Ashley has her hands full with that one, I can tell you. So, that's that. Now, tell us all about the mysterious boy."

While Grace was relieved that they hadn't heard about Ashley's earlier visit, the box, or the kiss she'd planted on Mac, she was still left with David's bombshells.

Avril didn't do waiting well. "Of course, if you and that cretin you used to be with have secrets—"

"What have you heard?" Grace spit the words out, irritated by the subterfuge required to keep any personal matter under wraps in Mallard Bay.

"Well." Avril seemed to consider which bits of gossip to share. "David was at your house stomping around in the yard and yelling into his phone, then you came home, took him inside, and after a while, he came out still yelling in his phone and drove off."

Grace wasn't fooled. "And?"

"New people arrived at the river house over the weekend," Avril said, using the name David had given the estate he owned outside of town. "They're staff, not guests, and they're as tight-lipped as Secret Service, except for the housekeeper. She's been throwing David's name and money all over town, and her grocery order included diapers."

Although she knew very well how Avril's local news network operated, Grace took a moment to regard her friend with awe. "Have you been over to visit?" she finally asked.

"I thought I'd wait until you checked everything out. Except, now I'm tired of being patient. Spill it, girl."

There was a time when Grace would have resisted, but Avril had burrowed into her life, bypassing the role of friend, and setting herself up as a mother figure. It was better to tell her what she wanted to know now, instead of trying to straighten out the gossip she would hear later. But when Grace started explaining Peter Carlton, David's marriage, and his other daughter, she realized the grapevine would have a hard time making this little soap opera any more convoluted than it already was.

CHAPTER NINE

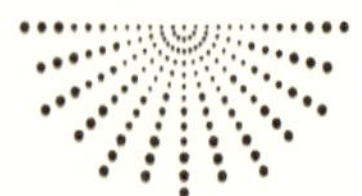

After her lunchtime entertainment departed, Grace began knocking chores off her list, and for a little while, her professional life was moving in the right direction. She was looking ahead to resurrecting her dinner-proposal plans when David called. A few minutes later, she disconnected and slowly lowered her forehead to the desk.

It was three forty-five. There would be no romantic dinner tonight, either. Somehow, in three short hours, she had to wrap up here, clean up and change her own clothes and Fiona's, and persuade Mac to accompany them to dinner at the river house. They were going to meet David's new family.

Thankful that she was still on a flexible schedule for a few more days, she shut everything down, locked up the office and raced down the steps, jerking to a halt right before plowing into a woman who was stepping onto the front porch.

"Watch it!" the thin blonde said as they missed a collision by inches.

Grace apologized, but kept going. Whoever her almost victim was, she'd get sympathy in Cyrus's office. It didn't take much imagination to hear Marjorie saying, "Oh yes, that's our second-tier attorney. We usually keep her in the attic."

Better, Grace told herself. She had to do better than this.

Her mood improved when she got home and found Mac waiting for her. He even agreed to the dinner invitation.

"Why?" she asked, suspiciously. "You're way too laid back about this."

"The only thing I can control here is how I feel about it, so I'm choosing to be entertained. Ordinarily, I'd see an evening like this only on Netflix." He kissed her, then laughed at her expression. "Better follow my lead. If you don't grow a sense of humor about our life, it's going to be a long couple of decades until we can officially dump David and whichever wife he has by then. You do realize we'll all be together at Fiona's school events and graduation, right? Correction, graduations. That child is so smart, there'll be one PhD, at least. And just imagine her wedding. She'll have a blowout, I'm sure."

"Maybe at the National Cathedral?" Grace asked, finally giving into a smile. He was talking as if their future were all set. Maybe all she had to do was ask. "How about if we made it—"

The phone in his pocket went off, making them both jump. The look on Mac's face told her it wasn't good news. He'd removed Ashley's photo from his list of contacts, but Grace saw her name on the screen. She pushed the phone away, gave him a fierce kiss, then said, "Now you can talk to her," and left the room, closing the door behind her.

Dinner, she vowed as she stalked off to feed the baby. A steak dinner, wine, no phones. All of it as soon as possible.

"I'm scared, Lee."

Mac had never told Ashley that it annoyed him when she called him by his first name. There were so few people left who did, and they were all women who'd known him since he was a child. Even Cyrus Mosley, who was older than God, called him Mac. Lee McNamara had been his father, as well as his father's father, a stern-looking old man in an oil portrait that hung in the Mallard Bay Library's Founders' Room.

But while they were first dating, Ashley had heard Avril Oxley call him by his given name and had immediately appropriated the privilege for herself. He'd been too interested in her at the time to object, and now it was too late. It was especially irritating because he didn't want her to call him anything at all; it only caused problems with Grace. Especially after yesterday.

"What's wrong, Ashley?" He didn't try to sound sympathetic. He wouldn't encourage these "save me" episodes, no matter how upset she was.

"It's Mona. She's disappeared. Somehow, she was released from the clinic in Towson yesterday, and she spent the night here with Simone and me. She's a mess, Lee. Like I told you, Henry's behavior is devastating, and this screwup at the clinic couldn't have come at a worse time. I was up most of the night with her and went into work only when I thought she was sleeping. I just got home, and I can't find her."

When they were dating, he'd thought Ashley was a smart, beautiful, and self-sufficient woman. He'd never seen her upset. She'd even accepted the news graciously when he told her he was in love with Grace. It had taken a while for him to realize she'd never given up on their relationship. But then, even when he knew what Ashley was doing, he'd taken the impractical approach of ignoring her. When she became bolder, he made a joke of it with Grace, who found nothing amusing about the behavior. He'd never, to his knowledge, had two women battle over him, and he had to admit that while it was juvenile, it could be fun. Except for now. Now was not fun. Fun was waiting in the other room.

"What does the clinic say?" he asked Ashley, wondering why she was so panicked. Mona was in her thirties and apparently had been judged ready for release by the rehab center. He knew Grace would say this was another play by Ashley for his attention, and the novelty of the situation was wearing thin.

But Ashley's concern seemed to grow as she answered him. "She wasn't at the clinic under a court order, so she technically could leave, but she never has before. She really wants to be well. And the clinic office won't tell me anything."

"Did they say she'd finished treatment?"

"They won't tell me! When she went in this time, she didn't list either Simone or me as her medical contact, so they won't admit she was there at all, even though I personally delivered her to them three weeks ago. She's supposed to be in a three-month program."

He could understand her worrying, but her niece was an adult. He had no authority to inquire into her whereabouts. "What does her mother say?" he asked.

"She's out of ideas. After Grace refused to help us yesterday, she said she can't do anything but wait and see what happens. I still can't believe Grace was so cruel. She was that awful Bryce's girlfriend, so she should have been sympathetic, but she was horrible to Simone."

Mac glanced at the bedroom door. Still closed. "I'm not discussing that."

But Ashley wasn't finished with Grace. "I tried to talk to her this morning, but she was rude to me, too. I was so upset, I was useless at work, so I finally went home, and that's when I discovered Mona was gone. Simone was on her way back to Baltimore, and she'll drive around and look for her, but I'm just frantic. I don't know what to do."

Mac couldn't believe that in all the time they'd dated, he'd never heard the whine in her voice. "I'm with Grace, right now," he said. "I'll tell her your concerns, and if she knows anything, I'll ask her to call you. Other than that, there's nothing I can do. Mona's an adult."

"Please! I need you."

He felt a bit of the old tug, a call to help. But what Ashley wanted, he'd already given to Grace. "I'm sorry," he said.

The click as she disconnected sounded final, but Mac didn't kid himself. This situation wasn't over.

Grace shook her head when Mac told her about the call. She looked disgusted at hearing Ashley had dragged up her brief relationship with Bryce Cutter, but only said, "That's a fairy-tale version of attempted murder. Too bad I lived and ruined her plans for you."

Ignoring the smile behind her words, he pulled her to him and whispered, "Sometimes you scare me to death." He knew what she'd gone through when the town, led by Bryce Cutter and aided by Henry, had turned against her. It was a short-lived period, but an ugly one. Grace had moved on, excusing most of the bystanders' behavior as human nature. He'd thought her wounds from that time had healed, but now Ashley and her family had ripped them open again. Any sympathy he'd had for them was gone.

They were dressing for dinner, or rather, Grace was trying on outfits, and he was watching. He loved living with her for many reasons, but scenes like this, intimate, casual, and unguarded, were unexpected bonuses. She kept rejecting outfits, declaring that her remaining baby pounds made her whole wardrobe too small, so he reached out and pulled her down beside him.

"I'll never get ready if you keep doing that," she said after he'd kissed her.

"You should just wear this." He ran a finger under the lace strap of her camisole, making her shiver. "The dinner conversation will be much more entertaining."

They were late leaving, and she never got around to telling him about Ashley's box.

CHAPTER TEN

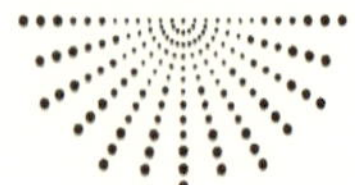

As they drove down the lane to David's home, Grace was reminded of why she disliked it. The squat concrete-and-glass structure was just plain ugly, and so large it reminded her of a warehouse. A warehouse perched on the bend of a particularly lovely branch of the Wye River and within shouting distance of the beach on Mac's property. David had wanted to make a point, and he'd succeeded. This house was bigger and the property more valuable than Mac's family home, which sat on the other side of the river.

"Looks like it's a party," Mac said as he parked his truck behind a line of cars in the circular drive.

"I don't think so," Grace said. "The Porsche is his, and the wife has to drive something. The housekeeper, nanny, and caterer will own the others."

"What? No gardener?"

"He has a service for daily landscaping and maintenance chores." She laughed at his expression. "There's also a Land Rover around here somewhere. David calls it 'the house car.'"

"Well, what else would a Come Here drive on the Eastern

Shore?" Mac asked as he maneuvered Fiona out of her car seat. He stepped back, looked at his Ford pickup, and grinned. "I'll bet he's all nervous with this in his driveway."

She wanted to kiss him right there for making her laugh in this awkward situation, but settled for taking the sleeping baby from him so he could unload the Pack 'N Play. Then, there was nothing else to do but go knock on the door of the house she used to own and meet her daughter's new stepmother.

If there had been a lineup of a hundred beautiful women, all shapes, sizes, colors, and accents, Grace would have never picked the voluptuous brunette wearing a sequined tank top and pink streaks in her ponytail to be David's new wife. He had a type, and this woman wasn't it.

Grace liked her immediately.

"Hey there! I'm Krissy Farquar. So happy to meet you!" The husky voice and sugary tone completed the Southern Girl persona.

"They know we're married, Kristen," David said, coming up behind her.

"I need to practice my new name," she said with a giggle. "It takes some getting used to, doesn't it?" This was directed to Grace, who grinned.

David ignored the exchange and introduced Grace as Fiona's mother and Mac as the local chief of police. "Putting us in our place" was how Grace would describe it later.

"And this is my daughter," David said as he took the baby from Grace, waking Fiona in the process.

"Mercy, David! Don't hold that child like a salami! Give her to me." In a flash, Krissy had Fiona in her arms and was cooing to her in an exaggerated drawl, leaving David empty-handed and embarrassed. Krissy didn't spare him a glance. "I wish you could meet your big sister, honey, but that little girl was so tired she fell asleep during her dinner. Somebody"—David got a squinty look—"decided she could stay an extra half hour at the park and just wore my baby doll out." She swayed as she talked to Fiona, who seemed transfixed by the conversation.

"Well, it's one less crying kid at dinner," David said.

"Oh, you hush." Krissy shook her head and smiled conspiratorially at Grace. "Just a big old grump, isn't he? Come on in and see what we've done to the place. I hope you like it."

Grace followed her across the foyer and into the large, open living area.

"How about a tour?" Mac said, aiming the comment at David. "This place is huge. Any chance there's a pool table somewhere?" He turned to wink at Grace as he followed David out. He knew very well there was a library with a pool table.

"Has our David always been this way?" Krissy asked as she and Grace watched the men leave.

"He's all yours," Grace said, assuring her, and was rewarded with a smile. "I'd like to say no, but you seem to know him pretty well." She stopped as a man in a chef's coat came in carrying a tray of shrimp hors d'oeuvres.

Krissy thanked him and said, "Larry, my husband disappeared without offering our guests anything to drink. Can you please bring us some of that wonderful sparkling cider I picked up at the farmers market?" She looked at Grace and said, "Unless you'd like something else? Believe me, we have everything. Just name your poison."

Grace said the cider was fine and joined Krissy in a seating area in front of a wide glass wall. She debated asking for her daughter back, but Fiona was dozing peacefully, and it was nice to see how Krissy handled her.

"This is my favorite spot," Krissy said as they settled in overstuffed swivel rockers. She nodded at the river view and added, "I can't believe you gave it up."

So much for awkward transitions, Grace thought. She was liking Krissy more and more. "It is beautiful, but it doesn't have good memories for me. I hope you'll be happy here, though." Grace smiled with the words, realizing she meant them sincerely.

"I'm sorry," Krissy said. "My mouth works overtime when I'm anxious. Look, I want us to be friends, and I want you to know this was all his idea." She lifted her left hand to wiggle a large diamond that Grace recognized from five feet away. "Did this sucker get in your way when you had it? It's like totin' a bowling ball around."

That did it. Grace covered her mouth to keep from startling the baby with her laughter. "Where did you find him?" she asked. "And why . . . ?"

Krissy jumped in to answer both questions. "The where was a riverboat on the Mississippi about ten miles out of New Orleans. But, honey, I ask myself why every day. Still, I've got the cutest little girl you ever did see. Just as cute as her sister, here. Wait till you see my Amalie. She doesn't look any more like her father than this baby does. Can you believe he wanted me to have a DNA test run on her?"

When she took a breath, Grace dived in. She'd thought it would take longer than five minutes for David's wife to give up the details she wanted. And to think she hadn't wanted to come tonight. "Oh, I believe it," she said. "Were you shocked to learn about us? I mean, that David had another baby?"

Krissy peered around Grace to check the doorway before saying, "I'm not supposed to discuss this with you, but I know he has three children." Her eyes twinkled. "There may be even more, you know. We might have a club. The David Farquar Mothers' Sorority. What do you think?"

Grace shook her head, suddenly not so amused. She and Mac

had joked about this very thing, but hearing it from Krissy made the possibility sound more real. There wasn't much she could do about it, except give in to the humor. "I guess we may as well laugh about it. What's done is done. How'd you find out?"

"About his son? Oh, please. Who do you think the staff works for? I brought most of them up from Louisiana with me. The walls in this place have ears, honey, and they're all mine."

Grace didn't hide her surprise and was rewarded with a sly smile from Krissy, who added, "Tell the truth. You thought I was a floozy who snagged a big fish when she got pregnant by your ex. Right?"

"No!" Grace was able to say this with honesty only because she didn't think she'd ever used the word *floozy.*

"Oh, please. It's a logical assumption. See, my parents thought I needed to learn the value of their money. They made me work every summer while I went through Tulane. I've done just about everything in the hospitality industry. Cleaning rooms, waiting tables, bartending—and I did it all on the biggest riverboat out of New Orleans. Even tried my hand as a prep cook and then as a dealer in the casinos. Drove Mother wild. She wanted me to quit, but I liked doing it, and I have a lot of friends still working on the *Princess Belle.* I was fillin' in for one of the girls in the main bar the night I met Mr. Wonderful. I can assure you I'm never gonna hear the end of the 'I Told You So' song from Mother. She said I'd fall in with the wrong crowd, and she was right. She's absolutely livid that I married David, who is fifteen years older and not nearly as rich as the investment broker she'd picked out." Krissy's smile faded a bit. "I'm gonna tough it out, though. Can't go running home too soon."

Grace's head was swimming. She couldn't wait to tell Mac that David's wife thought he was socially and financially inferior.

"Let's have lunch soon so we can really talk, okay?" Krissy whispered as the men came back into the room.

Grace quickly agreed. If Krissy was just getting warmed up, she wanted to be there for the main event.

Dinner was delicious. Grace said she'd never tasted better bouillabaisse and had to restrain herself from asking for seconds. David said good food was a bonus to having a beautiful French Creole wife. Krissy gave an unladylike snort and said that her family was originally from Wisconsin and the only thing she had to do with dinner was select the menu. Mac smiled so much he told Grace later that his face hurt.

Fiona woke during dessert, but Grace still got a taste of the pecan pie before getting up.

"Alexandra is sleeping through the night," David said with a hint of disapproval when Grace asked where she could feed the baby.

"Amalie is a year old, David," Krissy said as she stood and joined Grace. She led the way to a guest room with a comfortable easy chair, closing the door behind them. "He's on my last nerve with that 'Alexandra' nonsense."

"Yeah, he tried to name Fiona that, too," Grace said.

"Seriously? Well, do you know why?"

Grace shook her head, then said, "If it's a name in his family, he probably would have said so. I think he just wanted to be a part of Fiona's birth, to make some decisions, you know? But the name was set as soon as I knew I was having a girl."

Krissy sighed and shrugged. "Same with me. He's filing papers to add his name to Amalie's birth certificate, and he wants to tack Alexandra on when he does it. I told him I named her when he was still up here insisting he was sterile, and she's staying Charlotte Amalie. Do you know the town on Saint Thomas?"

Grace said she did, not adding that she and David had vacationed in the Virgin Islands several times.

"I led a pretty sheltered life until I went to college, and the first time I ever traveled without my parents was a sorority cruise. I told the other girls that I had never seen a more beautiful place, and that I was naming a daughter after it. I pronounce her name Ahm-a-lee, like Emily. It's just prettier, don't you think?"

Grace said the first thing that occurred to her. "Did you play with Barbies?"

Krissy laughed. "Oh, of course I did. I just love all that froufrou frilly stuff. I'm guessing you don't?"

"To each her own," Grace said with a smile. "But you're gonna love my cousin, Niki."

Krissy looked stricken. "Please don't tell me you're anti–baby dolls?"

It was the first time Grace had ever considered that she might have a girly-girl for a daughter. Or that Fiona might have a sister to play with. And a big brother. And maybe others . . .

"Goodness, girl. Don't panic. We'll work it out."

Grace refocused on Krissy's anxious face. "Sorry. Every once in a while, this all rushes in and I panic. I'm thrilled Fiona will have a sister. I was an only child, and I'm so glad she won't be."

"We'll take things slowly," Krissy said. "I'm so glad that I like you. We're gonna be like family for the rest of our lives. Isn't that awesome?"

When she was gone, Grace said, "I think we got lucky, Sweet Pea." She stroked Fiona's cheek, then whispered a thank-you to the goddess of fractured families for sending her an ally, even if Krissy came with Barbie dolls in tow.

CHAPTER ELEVEN

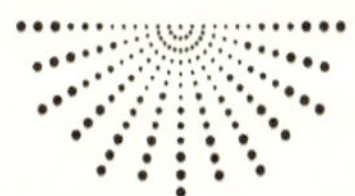

Mac drove through a quiet Mallard Bay early on Wednesday morning, making the trip to his cottage on autopilot, not seeing the sunrise over the farm fields to the east of town or hearing the birdsong from the waterfront park. He was short on sleep and uncomfortable about a decision he'd thought was already settled in his mind. Before last night, he'd planned to sign off on the final blueprints for a new bedroom wing that would turn his small waterman's cottage into an equally charming, but larger farmhouse-style home that would meet the needs of a family. Somehow, David Farquar had ruined that, too.

Dinner the night before had become awkward as it drew to a close. David clearly had something on his mind, and Mac watched both women tense up as the small talk waned. When the subject of Peter Carlton came up, introduced by David himself, all pretense of hospitality ended. The memory of the last half hour of the evening made him angry all over again.

David had started calmly enough, reiterating what they all knew about Peter and adding that he and the boy's mother had been together off and on through college and for nearly a decade after. But after saying that he'd never known she'd had his child, he announced he needed time to figure out how to move forward, and he needed to do it without interference, no matter how well intentioned.

Grace, of course, was not deterred and asked if he was sure this Bethany was Peter's mother. "After all," she said, apparently oblivious to David's angry expression, "she denies it. Why would she do that?"

Sometimes Mac wondered if she did it on purpose. He'd even asked her once, and she'd answered him without hesitation, saying she had long ago decided not to tiptoe around sensitive subjects just to keep David on an even keel. "His temper is not my problem," she'd said. "I won't provoke him without a good reason, but I won't shut up when I want to talk, either." And that had been the end of the discussion.

He wished she'd made an exception last night.

David had looked each of them in the eye and told them in no uncertain terms that the situation was none of their business, and forbid them to have contact with the boy. Mac had stood, hoping to get Grace moving toward the door, but he needn't have bothered. The new Mrs. Farquar informed her husband he wasn't God and told him to get over himself. David had stalked out of the room without another word. Then, as if nothing had happened, Krissy walked them out, thanked them for coming, and waved goodbye from the front porch.

Mac hoped Krissy hadn't killed David when she went back inside that concrete boxcar of a house. Grace had talked all the way home, and he was pretty sure she was still at it when he'd drifted off to sleep several hours later. The last thing he'd heard her say was, "Good thing we're staying at my house—we'd be able to hear them yelling from yours." Oddly, this reminder that David's house was just across a narrow branch of the Wye River from Mac's property hadn't kept him awake, but it was the first thought into his aching head when he woke.

Of course, she wouldn't want to live that close to David and his family. He didn't want her to want it, did he? He was still wrestling with that when his cell rang, dragging him from his glum thoughts and into a mess of a different kind.

"I want to apologize," Ashley said in the silky voice he'd once believed was natural for her. "I was out of line yesterday, and I should have just called Grace myself. I hope you'll forgive me."

Mac thought this might be more uncomfortable than yesterday's call, and he had even less patience for her now. He pulled into his driveway and parked in front of his cottage, watching a crew of construction workers unloading equipment.

"Don't worry about it," he said. "But I have a meeting, and I need to go." Leaning down, he unclipped Rocky from her leash, and the puppy tore around in circles before dashing after a squirrel she had no hope of catching.

"But, Lee," Ashley cried, "you have to help me. She's still missing."

That set him back for a moment. "You haven't heard from your niece at all?"

"Not a word. Her phone goes to voice mail. She's been gone nearly twenty-four hours."

"And you're sure your sister hasn't heard from her?"

There was a hesitation, then a sigh. "Simone is refusing my calls. Yesterday she drove me crazy, and today she can't be bothered to talk to me."

The whine was back in her voice, and it made his headache worse. He couldn't help her, and it was time to end this. "Mona's an adult, Ashley. For all you know, she and her mother are together. The only thing I can suggest is that you call the clinic again and tell them what you've told me. If they have concerns about her mental status, then they'll contact the authorities. Also, Simone may not be taking your calls because she knows where Mona is and doesn't want to discuss her daughter with you." He knew that had been unnecessary and felt bad when he heard her gasp. "There are a dozen other possibilities I can think of," he went on to say, hoping to ease her mind, "and none of them involves the police. Now if neither you nor Simone has heard from her in forty-eight hours, call the state police—she lives in Baltimore, not Mallard Bay."

"So, you're saying I should call you back in the morning if I haven't heard from her?"

"No."

"But Lee!"

"Ashley, stop it." He wanted to say, "Stop all of it. Stop the phone calls, the accidental meetings, and the bitchy behavior to Grace." But what came out was "You're better than this." Then he hung up.

It was a huge relief to join his contractor, Benny Pannel, and finally have a conversation about a subject he understood with people who wouldn't cry if he disagreed with them.

Back in the winter, Benny had given him the bad news that a roof-replacement project was going to require substructure work, too, because of an old termite infestation. That news was the push he needed to remodel the eighteenth-century cottage that had been in his family for generations. Since the central portion of the first floor would have to be replaced, he decided to remodel the space for Grace. She loved large rooms and open spaces, and now he could give her the design she wanted.

What he hadn't considered when he devised his big surprise was how hard it would be to keep a secret like that from her. She knew more about construction and renovating old structures than he did, but she consistently allowed him to get away with the "termite damage" charade as an explanation for the length of time the new roof was taking.

Now the project had reached a crossroads. If he told Benny to wrap up the work in the original footprint of the house, the result would be a fresh, updated cottage with a new sunporch and open floor plan. But Benny had suggested an addition, an L-shaped, first-floor wing with a large master suite and another bedroom. As soon as he saw Benny's sketch, Mac thought it might win Grace over. The cottage would become a modern-style farmhouse, something his parents and grandparents wouldn't recognize. But there was the not insignificant matter of money to consider.

He and Grace discussed finances from time to time, and each knew the general parameters of the other's income. She would know he'd need a significant mortgage for the addition and would insist on contributing. Then they'd be into a whole new relationship when she wouldn't even commit to the one they already had. And it was possible she wouldn't like the house even if he bulldozed it and built her dream home. It was his history here with Meri that made Grace uncomfortable, and no amount of renovation would erase a ghost.

He'd once asked her how she expected him to tolerate a live, irritating David when she couldn't ignore someone who'd been dead for more than a decade. Even Avril, who rarely criticized him, called him an idiot over that one.

"All Grace's ever heard is how beautiful, dignified, and kind Meri was," Avril had said, as if explaining a basic element of female emotions. "And whenever you speak about the past, you look wistful, and you need to knock that off, Lee. Grace will always be envious of Meri's time with you, but she deals with it."

"So, you're taking her side?" he asked, trying to make light of the sting her words carried.

"Hell, no. I told her she was an idiot, too. You two are ridiculous together and deserve each other."

He was pretty sure that wasn't meant in a loving way, and the intervening months had only reinforced Avril's opinions. He was slowly accepting that while he couldn't give Grace up, it was unlikely he could make her completely happy, and there was no point in bankrupting himself. David had already shown the lack of effect extravagant gifts had on her decisions.

"Glad you could make it," Benny called as he came out of the house to join Mac in the bright spring sunlight. When they'd exchanged pleasantries and Benny had gotten an update on Rocky, he said, "Well, it's that time, Chief. Have you decided on a final floor plan?"

"I think so. Go ahead and finish the exterior, but only frame in the extension. It'll probably be a three-bay garage instead of a bedroom wing, but leave the interior open, and I'll decide how to use the space down the road. Sound okay?"

Benny, who was extraordinarily fond of Grace, looked surprised. "No new master bedroom?"

"Just a garage for now," he said. "And the bedroom-wing plan stays between us, okay?"

"You didn't even ask her, did you?"

Mac shook his head. The day was off to a bad start, and it didn't help that Benny was right. It was time to tell Grace the truth about the renovations. The limbo they'd been living in had to end, and he couldn't see the resolution taking place in the old McNamara family homeplace. She'd never be happy here.

On the drive back to the office, he tried to decide how to tell her he'd remodeled just for her. The open kitchen and family room were as close as Benny could get to what she'd said she wanted in a dream floor plan, and the long sunroom was modeled after the one she loved at Avril's house. The bathrooms were updated, and new window seats with storage turned Meri's former sewing room into a playroom for Fiona. The hard part would be explaining why he'd stopped short of the full plan. He had no doubt that sooner or later she'd learn about the vetoed downstairs bedroom wing. "I didn't expect you to agree to live here" wasn't a winning explanation.

He gave up on the useless line of thought as he entered the town limits. Out of habit, he scanned the sidewalks and passing vehicles, but instead of just checking things out, he also looked for Mona Cutter. He hated to admit it, but Ashley might be right. The longer her niece was gone, the better the chances were that something was wrong.

CHAPTER TWELVE

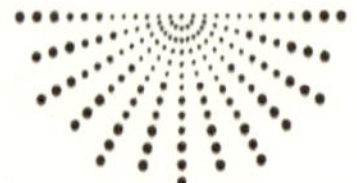

Grace wondered if every workday morning was going to be a tangle of priorities, with hers always coming in last. Mac's early meeting with Benny was obviously a ploy to escape the turmoil of her household, but she didn't hold it against him—she'd escape, too, if she could. At least he'd taken Rocky with him. One demanding infant in the house was enough, especially since Hallie wasn't scheduled for nanny duty until noon. That very poor decision on Grace's part would derail her morning work schedule, but served as a fine reminder that plan-as-you-go baby care had serious pitfalls.

By the time she and Fiona were finally fed, dressed, and ready to leave, it was nearly nine, and that's when she remembered she'd told Aidan he could get into the office at eight thirty. He didn't answer her call, and when she finally arrived at work, she found him sitting on the front steps with a tower of boxes stacked next to him.

"I'm so sorry, it's been a crazy morning," she said, skipping a greeting and going straight to groveling. "But why are you sitting out here?"

"Mr. Mosley's attack human wouldn't let me wait inside their office because I told her I wasn't a plumber and couldn't fix their leak." He stood and made a show of dusting off the seat of his jeans. "There's a tiny water stain on the kitchen ceiling and she's having a fit. The old b—"

"Aidan!" Grace handed Fiona to him as she rummaged for her keys.

"I was gonna say 'bat,'" Aidan explained to Fiona, giving her one of his rare smiles. "That's what your mom calls her."

"We're setting a good example these days." Grace swapped him keys for the baby and told him to go on upstairs. "I'll just have a word with Marjorie. Will I need to apologize for anything you've done?"

Aidan looked offended, but as he picked up the boxes, she heard, "Not unless she saw my finger." Then, balancing the teetering stack of cameras and AV equipment, he disappeared through her front door.

She groaned and said, "Get ready to charm Miss Marjorie, Sweet Pea." But as she opened the door of Mosley and Associates, she heard footsteps thudding down the staircase on her side of the building.

Aidan, minus boxes and keys, burst out onto the porch, yelling, "Get the baby inside and lock the door behind you."

"Why?"

His phone was in his hand, and she heard the three musical beeps, then, "Nine one one. What is your emergency?"

Grace did as she was told when she heard him report a dead body.

She and Fiona weren't locked in long with Cyrus and Marjorie. In short order, Mac arrived, followed by an ambulance and the state police. Main Street was blocked off, and people gathered at the barricades.

It was Mac who broke the news that Mona Cutter's body was on the staircase leading to the second-floor landing. Grace doubted he would have parted with the information so quickly if they weren't trying to find Henry, Ashley, and Simone. Mac's call to Ashley's sister went to voice mail, but Henry soon arrived with Ashley on his heels.

Grace thought Mac was gentle and compassionate as he broke the news, but she also saw the cop in him who didn't miss a single detail of the reactions of the dead woman's husband and aunt.

Cyrus, while as shocked as the rest of them, went into legal mode as soon as Mac started asking questions. Age may have rendered the attorney a little unsteady on his feet, but hadn't touched his mental reflexes. He went to his client, and didn't leave Henry's side.

Left to fend for herself, Ashley stood off to one side, crying, until Marjorie jumped into rescue mode.

Statements were taken by Maryland State Police Detective Sergeant Desiree Marbury, who, for once, didn't comment on finding Grace on the witness list of a homicide. The usually terse detective even softened enough to admire Fiona, but only when she and Grace were alone for a moment. Grace thought they were making personal progress until Desi told her to stay put and be ready to answer more questions. Apparently, it was only Fiona she liked.

Marjorie prepared a list of people who'd been in the office that morning, then was stunned when she was told to include everyone from the day before.

"I can't believe this. I talked to that poor girl! Showed her where to sign her divorce documents. Are you saying she died in this building yesterday? Was she d-dead in that hallway the whole time I was here alone this morning?" Already pale and jittery, the secretary sank into her chair behind the reception desk.

Eyeing her like a lab specimen, Desi said, "Can you explain what she was doing out there?"

"No! I mean, she wanted to talk to an attorney and Mr. Mosley wasn't here, so I sent her upstairs to Grace, but I didn't check to make sure she made it. I mean, I can't be expected to cover two floors at the same time. I locked the connecting door to the hallway after she started up the steps. If Grace had been working like she was supposed to, none of this would have happened, right?"

"I don't know." Desi leaned a bit closer and added, "Why would you say that?"

Despite the circumstances, Grace had to struggle not to smile, then she had an unsettling thought and interrupted, asking, "Was Mona Cutter the woman I almost ran into yesterday?"

"We'll talk about you in a minute," the detective said, still watching Marjorie, who'd gone pale.

"I don't understand," Marjorie said slowly. "All she had to do was go out Grace's entrance. The outer door opens from the inside even when it's locked. But if she died yesterday . . . Does that mean I sent her up to her killer? Was someone waiting on the staircase?"

Grace jumped in before Desi Marbury could answer. "Here," she said and placed Fiona in the distraught woman's lap. It was that or pat The Bat's shoulder, and neither one of them was ready for that. She held on to the baby until Marjorie gathered the child up and began to rock.

To the detective, Grace said, "Let's go into the kitchen." She was relieved when Desi followed her without complaint. "You know, for all her bluster, Marjorie is pretty naïve," she said as she poured coffee for both of them. "To the extent you can, please go easy on her. She's traumatized, and she's older than she looks.

Well, I think so, anyway. I'm not sure anyone but Cy actually knows her age."

"I'll be sure to do that." Marbury's tone said, *get real*. "But I don't have to worry about you, do I? You must be used to having people knocked off wherever you go."

"I'm sure you mean that in the kindest way." Grace suddenly realized it was quiet for the first time since Aidan had found Mona Cutter. "What's going on outside?"

"Nothing that requires me, which is why I get to keep an eye on you and the fragile flower out there. Medical examiner is finishing up. The only thing we know for sure is the vic's been dead a while, so if you remember anything that might be pertinent about yesterday, better tell me now."

"I'll have to give it some thought," Grace said. So much had happened in the last twenty-four hours, it would take time to sift through all of it, but nothing came immediately to mind.

"Sure," Marbury said, as if she hadn't expected any help. "Transport's waiting to load the body. The chief, Mr. Cutter, Dr. Greenburgh, and Mr. Mosley are at the station. Everyone else is looking for the vic's mother."

Grace didn't have time to consider the unusual sharing of information before Aidan came into the kitchen through the back door. During his law enforcement career, both with the state police and the Mallard Bay Police Department, his relationship with Desi Marbury had been acrimonious at the best of times, but he didn't seem unhappy to see her.

"You, again?" he asked as he helped himself to the last of the coffee.

Grace thought his gibe lacked its usual acid, but she reasoned that even Aidan would be off stride after nearly tripping over a dead woman.

"Well, if they've turned you loose, they must be ready for Grace," Desi said.

"Me?" Grace said. "But I—"

"The victim is on the interior steps of your office," Desi said, breaking in. Apparently, friendly had been a fleeting emotion on her part. "You need to see if anything's out of place in the down-stairs area, then check upstairs after the body's been moved." To Aidan, she added, "Would you look in on Ms. Battsley and Grace's baby?"

Grace didn't stop to ponder the unusual alliance unfolding in front of her. For all her talk about Marjorie being naïve, she'd been up close to the victim at only one other unnatural death scene, and that experience had haunted her for weeks. Reluctantly, she followed the detective.

The sight of the body stopped her cold. She didn't want to look and yet couldn't look away. Her first thought was that the scene was staged. It wasn't, couldn't be, a real person who lay upside down on the stairs, arms and legs at angles like a skier who'd wiped out.

She became aware of Desi holding her left elbow in a firm but gentle grasp.

"You're okay," she said as she handed Grace a paper face mask. "Put this on and breathe through your mouth."

"I saw her yesterday as I was leaving," Grace said, and described the encounter for Desi.

They went outside while the body was removed and the area where it had lain was photographed and processed. Grace was relieved to see the technicians take the carpet as well.

An hour later, she was upstairs in her office, confirming again that nothing was amiss. The door at the top of the stairs had been locked, and everything in the office was as she'd left it at four o'clock the afternoon before. There were no obvious clues to shed light on Mona Cutter's death, just a lot of uncomfortable ques-tions with few answers.

When she and a cranky Fiona were finally home, she couldn't relax, and the rest of the day seemed endless, despite countless calls from everyone except the one person she desperately wanted to talk with. It was after midnight before Mac arrived, not that he told her much.

"It didn't look like an accident," he said in response to her barrage of questions.

He wouldn't say anything more, so she settled for the comfort of sleeping wrapped in his arms. It was what she'd been waiting up for, anyway, and it was enough—for tonight.

CHAPTER THIRTEEN

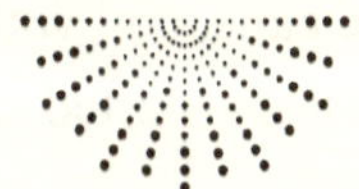

For once, it wasn't Fiona who woke her. Men's voices outside her bedroom window pulled her out of a fitful sleep. Grace recognized David's strident tone immediately, then Mac's lower, but equally harsh, response. After a quick check of the nursery where Fiona slept on, knees and elbows tucked under her chest and bottom in the air, she threw on a robe and scooped Rocky up as she ran out to the driveway where the men were squared off.

Mac's only reaction to her arrival was a warning glance, but David turned on her immediately. Rolling his eyes at the sight of her wrestling the squirming dog, he said, "What did you tell Peter?"

"We'll talk in the house," she said. "And if you wake Fiona, you won't have any more problems because I'll kill you myself."

"Not a good idea," Mac said. "I think David and I should go down to the station. I can answer all his questions there."

That was when she noticed Mac was wearing his uniform and had his keys in his hand. David's Porsche was in the driveway, blocking Mac's truck. The Porsche's engine was still running, and the drivers-side door hung open.

David's face was an unhealthy shade of red, and he took a step toward them. "You will tell me now why you arrested my son, or it will be the last time you take anything from me."

"I didn't arrest anyone," Mac said calmly. "You have my word. But I can help you find out what happened. Come with me to the station. I'll make the calls, and you can hear everything."

"You'll do it now—" David started saying, but Rocky cut him off with a growl.

"Good girl," Grace said, and slipped her a treat from the stash in her robe pocket.

"Not inside," Mac said to her. "And David, let's not entertain the neighbors, okay?" Mac lowered his voice. "Let's go to the station and find out what happened to Peter. I'll ride with you if you like. You'll hear and see everything I do as I get information about your boy."

The moment stretched while Grace hung on to the tense dog and David glared at Mac. Finally, he said, "You and your gun can ride in your piece-of-crap truck. Don't make me wait on you." He stalked back to his car and seconds later, peeled out of the driveway, grinding the gears, and taking a chunk of the lawn with him.

"What happened?" Grace asked as she followed Mac to the truck.

"I got a call from Desi. That's why I'm going in. Peter Carlton was picked up in Chestertown last night. It was only a speeding stop, but the 'Person of Interest' alert she had out for him showed up when the patrol officer entered his information. Unfortunately, Peter tried to run. I'll tell you more later."

"Wait!" Grace grabbed the door handle. "At least tell me why is Desi looking for him."

He started the engine before saying, "Eyewitnesses identified him running away from your office at four forty-five yesterday."

Grace stood looking after him as he drove off. Despite his despicable behavior, she sympathized with David. He was afraid, and so was she.

———

The ringtone she'd assigned the forwarded calls from the office went off fifteen minutes after Mac and David left.

If Peter had looked older than eighteen when she met him, he sounded much younger than that as he asked her to represent him. The shock of going from high school student to accused felon had clearly rattled him.

"You still take clients who can't pay, right?" he asked with a tremor in his voice. "I promise I'll make good on the bill. I'm eighteen, you know, I'm responsible for myself."

His voice broke on the last words, and Grace felt her heart go with it. She asked questions until she could sense that he was calming down. The boarding school's headmaster had sent an attorney to help him through his initial processing, but as soon as the boy had asked for Grace, arrangements had been made for a phone call, and the school had withdrawn its representation.

"All right," she said with more confidence than she felt. "I'll act as your attorney until we know exactly what you're dealing with. Then we can decide the best course of action. You aren't alone, Peter, I promise." The P word was one she never said to a client, but it flew out of her mouth, and she didn't regret it. "You haven't said if you were injured in the wreck, or during the arrest. Were you?"

"Not much. I'm sorta banged up, but nobody touched me. I hit my head when I crashed the car. It's my fault. All of it is—"

"Stop." She shut him down. "Don't say anything like that, no matter what you're referencing, understand?"

"But, I—"

"Stop talking. Don't admit guilt for anything. Not on the phone and not when you hang up. In fact, no chatting with anyone, not even the other people who are in the cell with you. Answer questions with yes, no, or 'My attorney said I can't answer.'"

"Won't the guards and police get mad?"

"Probably. But they won't be surprised. This is standard procedure. Can you handle it?"

"Of course."

Despite the situation, she smiled at hearing the bravado returning to his voice. "Good. I'll find out what's happening, and I'll come to you. You'll probably stay at the state police barracks there in Centreville or be moved to the detention center near there. Wherever it is, I'll find you. Do what you're told. Cooperate, but don't talk details with anyone." Then remembering whose son he was, she added, "And don't argue with anyone."

He gave her the contact information for the Howard Military Academy's headmaster and the school's attorney. After a brief hesitation, he said, "I don't want you to tell David Farquar I've been arrested. You can't unless I say so, right?"

"No. That's not right. I can explain attorney-client privilege when we have more time, but in short, I can't share your confidences related to the crimes you're accused of, or anything pertaining to your case that might hurt you. If you want an attorney who doesn't have a personal connection to you, I completely understand. I'll help you find a good one."

"I want you. I need someone who understands my situation, but why do you have to tell him anything?"

"You're aware of my personal relationship with David. He knows who you are, and that you came to see me." She let that sink in. Peter had to decide if he wanted her representation after hearing she'd already discussed him with David and would have to again.

There was only static on the line, and she wished she could see him. Finally, she said, "Let's just take things one step at a time. I'll get you through today and help you find another lawyer if you want one. But you should know David's already been to see me this morning. He told me about the trouble you're in."

"I don't want to see him!"

"Peter, get a grip." She was already jotting down a list of things to be done before they met. There was no time for him to backslide. "Put your family issues out of your mind. You have a lifetime ahead of you to handle them, but right now, your only job is to get out of jail. That's it. And it's all up to you." She stopped and waited for him to decide the next step.

"I guess I sound crazy," he said. "But once I found out you weren't dead, I knew you would be the best one to help me. Thank you. I'll try not to make it harder for you." A male voice interrupted at his end and said something she couldn't make out. Then Peter said, "They're transporting me to the detention center in a few minutes. I have to go."

"Wait! Why did you think I was dead?"

He hesitated, then in a lowered voice said, "I came back to see you yesterday afternoon. When I looked through the window of the door to your office, I could see part of a body. I couldn't make out much, but all I could think was that he'd killed you."

"Who?" Grace said, struggling to understand him over the background noise.

"David Farquar. That's why Bethany hated him and why she took me to raise. She wanted to keep me away from him because he used to hurt her."

CHAPTER FOURTEEN

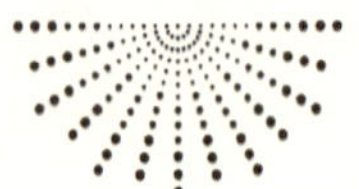

Mac expected to find an unhinged David waiting for him at the police department, but the only person in the room that comprised the reception and booking area was Patrolman First Class Tremaine Harper. The newest officer in the MBPD was on the phone, displaying admirable restraint as he worked to calm an elderly woman whose property faced the parking lot behind Cyrus Mosley's law office. Harper ma'am-ed her even as she used words that made the young officer's eyes widen. Mrs. Edith Pratt was not pleased at having a murder occur across the street from her front porch.

Mac thought he might have the better deal with David.

By and large, the citizens of Mallard Bay were Locals—born-and-bred natives who resisted the intrusion of big-city ways and big-city crime. Any property owner who wasn't a Local was usually called a Come Here. Locals blamed Come Heres and tourists for everything from rising prices to the erosion of farm-land and pollution of the bay. Edith Pratt was a Local who wanted her police department to find the murdering outsider and string him up.

Mac winced at the thought of tourists walking past Edith's house over the next few days. Her vocabulary would undoubtedly be on full display. He made a mental note to stop by and visit her later. Assuming, of course, that the scene he still had to have with David was settled amicably. If he had to arrest Fiona's father, he wouldn't have time to soothe a taxpayer's angst. The morning shift didn't officially start for another ten minutes, and so far, they had a raving great-grandmother and an angry father breathing down their necks. This didn't bode well for the rest of the day.

As if cued by Mac's morose thoughts, David appeared, looming in the doorway until Mac invited him in. Tremaine left on an unscheduled foot patrol, and when the door shut behind him, the room was very quiet.

"I'm having a coffee," Mac said. "Join me?"

"If you didn't arrest Peter, who did?"

Mac poured his coffee, but kept David in his peripheral vision as he said, "The Chestertown Police Department." He was surprised David hadn't known at least that much. "The state police are investigating a murder that occurred outside Grace's office sometime late afternoon or evening on Tuesday—"

"I know that. Get to the point."

Mac nodded as if it were a reasonable request. He was determined not to engage the volatile man if he could help it, but he also knew he might not have a choice. "Maryland State Police issued an all-points bulletin listing Peter as a person of interest in both a property-damage incident and in the death of a woman named Mona Cutter." He sat on the edge of the reception desk and motioned to a nearby chair.

Ignoring the gesture, David leaned in. "That's insane! Why would that happen? What are you claiming the boy did?"

Mac didn't stand. Grace's ex had at least three inches on him and standing wouldn't help his position, only escalate the tension. He wouldn't move unless he had to subdue David. Experience told him to just let the tantrum play out, but he had to work to suppress the fury he felt as he thought of all the times Grace must have faced this bully's wrath.

None of his feelings showed as he said, "I'll skip the part where I repeat that I have done nothing at all with respect to Peter Carlton." His next words were lower, colder. "Three individuals passing the building where the murder occurred reported seeing a young man trying the locked front doors around four forty-five on Tuesday afternoon. Two of the three witnesses picked Peter's photo out of a selection of fifteen men of similar coloring and age. One witness said Peter acted erratically, then ran away. Ten minutes later, other witnesses saw him back his car into a fire hydrant two blocks from away from the office and speed off. They took photographs of the car tags, which came back registered to Bethany Carlton."

"It's not a crime to touch a doorknob," David said. "All you've got is sun-drunk tourists who saw someone who might have been Peter—"

Mac cut him off. "He's clearly identifiable on the film from the security cameras at Cy Mosley's office building. But that's not why he was arrested. A patrol officer in Chestertown stopped him for speeding last night. The APB showed up when she ran his tags. He was asked to get out of the vehicle, but he drove off, clipping the officer, and causing an accident involving two other cars. He was arrested at the scene on a string of charges, the most serious of which was assaulting a police officer with deadly force. You'll find all of that reported online now, and on the front page of tomorrow's paper."

David's face paled with the recital. This time, his only response was to ask where his son was being held.

"The Kent County Detention Center in Chestertown, and we're not likely to get him moved any closer. Right now, their charges outweigh our interests." Mac took one of his business cards from a tray on the desk and jotted down a name and telephone number. Holding it out, he said. "Sergeant Merkle at the Detention Center will help you. Call me if I can help." He knew David would never use his name or call him, no matter how much easier it would make his introduction to the intake director of the center.

David left, tossing a grudging "Thanks" over his shoulder. Mac knew that paltry bit of civility was painful and hoped it irritated the arrogant loudmouth for the rest of the day.

CHAPTER FIFTEEN

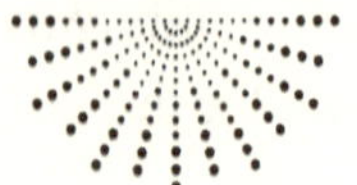

Grace's call to the Mallard Bay PD line rolled over to the Kingston County Dispatch Center. There was no message she could leave for Mac on that emergency line that wouldn't cause more problems than it would solve, and he wasn't answering his cell. She'd try him again after she'd seen Peter.

Her thoughts kept looping back to the boy's last startling comment. Could it be true? Had David been physically abusive to Bethany Carlton? He'd certainly been angry enough with Grace at various times over their years together to hurt her. But he never had. Well, not physically. Much. Nothing beyond bruises from grabbing her arm. Did that count?

She knew it did. She knew it all counted, and she felt sick.

As she tucked her blouse into the back of her skirt and reached for her suit jacket, she wished there was time for one more cuddle with Fiona, but Hallie and Avril urged her to the door. They were double-teaming the babysitting today, and that included supervising Grace's preparations. It had taken all three of them to get her ready.

"Go," Avril ordered, when Grace turned back at the door. "If you wait any longer, that boy will be convicted."

"If you need . . ." Grace started saying as she stepped onto the porch, but the door closed in her face, and she heard the lock engage.

She was on her way to work. Her feet were in real leather pumps, her hair in a neat, tucked French braid, and Avril's final inspection had found no stains, drips, or dried cereal on her navy pinstripe suit. She even wore a little makeup and lipstick, none of which would matter to Peter Carlton. Charges were piling up against him at an alarming rate, and what he needed was a good attorney.

She used the half-hour drive into Chestertown to run through what she needed to accomplish and how best to handle the awkward relationship with her new client. She also prepared herself to handle a raging David. She had first-day-of-school jitters, but knew they were nothing next to what Peter must be feeling.

Get a grip.

She gave herself the same advice she'd given her client and kept her mind on work.

David beat her to the detention center, but it didn't do him much good.

As Grace was escorted to a tiny interview room, she could hear David two doors down the hallway. The officer who accompanied her said, "Parents. It's never their kid's fault, is it?"

Outwardly, at least, Peter was much calmer than his father, and he impressed her with his attention and manners. As they finished the paperwork and she started to explain the next steps, he stopped her, saying he'd been told what would happen in the preliminary hearing scheduled for the next day. He asked intelligent questions and seemed to understand her answers. She was relieved to hear that he'd been sober at the time he was stopped in Chestertown, and asked if he had any kind of record.

"No. Ms. Reagan? I heard a guy yelling a while ago, and I heard my name. Was that him? David Farquar?"

"I think we're past the formalities, Peter. I don't know how to label our relationship, but we have Fiona in common, and we'll always be family. Call me Grace, okay?"

His eyes filled, then he rubbed his face and mumbled, "Sounds good."

Grace said, "I heard the yelling, too. Yes, it was David. He wants to see you, but they won't let him because he isn't legally your parent or your attorney."

Peter looked pensive. "What do you think will happen now? Will I be able to go home? I mean, back to school. I get that there'll be some kind of trial, but I don't have to stay here until then, do I?"

"I'm afraid so, for now, anyway. But I'll try to get you released tomorrow. So far, no one is hospitalized as a result of what happened last night. The officer was only brushed by your car. She lost her balance and fell, but wasn't hurt—at least as far as I know. However, she may have visible bruises, and you can be sure she'll be in court tomorrow. The two cars that wrecked are probably totaled, but fortunately, none of the three people involved were injured, although odds are whiplash symptoms will show up in the coming days."

His groan sounded just like David's.

"Don't do that again," Grace said, her tone firm. "An inch or two closer to the officer and you'd be in prison for years, do you understand? And those people in the cars? Do you have any idea how lucky you'll be if they sue you only for whiplash? Which, by the way, is a real thing."

"Okay, jeez. I'm sorry. I just can't believe any of this is happening. I never meant to hurt anybody. I was just really scared, and I panicked."

"That's what you need to tell the judge tomorrow."

Peter looked uncomfortable. "Are you sure? You want me to say what I thought I saw at your office and why I ran? Won't that get him into trouble?"

She knew he was referring to David and was touched that the boy was struggling with what to call the father he'd just found. And his question was valid. Letting Peter testify that he'd thought his estranged father had killed Grace would be like swatting a fly with a hammer—unlikely to kill the fly, but very likely to cause serious collateral damage.

"Where were you going last night?" she asked, ignoring the matter for the moment. "Why were you in Chestertown?"

"I wasn't running away! I know that's what everyone thinks, but I wasn't. I was just riding around, trying to make sense of everything. It felt good to be away from everyone. God, I sound so stupid. I felt safe, okay? I felt safe out there in the dark."

"Safe from whom?"

"The cops. About the hydrant. I mean, I was freaked about seeing the body, too. I thought I was looking at you and I felt terrible. I thought he'd killed you because I came to see you. He and Bethany had awful fights. She told me about them so I'd know what kind of man he was. Is. Jeez, was that really him down the hall, yelling for me?"

Grace recognized the signs of prolonged stress. "When did you eat last?" she asked, pulling a protein bar and cheese crackers from her briefcase, then walking over to the door without waiting for an answer. The guard who appeared checked the food and agreed to let Peter eat, but stayed outside the door to watch through the window.

When they were alone again, Peter said, "I ran because I

thought you were dead and it was my fault. The hydrant was an accident. I shouldn't have driven off, but I was scared, and I didn't think it was a mistake until later. When the cop pulled me over last night, I knew she'd seen the damage to my taillight. I was doing okay until she went back to her car and I heard her talking, I guess on a radio, and then she was all like, 'Outta the car, keep your hands where I can see them,' and I knew it wasn't about the hydrant. I never meant to hit her. She stepped forward just as I started the car, and she had her hand on her gun. I should have stopped, I know, but I didn't. I didn't see those other cars coming toward us, either. I was just trying to get away."

He sounded sincere, but there was one other problem they had to hash out. Grace said, "I need you to trust me and answer my next question with the whole truth. I'm going to talk with the state's attorney before the hearing tomorrow. I'll try to get you released on bail, but I can't get hit with any surprises in that meeting. Other than this arrest, is there anything else on your record?"

He sat motionless on the other side of the smudged plexiglass window. After a moment, he nodded. "You'll need to know about the fire," he said. "But I promise it wasn't my fault."

CHAPTER SIXTEEN

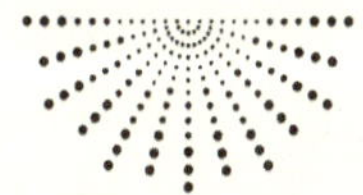

A simple Google search for Bethany and Peter Carlton brought up a string of articles. Grace hadn't had time to read them before she left home that morning, but the first headline gave her the pertinent facts. Peter's mother had died three months ago in a house fire Peter was initially suspected of starting. He hadn't been arrested and was eventually cleared, but not before intense public interest had driven news reports for several weeks.

Peter's account matched what she'd read, but he sounded wooden as he told her about Bethany's death. While he handled his emotions well outwardly, she thought he hadn't processed the tragedy internally. There was no time to help him with that now; she just hoped he could remain this calm in court.

She was sure David had the details. It explained why he'd ordered her to stay away from the boy. She wished she had a paralegal to assign the research that needed to be done and briefly considered calling a temp agency. The idea was discarded as soon as she considered the complications. She had to find permanent staff, and soon.

A check of the police station parking lot showed a black

Chevy Tahoe sporting heavy-duty antennae and dark windows parked between the Mallard Bay Police cruiser and Mac's pickup. Frustrated that her access to Mac was cut off by the state police detectives, she went on to her office, only to find a work crew blocking her entrance as they wrapped up the installation of new carpet on the stairs. It seemed Marjorie had worked one of her miracles. All traces of Mona Cutter's death had been erased.

Home, Grace decided. If she couldn't work, at least she could grab something to eat.

Just then, someone at the top of the stairs said, "Sorry to bother you guys again, but no one's up here."

She hadn't heard that voice in more than two years, but she knew who'd been in her office. The workers shifted around to let a large man make his way awkwardly down the steps. Henry Cutter. She felt queasy as she watched him stepping over the exact spot where his wife had died two days ago.

She moved out to the front porch and Henry followed, saying, "Well, this feels odd."

"I was just thinking the same thing," she said.

The last time they'd talked, she'd begged him to believe that she'd been assaulted by his cousin. She'd desperately needed help, but he'd hung up on her. Months later, after Bryce had been convicted of illegal drug distribution, she'd gotten a short note from Henry. Two words on a plain white note card: *I'm sorry.* She'd thrown it away.

"I guess you're still mad, and I don't blame you." He paused, then sighed when she didn't respond. "I was looking for you because we need to talk, if you can spare a minute. I'm sorry, of course, about everything that's happened between us, but is there somewhere we can go?" He gestured to Mosley's office door. "Maybe in there?"

"I'm sorry for your loss, Henry. And I'm fine. Thank you for asking." She watched with satisfaction as he turned red. "Say whatever you need to right here. It's not like I can hang up on you, right?"

"I deserve that." He looked around uneasily, then said, "Over there?" and pointed to the far corner of the porch, where a trellis bearing a budding morning glory vine offered a little privacy.

She gave him that concession, then folded her arms and waited, saying nothing to make his speech easier.

When he finally spoke, he sounded nervous. "Mr. Mosley says the kid that killed Mona is related to you?"

"Not right," she said, wishing she knew exactly how Cyrus had described the situation to Henry. She felt sure it hadn't been in such absolute terms. "Peter Carlton is my daughter's half brother, and I am representing him, but he didn't kill your wife."

"Well, of course you'd have to say that."

His assumption infuriated her. That and the unctuous look that said, *Come on, now. You can be straight with me.*

"Yes," she said, enjoying his hopeful look. "I do have to say that, because it's true."

As her words sank in, he looked alarmed. "But Grace, he killed Mona. He's the only one who could have."

"No. Peter's innocent. I wouldn't be talking with you if he weren't." Henry was the one who shouldn't be talking, but she guessed he must not have listened to that part of Cyrus's standard warning.

"But that only leaves Simone and Ashley," he protested. "Or some random stranger, other than your kid."

Her kid. She let it go. To some degree, that was how she was feeling about Peter. She'd known him less than a week, but they had a connection that felt real. "Ashley, her sister, and a stranger aren't the only possibilities," she said.

He recoiled as if she'd slapped him. "You can't think it was me!"

"It wouldn't be my first guess," she said, truthfully. Henry

Cutter was a timid soul, and loyal to a huge fault. But just because he didn't look, act, or give off the vibes of a killer didn't mean he wasn't one. She decided to push him a bit. "What do you think happened? You say you didn't do it, and I know Peter didn't. So, who do you think killed Mona?"

He floundered for words. "I . . . I don't know. I mean, all of us who knew her loved her. Are you sure, Grace? About this Peter? Mona had problems, she, uhm, she was addicted to painkillers. Bryce got her on them." He choked on his cousin's name.

Despite her own painful memories, she was reminded of Simone's story and all the other people who had been hurt by Bryce Cutter. "I'm sorry," she said, and meant it.

He glanced around, as if remembering they were still standing outside in the middle of town. "I keep thinking everyone's staring at me. It's happening all over again, the looks and whispers. Bryce was old news, and I was moving on and now . . ."

"Yeah, that's uncomfortable, isn't it? You know, when innocent people are scrutinized and their reputations damaged."

"But, Grace—"

"I asked who you thought killed your wife."

"She was on her way to your office," he said without hesitating. "And that boy was visiting you earlier. She could've been meeting him. You know, to buy, or maybe even sell, some pills."

Grace made herself hear him out. His theory would probably be brought out in court no matter who was charged with Mona Cutter's death, and it was better to know it now. As he talked, though, she found herself listening to the man who'd given her encouragement and helped her save Delaney House. A kind man who spent his free time with animal-rescue work, and always had a kind word and a helping hand. Her friend Henry described his broken marriage and told her Mona had agreed to an amicable divorce because they'd both moved on. He picked up speed and animation as he described his new life and a new woman he'd fallen in love with. A woman he wanted to marry.

She'd asked who he thought had killed Mona, but all he told her was that he was finally happy—as if that made it impossible for him to commit a crime as violent as murder. She let him talk uninterrupted and made note of all the reasons he'd want his drug-addict wife to be gone for good.

"It wasn't me, Grace. I swear it," he said, the passion fading from his voice when she didn't respond. "You know me," he pleaded. "You know I couldn't hurt anyone."

But he had. He had hurt Grace, and that memory lay between them, unresolved.

"I can't help you," she said, aware it was the same response she'd given Simone Lancer. Still, despite all that had happened, and how angry she still was with him, she thought he might be telling the truth. And if he were, the only suspects left were Ashley, her sister, and the always-popular Random Stranger. That thought nagged at her as she'd made her way up to her office, stepping carefully around the area where Mona had died. She was so preoccupied that it took her a minute to realize what was wrong at the top of the stairs.

Her office door was standing wide open.

CHAPTER SEVENTEEN

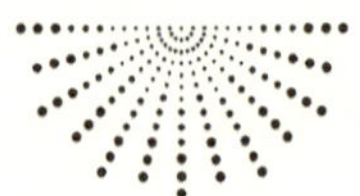

"You need to keep this locked," Mac said as he tested the latch on the outer door of Grace's office. He'd appeared as she was checking to make sure nothing in the office had been disturbed, and she'd been startled enough to tell him about the open door.

The day had been one long test of her patience and fortitude. Neither would last much longer, and she didn't want to lose her temper with him. He was right, of course, but telling him that the door had been locked when she left wouldn't lift the tension between them. Right before he walked in, she'd realized her phone was still on silent from her morning meetings and she'd missed two calls from him. He would have worried about her when she didn't respond. Unless, of course, he'd known what she was doing.

"I guess you've heard my news?" she asked, and got a curt nod for an answer. "I tried to call you before I left to meet with Peter, but I missed you," she said, and then because he looked tired and he didn't have a smile for her, she added "I'm sorry" to the hug she gave him. "Come sit down with me." She tugged him toward the bench that still looked like a church pew, no matter how many pillows she added.

He pulled away, gently, and tucked a stray curl behind her ear before walking over to examine the new draperies.

She forced herself to be patient. "Look, Mac—"

"I stopped by the house to check on you. Hallie and Avril told me where you'd gone. They're quite the comedy team, aren't they?"

"Like I said, I called, but you didn't answer, so I called dispatch, but you were unavailable, and I couldn't leave a message." She joined him at the window, but didn't touch him this time. "You wouldn't expect me to, would you? I mean, I could hardly say, 'Hey there, can you tell my boyfriend I have a new client and he's not gonna like who it is?'"

Her teasing fell flat. He looked at her for a half second too long before saying, "Place looks good. I didn't know everything was done."

She hadn't told him about Avril's outrageously expensive gifts or the decorating frenzy. Or about Ashley and her box. Now was definitely not the time to bring that up, not when he was already upset about Peter.

Her guilt ran smack up against a wall at that last bit. She was not, not ever again, going to ask for permission to do what she felt was right. It was her career, her work, her client, and she wasn't clearing her decisions with anyone. She started to tell him just that, but he turned to look at her, and her heart did that thing it did. Her anger died, leaving an awkward sadness in its place.

"I thought these looked familiar," he said, as he ran his fingers across the pale gold drapery fabric. "They used to be in Avril's front sitting room." He looked around the room and said, "I'm glad she gave you the good stuff."

"I'm glad you like it," she said, matching his formal tone.

He sighed. "We need to talk."

Well, there it was. She pushed back alarming thoughts of the many things he could say, all of which meant they were through. Unless . . . "Are you all right? You aren't sick, are you?" He certainly didn't look well. Why hadn't she asked that first? Ashley would have. "Tell me what's wrong," she said, more firmly this time.

"The state police are handling the investigation of the murder," he said.

This was not news, but Grace thought she knew what was coming.

"Desi is in charge at the moment, but this is a complicated situation. I could have handled things better if I'd had a heads-up from you before I got a cautioning call from the state's attorney. I was embarrassed, to say the least."

Of course, he would have been, she thought. Why hadn't she given his professional responsibilities more consideration? She doubted he'd ever been in a situation like that before she started complicating his life. "I'm sorry, but I did try to call, and I should have checked my phone for messages. Was it our SA who called you, or Kent County's?"

"It was Emily, and it wasn't official, but still."

Kingston County State's Attorney Emily Haskin, would have gotten all the details from her Kent County counterpart. One of her first calls would have been to Mac to get the ground rules straight with Mallard Bay's chief of police. When Peter was turned over for questioning in Mona Cutter's death, the nature of Mac's relationship with Grace, and hers to Peter, would be awkward, to say the least. Now she knew why he'd put distance between them for this conversation. It wasn't a problem that could be helped with affection.

"I couldn't tell him no, Mac. He's a kid. And he's in trouble. When you hear the whole story, you'll see I had no choice."

His smile looked as tired as the rest of him, but she was happy to see it.

"I'm not asking you to stop trying to save everyone, honey. But Peter Carlton is a suspect in a murder that occurred in my town. I'd just like a little warning when you're about to blow up my job, okay?"

It most definitely was not okay. "Mac, that's ridiculous! You can't expect me to check in with you like I'm a delinquent. Besides, Peter's being charged only in the Chestertown incident, which doesn't involve you. At most, he'll be a witness in the murder trial. When you hear everything—" She stopped, realizing that she was begging.

She got a raised eyebrow and a level stare. Then he said, "Are you telling me his actions last night have nothing whatsoever to do with him being outside this building during the time the murder could have occurred?"

"You know I can't talk about that," she said stiffly.

"Well, if he's caught up in the investigation of Mona's murder, will you represent him?"

"It depends. I can't leave him, Mac. He's Fiona's half brother. As long as he needs me, I won't abandon him. He didn't kill Mona Cutter."

This earned her a real, not so tired, smile. He crossed the space between them and pulled her down to sit beside him on the bench. "I love you." His voice was gentle as he took her in his arms. "But that doesn't make the hard parts of our life together go away. Emily and the investigative team will rightfully expect me to turn over any evidence or information I get in the course of my daily life with you. We can't live like that."

"So, we won't talk shop."

"Grace, we always talk shop. I'm upset, mostly, because I don't see an easy way to handle this. I'll have to move back home. At least Benny's mostly got the house enclosed now."

"No!" She pushed away but held on to his arms.

"I have to go sometime, and this seems like the smart thing to do for now. Besides, the renovations are at a critical point and I'd like to be there to see how things go."

She said nothing because she didn't want to overreact, or worse, cry. Couldn't they settle this issue without him bringing that damned house up? She pushed her welling anger aside. His house was the least of her problems. She'd known there'd be situations like this, in which her work and his would conflict, but she'd never guessed he'd react this way. It was so unfair, and she told him so, winding up with, "If we get married, are you going to leave me every time I have a criminal case and you don't like my client?"

The M word landed between them like a bomb. A flush crept up from under his collar. He'd brought marriage up in the beginning of their relationship, when Fiona was born, and again on New Year's Eve. Every time, she'd broken out in hives and put the conversation off. Now that she was ready and had elaborate plans to propose to him, she'd ruined everything by dropping the subject into the middle of an argument.

"Grace . . ." He drew her name out. "*Now* you want to talk about marriage? I feel as if I'm always one step behind you, and that's not working for me. I never know what you're going to do or say next."

She froze. For months she'd avoided the subject of a formal, public commitment. Had she waited so long, he'd had enough time to change his mind? Did he want his freedom, after all? She had to get out of this conversation before she made it worse. "You need to go. We'll talk later."

"No. We should talk—"

"No, we shouldn't," she said, getting up and straightening her clothes in order to have something to do with her hands besides scratching her arms. "You should go to your home and take care of whatever secret thing it is you're doing there. In the meantime, I'll do my job and try not to compromise you while I'm at it. When all of this with Peter is over, we'll see."

"See what?"

"Where we are."

Her voice was strong, and she knew it was because the words came from the core of her feelings. She loved him so much her heart was breaking, but ten years with David had taught her that refusing to acknowledge an oncoming disaster only made the pain worse when it hit. She couldn't change Mac. He would have to decide if she was worth the trouble she caused him. She wouldn't change herself for him. She was never doing that again. Still, she held her breath, willing him to come to her, to make everything all right.

He left without another word.

CHAPTER EIGHTEEN

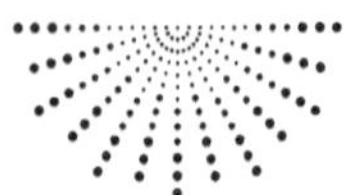

There was no time to contemplate the sad state of her love life. She barely had time to put cortisone cream on her arms before she was summoned to another argument by her almost partner.

"I've just gotten an earful from David Farquar," a furious Cyrus Mosley said. "He seems to think I have some control over what you do. I assured him you ran your own practice, and that I had no say in whom you represented. I didn't add that you hadn't told me and I knew only because Emily Haskins called me."

Grace wondered who else the SA had called, but she kept her thoughts to herself. The old lawyer's bald, freckled head had a gleam of perspiration, and his face was pink. She chose her words carefully, hoping to calm him down. "I guess David called you because he couldn't reach me. We had a tense conversation this morning, and I haven't taken his calls since. Everything happened very fast, but you were next on my list to talk with."

The list of angry people who thought she'd ignored them was growing.

Mosley was not appeased. "Why would you do it? Can't you

see the conflict? You can't represent our client's wife's killer! What are you thinking?"

Tired of standing in front of his desk like an errant child, she sat and waited for him to sink back into the huge leather swivel chair that always looked as if it were swallowing him. He remained upright, waiting for an explanation. To anyone else, she'd have said there could be no partnership if this was how things were going to be handled, but this man had acted as her grandparent from the day she was born. She wouldn't hurt him, but despite how her last stubborn stance had turned out, she couldn't back down, either.

"Peter is a teenager, Cy, and he asked me for help. He isn't charged with anything to do with Mona Cutter's death."

"But—"

"And he didn't kill her."

Mosley looked at her for a few moments, then his shoulders sagged. "You're sure?"

"The evidence is strong in his favor. I can't prove it absolutely at the moment, but I believe he's innocent."

"Henry will require extended representation, then."

She nodded. "So will Ashley and her sister."

Mosley jotted a few notes, then sighed.

Trying to lighten the situation, she said, "Please tell me you have an alibi."

Her weak joke fell flat, but eventually he said, "Golf course. At least three people talked to me, and two of us went from there to dinner. Marjorie locked up early and a friend picked her up, so she's probably in the clear, but just barely."

Grace didn't tell him that Peter's testimony would place the time of the attack within minutes of Marjorie's departure. It felt strange to keep anything work related from Cyrus, but she had no choice. "Well, Mac and I were together, and so were Avril and Hallie. Aidan had a job after mine, so he's okay."

She expected him to go off into one of his how-did-we-come-to-this speeches, but instead, he said, "Right. Well, we both know where we stand. Do you agree that for the duration of our conflict, we'll operate independently?"

She'd come to the same conclusion, and she knew she wasn't ready. How could she handle Peter's defense alone? She needed administrative help, and someone to cover the other clients who expected her to be functional on Monday. But she said, "Yes. And I am sorry we're starting like this, but I can't turn him away."

"I at least have Marjorie. How will you manage, m'dear? Under the circumstances, I don't see how we can share her."

"I can't think of any circumstances where we could share her, Cy." This got her a weak smile. He knew as well as she did The Bat was his gatekeeper, not hers. "I'll find a secretary. In the meantime, I'll limp along. And I hope you'll understand that I need to have the locks changed on my office door. Marjorie opened it up for the carpet installers to replace the threshold, and Henry had a walkabout up there before I arrived this morning." She waved his apology away, saying they were all under stress, then added, "I know this kind of haphazard operation isn't what you had in mind for our partnership."

"Au contraire," he said as he walked her out of the office. "This is exactly what I expected, but I thought I'd have a week or two to adjust."

She hugged him and said, "I'm just upstairs."

"Please be careful, Grace."

The trek back upstairs was a slow one. She was on her own. No Mac and no Cyrus. She wouldn't be surprised if Fiona packed her bags and moved over to Avril's with Hallie and the dogs. She gave herself a mental shake as she stepped over the spot where Mona Cutter had died. She needed to work on a new game plan, and she needed it now.

It was only three thirty, but Grace felt as if it had been a week since she'd awakened to David's and Mac's angry voices. Her life had been altered twice in the last few hours, and now she was numb. If bad things came in threes, she was due another disaster before the day was finished with her. Trying to stay positive, she told herself that at least she didn't have to rush home, clean house, and try to pull off a steak dinner and marriage proposal, but that had her dashing away tears.

Retreating to her own office, she stood by the window looking out across the rooftops of Mallard Bay and tried to process the events of the last few days. David's news was shocking, Peter's arrest potentially disastrous, but knowing Mac was angry with her at the same time Ashley was chasing him was horrible. Why couldn't the blasted woman just go away?

Because you waited too long and she has the perfect opportunity.

"I trusted you, Mac," she whispered into the empty room.

He was one of the few people who would know what a huge step that trust had been for her. Her never-married mother had been a living, breathing warning against permanent attachments. Men were to be enjoyed as friends and lovers, but no commitments. Julia Reagan had despised David, but Grace was sure Mac would have charmed her. Before today, anyway.

Her mother had summed up her advice on romantic relationships in one sentence: "Keep the upper hand, and never be the one who loves the most."

"Well, that ship has sailed," Grace muttered. Apparently, she not only loved the most, she was only one of the women who did.

The ruby on her finger sparkled in the sunlight, catching her eye just as it had weeks before when she'd seen it in a jeweler's window in downtown Annapolis. She'd shown just enough interest for Mac to notice, and as she'd hoped, the ring was his birthday gift to her. The ring and nothing else. Now she felt like a fool. She must have missed some sign that he was cooling off.

She tilted her hand, studying the ruby. She was finally ready for marriage. So, of course, Ashley was back in the picture.

"Over my dead body," she said out loud.

It didn't help at all.

Mac's things were gone when she got home. A note on the kitchen table said he would call in the morning. She felt bad about the position she'd put him in, and even sorrier for herself. They'd have to work something out, or one of them would be looking for a new job, and that was the happiest outcome she could imagine at the moment.

She needed a break from the worry. She might not have the same support system as when she left home that morning, but she wasn't without resources. She couldn't discuss Peter's situation and didn't want to talk about her suspended relationship with Mac, but that still left an alarming number of issues that required input from rational people who didn't have a boatload of trauma to work through.

Fortunately, Avril and Hallie were quick to agree to dinner, and her cousin, Niki, insisted that they all come to Delaney House. Grace didn't miss living in the house she'd restored as much as she'd thought she would, but visiting always filled her with a sense of accomplishment and awe, and something she'd wanted all her life—family history. Her family history. Plus, it had been ages since their last girls night.

As the house had emerged from its state of near ruin, stories of its history of her mother's family emerged. At its core, the Delaney family's story was a universal one of love and loyalty, greed and selfishness, and mistakes. So many mistakes. There were still a few family members left, but only one that Grace was tied to without reservation.

Niki stood in the doorway of the grand old mansion and held her arms out for Fiona.

"Here's your mini-me," Grace said, handing her blonde baby over to her equally blonde cousin, and giving herself a moment to enjoy the thrill she felt every time she stepped over the threshold.

She was responsible for the building's restoration, but many people had worked to make her dream come true, and she was grateful for all of them. From the soaring three-story ceiling and cantilevered staircase in the entry hall to the state-of-the-art, Victorian-style kitchen, every space in the house had been brought back from near ruin to once more be filled with life. Thanks to Niki's tenacity and hard work, The Inn at Delaney House was a successful enterprise, and it always made Grace happy.

Niki gave her a tour of the changes she'd made to several of the first-floor rooms, and some of her tension eased as she admired new furniture arrangements that opened up the twin parlors for an upcoming party. As she relaxed in the atmosphere of the beautiful space, she remembered a time when this level of success with the derelict house would have been enough to make her happy. Now she had that success plus a beautiful baby, and she was restarting her professional life on her own terms. She was blessed with more than she'd ever dreamed of having, and she was surrounded by friends and family in this little town.

She knew it wasn't enough. Not without Mac.

CHAPTER NINETEEN

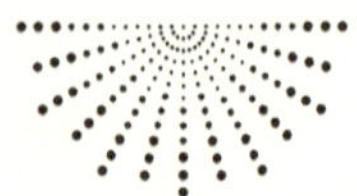

Dinner was served in the kitchen around a big pine table that had been in the family for generations. Niki had been testing the weekend party menu, and presented them with Maryland fried chicken and gravy, fresh asparagus, and beaten biscuits. Grace, who was the designated tester of Niki's culinary experiments, pronounced the meal perfect. The next hour passed with laughter, friends talking over one another, and good food. But despite the happy surroundings and her upbeat company, Grace couldn't keep her mind off the men in her life.

As usual, Avril didn't let her get away with it. As she topped off her glass of wine, she said, "I enjoy a good mystery as much as the next person, but this murder is too close to home. Tell us what's happening."

Grace repeated the details that were public knowledge and braced herself for a round of "poor Ashley," since that's how the victim's aunt was being referred to all over town. She was relieved when Hallie went in a different direction.

"I'll ask the dumb question. How do they know she was murdered? Couldn't she have tripped on the stairs somehow?"

The image of the corpse on the steps flashed through Grace's mind, but she pushed it away. "The medical examiner will have to make that determination, but until then, everyone who was in the vicinity at the time is of interest to the police."

The sanitized answer was met with skepticism, and Hallie changed the subject. "So, if they don't know for sure it's murder, why does David's son have to go to court tomorrow?"

Since both of Peter's legal problems would be in the morning newspaper, Grace briefly explained about the fire hydrant accident, but downplayed events in Chestertown.

Avril said, "Accident, my foot! And I don't mean the hydrant —anyone could have backed over it. I've lobbied for years to have it moved."

Grace and Niki grinned at each other. Avril had hit the hydrant herself on more than one occasion, and she scolded them for interrupting her.

"That boy could have killed the police officer in Chestertown, as well as the people in the cars he caused to wreck. If he wasn't so young, I'd say put him in jail."

Grace tried to keep her voice mild as she said. "He's my client, Avril. I can't discuss it, but you might consider the recent turns his life has taken. Anyone can panic and do something stupid when they're at a low point."

Avril looked thoughtful, and Niki jumped in to change the subject to David's new family. Grace's description of David's new wife and family soon had everyone chattering again.

"I can't believe David married some child named Kissy," Niki said, grinning as Hallie and Avril laughed at her deliberate mispronunciation.

Grace wagged a finger at them and said, "Now, now, ladies. Her name is Krissy, short for Kristen, and she's tall, gorgeous, and about twenty-six or -seven, if I had to guess. Her family sounds as if they own half of Louisiana, and she brought her own household staff with her. She fired David's nanny the first day they were here."

Niki looked shocked. "You mean we might actually like her?"

"Well, so far, Mac and I do. Very much. If she turns out to be as half as nice as she seemed last night, we've hit the jackpot. She wants our girls to be close, too. Think about it, Nik. I might actually have someone in David's house who I can trust with Fiona."

"So. We might love her," Niki said, then paused with a fork full of Smith Island cake halfway to her mouth. "But then, why did she marry David? How smart can she be?"

"I wouldn't go there," Avril said.

Grace started laughing. "Probably at least as smart as we are, Nik. I had a baby with him and you had a crush on him for a year."

"Did not!" Niki squealed.

"Did, too," Avril said, ending the subject. "We don't have time for that, anyway. Grace needs our help."

Everyone looked at her expectantly, and Grace sighed. "I really did want a girls night, and I didn't know it was a recipe-testing day, either, but I'm so glad it is."

Niki accepted another round of compliments, then told Grace to move on to the rest of the story.

"I need a secretary and a paralegal, and I need them now. I've been running ads since January, but only twenty people responded, and most of them wanted to work from home. Those who were qualified and came in for interviews wanted ridiculous salaries. So, in short, I'm on my own, and I'm hoping one of you knows someone who'd fit the bill, even temporarily."

Avril stood and started clearing the table, snapping, "Sit down," to Grace when she tried to help. "No wonder you're burned out. You and Niki are a pair of workaholics. It's good to stay busy, but you two overdo everything. I'm not office material, but I can pick up dishes."

"I'm fine," Grace said, refusing to relinquish her hold on the salad bowl. She noticed Niki was watching them with amusement.

"Is that why you have dark circles under your eyes?" her cousin asked. "You're taking on too much, and you haven't even started the partnership with Cy yet."

"Oh, stop being disingenuous," Grace said as she sat back down. "Who's been complaining—Cy or Mac?"

"Lee McNamara would never," Avril said, firmly. "And Cy wouldn't talk about your work. You should know that about both of them."

"Who blabbed?"

"Simone and Ashley."

Fiona began to fuss. Without being asked, Hallie dug a bottle of distilled water out of the diaper bag and picked the baby up.

"I guess you've already told her?" Grace asked as they watched the Baby Whisperer settle in the rocking chair that was tucked into a corner near the fireplace.

Avril shrugged. "She was with me when Ashley called and told me you'd refused to help Simone."

Grace groaned and put her head in her hands. "So that's how she's playing it. She's a vicious, vindictive . . . "

"Oh, stop it. You've never liked her," Avril snapped. "The important thing is, did you tell Lee?"

"Of course. And so did Ashley and believe me, our stories couldn't have sounded more different."

Avril came to wrap a bony arm around Grace's shoulders. "It's a misunderstanding, and it will blow over. We all love Henry, but what he did to you wasn't right, and Ashley couldn't have known or she'd never have asked you to talk to him."

"Sure," Grace said, trying to roll past a subject that would send them into another argument. "Now about the staff I need—"

"You need to clear up things between you and Ashley before

you do anything else. Tell her you don't wish her any ill will, but you can't get involved with Henry."

"I told her sister, and I'm not discussing the matter with Ashley. Case closed. Now, about the office, don't you know anyone competent who wants a good job?"

Avril leaned in and gave her the stink eye. "I know a woman who has a wonderful man that she's ignoring. And I know another woman with a big mouth who wants him. *That's* what I know." When the room fell silent, she added, "Meanwhile, how many people do you think Ashley's repeated her tale of woe to? You can come up with some way to make a friend out of her. Do it."

"That's ridiculous!" Grace said. She was thoroughly sick of the subject, but the astonished look on everyone's face shut her down. She'd made the same rude remark to Mac earlier and was ashamed of that, too. Softening her voice, she apologized. "I've had a rough few days, which is no excuse, but it is the truth. Ashley has behaved badly, beyond what you know, and that's all I'm saying about that. Believe her, or believe me, but I'm not getting into it."

Always the peacemaker, Niki said, "C'mon, now. Grace is as dumb as a stump about men, but she's not stupid enough to let Ashley take Mac, and he's not stupid enough to pick the wrong woman."

"Oh, thanks for that," Grace said. Then she felt a laugh coming on. A laugh or hysteria, she wasn't sure which, but when it proved to be contagious, the moment eased, then passed, with all four of them smiling.

Avril wasn't finished, but she gave Grace a speculative look before saying, "You do know, don't you, that Lee's doing everything he can think of to make you happy?"

"What do you mean?" Grace asked. She was out of mea culpas and didn't have another apology left in her. "Are you saying I should marry him?"

Avril looked irritated again, but said only, "I think it's time for us to go and let you get that baby home to bed."

Hallie looked up and said, "But you do think she should marry him, right?"

"I'm sure Grace remembers exactly what I said the last time we discussed this, and she doesn't need any more advice from me."

"No." Grace said, reaching out to pat her friend's hand. "My memory isn't as good as yours, but as I recall, you think I have an unhealthy fixation on Mac's first wife and I take it out on Ashley." Her neck started itching. It was all she could do not to scratch the spots that would soon be hives if she kept talking about Mac, marriage, and the women he'd loved before her.

Avril laughed. "Well, that's an improvement. You're calling Meri his first wife. And yes, I think it's time you moved her into that role. But I also told you that people arrive in our lives when we need them. Ashley isn't here just to irritate you, you know."

Grace said there was a long list of people she was sure had no purpose at all in her life except to boost her purchases of anti-histamine.

"That's it?" Hallie said. "I mean, he gave you a ring for your birthday. I thought you wanted to get together tonight to give us some news."

"It's just a ring," Grace said quickly, then felt ashamed at downplaying the ruby.

Despite everyone's efforts to resurrect the earlier good mood, the party wrapped up quickly after that.

Once she and Fiona were home, it took Benadryl and cold compresses to get the hives under control, but she still dreamed about a wedding in which she wore saggy yoga pants under a wrinkled wedding gown and Mac was a no-show. When she woke in the early hours of Friday morning to find herself alone, the dream felt like an omen for her future. She didn't know what to do, and there was no one else to turn to for help.

CHAPTER TWENTY

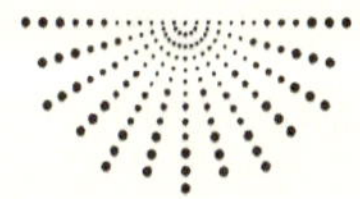

Since she was up early, anyway, Grace used the time to go online and order new, non-baggy slacks and several non-mom tops, none of which were sweatshirts. When Hallie arrived at eight to babysit, she found her employer ankle deep in a pile of clothes. Fiona lay on a blanket a few feet away from her mother, rocking furiously as she tried to get her knees in position to crawl.

"Goodwill donations?" Hallie asked, eyeing the mess.

"Trash can," Grace answered. "These passed Goodwill's standards a while back." She waited for some retort about her fashion sense, or lack of it, but Hallie had grown up with two mothers and an assortment of younger sisters. Apparently, she knew when to wade into another woman's clothes crisis, and when to scoop up the baby and head to another room.

Grace was ready to leave, wearing a dress that wasn't quite right for the office or for court, when Hallie asked for a promotion to personal assistant.

"What?" Grace was distracted, trying to convince herself she could make it all day in a pair of heels when she was already losing the argument with her feet.

Hallie took full advantage of her employer's lack of attention. "You said you need help, and I know how to do a lot. I could do a lot more than just care for Fiona. Although," she added quickly, "the baby would always be my priority. You haven't changed your mind about having her at the office, have you? I mean, this murder will be cleared up before long, right?"

Grace reluctantly paused at the bedroom door and looked back at the girl. Today's tattoo was a large Celtic cross with a flowering vine entwined around and through it. "You're already my assistant," she told Hallie. "I couldn't work if you and Avril weren't caring for Fiona."

"But she sleeps a lot. I can type and do research and stuff. And"—there was a dramatic pause—"I could shop for you. Groceries, clothes, shoes. I know you hate it, and I could do it for you. I shopped for Mom and Aunt Whitney and the kids all the time. And before you say you don't dress anything like them, remember I was shopping with their individual tastes in mind."

Grace shook her head. She had a vivid recollection of the Overton women's wardrobes.

Undaunted, Hallie argued on. "For instance, that jacket you have on makes your outfit too cocktail-y."

"Is that so?" Grace tried to sound insulted, but she'd already decided the same thing.

"Yeah." Hallie tossed around the rejected clothes that covered every surface in the bedroom and pulled a short sapphire blue sweater out a pile. "Try this, but flip the neck up like a shawl collar. And put this on." She held out a hammered silver link belt.

"A belt on this dress? On this waistline?"

"You wouldn't believe how many times I've dressed a pregnant or postpartum mother. I know what I'm doing."

After an exaggerated look at her watch, Grace shrugged off her jacket and took the sweater and belt. A moment later, she stared at herself in the mirror and said, "I can't afford to give you a raise."

"You buy lunches, and we'll call it even."

"You'll have to dress better when you work in the office," Grace said as she admired her newly visible waist. A closer inspection also showed that even with their perpetual shadows, her eyes sparkled next to the blue sweater, which somehow now looked like a jacket with the transformed dress.

Hallie hesitated. "Define 'better.'"

"Clean, plain jeans, no holes. No artistic renderings. No T-shirts. No visible tattoos of an offensive nature."

"I have never—"

"Last Friday?"

"You're too sensitive," Hallie said, but she was smiling. "Deal. I'll start today with this." She waved a hand at the piles of rejected clothes. "When I get things straight here, we can talk about the office. But before you go, wear these instead of those heels."

Grace obediently slipped on bone leather espadrilles, checked the mirror, and tossed the heels she'd been wearing to the back of the closet. There was only a quick moment of hesitation as she picked up her briefcase. Then she checked the mirror again and decided Hallie was seventeen going on a very fashion-conscious forty.

She kissed her baby and left the house feeling more hopeful. Later today, she'd be in court for the first time in months, but she was dressed for the part and knew she could pull it all off. That semi-Zen state continued for nearly three hours until David blasted through the door of her office.

"What are you doing here?" he demanded. "Why aren't you camped out in the state's attorney's office in Centreville until he releases my son?"

"I just finished a long teleconference with him."

"Has he been released?"

"No, I—"

David cut her off and began a tirade. Grace ignored him and went back to work. When he landed in the chair across from her, she looked up and said, "We can argue about any number of subjects, but you won't win. I have about fifteen minutes before my next meeting. Choose your topic accordingly."

"You're representing Peter."

"I am."

"He won't see me."

She waited.

"All right. I'll hire you. You'll have full use of my firm and staff. The boy doesn't have to know."

"Don't do this, David. Please."

"What? Act like a father?"

"No. Embarrass yourself. I work for Peter, and I'm not breaching his trust."

Frustration had never been a good look for him. "You know your face could freeze like that," she said, throwing him off-balance and, she hoped, resetting his attitude.

After a moment of icy silence, he said, "Let's be reasonable. I've checked everything out, and my son needs me and my connections. I can clear all his issues up in a day, two tops. I'm asking you to put your ego aside and let me do what's best for him."

It occurred to her he took every opportunity to refer to Peter as his son. Once, she would have thought it was his trademark arrogance to make sure everyone knew what and how much he possessed. But now that she had a child of her own, she knew the affectation for what it was. The first time she'd spoken of Fiona as her daughter, she'd teared up from the overwhelming emotion of that simple act. Even now, she rarely said the words without a smile. "My daughter" announced an unbreakable bond. David had lost Peter's childhood years. Suddenly, pity overrode everything else she felt.

"I'm not stopping you," she said. "If you can clear everything up, have at it. That's all any of us want. It doesn't matter who gets Peter over the finish line."

"He's refused to see me or talk to me."

"I can't help you with that."

"I won't lose him, Grace."

"You can't keep what you never had. He doesn't know you as a parent. Give him some time. Try to be his friend first."

"I'm his father."

She shook her head. "Only in the biological sense. He's still very angry about the way things ended between you and Bethany. That's going to take time and talk between you to heal."

David cocked his head to one side as he studied her in a way she knew all too well. "What do you mean? What did he tell you happened between his mother and me?"

Grace resisted the urge to kick herself. She couldn't tell him what the boy thought he'd seen when he'd found Mona. She might have to sacrifice David in order to clear Peter as a suspect, but she couldn't warn him. She could, however, possibly fill in a big blank in Peter's narrative. "He insists Bethany Carlton isn't his mother. Why are you so sure she is?"

Once again, anger transformed his face, and she had to force herself not to flinch. Even if she wasn't afraid of him, he still had the power to unnerve her.

"You've just been waiting to hit me with that, haven't you?" he said. "Are you planning to call me to the witness stand and humiliate me? Maybe you're going to tell the world I thought I was sterile and went around dropping baby bombs until you showed me how wrong I was? What do you think that will do to our children?"

Ignoring the provocation, she repeated her question. "How do you know for sure Peter is Bethany's biological son? Or, for that matter, that you are really his father?"

"So that's it." A slow smile did nothing to warm his expression. "You can't for a moment believe I would accept a child as my own without proof. Proof of my parentage and that of the mother's. Don't push me, Grace. You should know better than that," David said. "Fiona is only one of three, and there's no guaranteed inheritance for any of them. Besides, if you recall, your daughter already got her money. It's sitting in that trust fund you set up."

She'd gotten the answer she needed. David, as she'd expected, had somehow determined he was Peter's biological father, and that Bethany was his mother. It was time to wrap up and get on the road.

"I'm not getting into any of this. I have a meeting." She bent to pack her briefcase with files and her notes, but didn't tell him the meeting was a prehearing conference for his son.

David snorted and got to his feet. "Are you enjoying this?"

"You're the one with the vicious streak. Not me. You know better than that." Then, hating what she had to do, she said, "He's going to need bail."

"Done."

When he was gone, she called Niki. "That good-looking guy you dated last year? The one who owns a security firm over in Wilmington? Are you still in touch?"

She packed up her briefcase while her cousin revisited the physical attributes of a man she'd eventually decided was dull.

"Okay, okay," Grace broke in. "You said he was rich. Is that because he's good at his job? I need to hire an investigator."

She needed in-depth background reports on Peter and his parents, individually and collectively. She could use Peter's belief in Bethany's claims of abuse to argue for his release on bail, but to exonerate him, she needed the truth and had no time to do the necessary digging herself. Cut off from the resources of what was supposed to be her own law firm, as well as any of the investigators she'd worked with from David's firm, she was flying blind, and that had to end. If there was anything out there that could hurt Peter, she needed to know now.

CHAPTER TWENTY-ONE

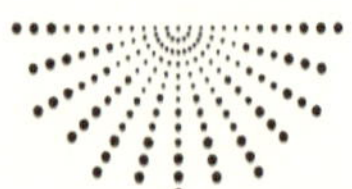

Grace had requested a prehearing meeting with the judge and the Kent County assistant state's attorney. With as little detail as possible, she explained who and what Peter thought he had seen on the staircase leading to her office and why he'd been so upset he'd left the scene of an accident—three accidents. She wrapped up with their complicated family relationship and after some discussion, got almost everything she'd asked for. She'd known going in that bail would be steep, but she hoped David wouldn't back out when he heard the number from the judge's mouth. At least neither the judge nor the assistant state's attorney had any interest in dragging David's name through the public records—yet.

In lawyer time, the details were settled fairly quickly. In sitting-on-hard-benches-in-a-courtroom time, people waiting for the hearing to start lost an hour and a half that they'd never get back. It was an uncomfortable scene when court was finally convened.

David sat several rows behind her, and Mac stood at the back of the courtroom with Desi Marbury and her partner, Detective

Wes Everly. All of them watched Peter and Grace as she switched their microphones off before whispering instructions to her client.

"Stand up when I tell you. Don't say anything except yes or no to the judge and call him 'Your Honor.' You'll be released, but I had to tell them why you ran when you saw the body. Don't object to any of the rules or restrictions the judge gives you, or you'll have to stay in the detention center until the next hearing. Can you do it?"

Peter's eyes widened, but he nodded.

Grace heard his sigh and hoped it was one of relief. She didn't want a family showdown wrecking the arrangements she'd negotiated in the judge's chambers. "One more thing. And this is crucial. Do not react when I discuss bail or payments. Not if you want to walk out of here today."

Again, he nodded, but this time, he looked over his shoulder at David.

When she addressed the court, she explained Peter had come to see her, then thought he was looking at her body through the window. He'd run because he'd been frightened and that fear had increased to overwhelming panic when he was stopped by the police a few hours later and ordered out of his car. She described his remorse for not obeying the officer's instructions and said he would cover all medical costs and property damage for the officer and the other individuals involved in the ensuing accidents. She wrapped her statement up with the assurance that he would finish his senior year of high school with honors in a few weeks, but could graduate only if he were not incarcerated.

Citing a request from the Kingston County SA, the judge delayed her ruling on the plea until Peter could be deposed in the investigation of Mona Cutter's death. Despite the fact that David posted his bond, Peter stalked off in a near run when David approached them outside the courthouse. Grace didn't follow.

They'd already agreed to meet later, and she knew he was at the limit of what he could handle.

David watched him leave, then said, "My people are contacting the police department and the civilians involved in the accidents. I'll take care of their expenses and settle everything."

At some point, he would learn why Peter was so angry, but for now, there was nothing more to say. The man Grace watched walk away from her looked older than the David she knew so well. She'd been furious and disgusted with him a few short hours before, but now she found herself hoping they would all make it out of this situation without any more damage.

Right now, that didn't seem possible.

Exceedingly awkward was how Grace described the experience to Avril and Hallie over dinner. They were having a broccoli-and-shrimp casserole and a large salad comprising all the leftovers in Grace's vegetable bin. She was touched that they were keeping her company for a second night, since Mac was still a no-show. He'd left the courthouse with Desi and Wes and hadn't answered the call she'd made on the way back from Chestertown. She'd told herself it was because he was with other people, but five hours had passed and she hadn't heard from him.

However, David had called twice, and she had three messages from him that she'd have to answer at some point. He was demanding a meeting with Peter. She couldn't make that happen, but she could delay delivering that news.

"You certainly lucked out with Daddy Big Bucks showing up," Avril said, still digging for details. "It would be bad luck to start your new practice with a nonpaying client."

As much as Grace hoped to someday be able to take on any client, regardless of their ability to pay, she was in no position to do it now. She said, "I'm sure it made a difference to the judge. Local support is always a bonus."

"David is local? Since when?"

"Since he switched his primary address to Kingston County last December. Lower taxes here, you know."

"It's always about money with him," Avril said, grousing. "On to your other problems—where does that leave you and Cy? Who's taking care of Henry and Ashley?"

Grace was glad her own mouth was full, so she couldn't let her initial reaction fly. She settled for a shrug and kept eating.

"I hadn't thought about them," Hallie said. "Grace, how are you working that out with Mr. Mosley? Is he upset with you?" Her earnest expression took the sting from the comment.

"Yes," Grace admitted. "But, despite how new the relationship is, Peter is Fiona's brother, well, half brother."

"Of course," Hallie agreed. "I don't like all my relatives, but family is family." She gave her guardian an apologetic glance and got a wink in return before Avril turned on Grace.

"Cy is family, too."

Grace knew this wouldn't be the last time she'd have to explain her choices. "Yes, he is. And I'm handling work for him that isn't related to this. What else would you have me do? Peter won't let David or his firm represent him. Besides, you know I can't represent Henry, and he doesn't need me, he's Cy's client. Ashley and Simone need their own attorneys. Ashley wouldn't want me, anyway."

Avril chewed for a while, but didn't give the subject up. "You don't know this boy, but you do know Cy needs you."

Grace pushed her plate away. She was full, but she wasn't sure if it was with dinner or frustration. "Big-picture time. If things go badly for Cy, I can help him pick up the pieces later. If things go badly for Peter, his life is ruined, and I will one day have to explain to a grown-up Fiona why I didn't do everything I could to protect her brother."

Avril said, "So you think Peter did it."

"No. I think . . ." Grace faltered, swamped with emotions. "It would be easy for an attorney who didn't sympathize with Peter's situation to let him slide into the correctional system. And a boy like him might not get out." She had to stop. The preliminary background report on Peter had come in just as she was leaving work, and she had no doubt the police and the court knew as much or more than she did. She choked up every time she thought of what David's son had been through.

Avril and Hallie were silent as they waited for her to start again.

"He has a lot of anger—anyone who lived through what he has would be angry at the world. But he's also scared. That's not a good combination. Another attorney might think he might be better off in a cell pending trial, if the grand jury doesn't go his way. I believe he's innocent, and incarceration could finish him off."

The room was quiet until Avril reached out to pat Grace's shoulder. "What can I do?"

"Be patient with me," Grace said. "I might have to bring Peter here to live with me if I can't work anything else out. I'm worried about him staying at school, and apparently, so is the headmaster. He talked to Peter today, right after court, and asked him to find other housing. Can you imagine? It's one more wound for the boy, and all of it is on top of his mother's death. It's a terrible situation."

"But here?" Avril glanced around the small kitchen that barely held the three of them.

"He's not allowed back in the classroom or in school activities, so his classes will be virtual. I'm sure he won't live with David, and I don't see him being allowed to stay indefinitely in the school's guesthouse, which is their solution to segregate him from the other students."

Avril looked thoughtful as she shoveled in another mouthful of shrimp. "It won't work," she said around the food. "This place is too small, and there's Mac to consider."

Grace's throat tightened again. "He's decided to spend more time at home. I would have told you last night, but it had been a long, bad day."

Avril and Hallie exchanged glances, then Avril said, "You don't know how this Peter is around babies. He can stay with me, and Hallie can move in here. There's no sense tempting a teenage boy's hormones."

"Hey!" Hallie protested before dissolving into giggles. "I guess that was a compliment. Kinda."

"Backhanded compliments are her specialty," Grace said. "It's a generous offer, Avril, but let's see if we even need to do that. This time last week we didn't even know Peter. Besides, he's eighteen, and I can't control what he does or where he lives. I don't know what kind of help he'll need or if he'll accept any at all. Let's wait and see what happens. Meanwhile, I know tomorrow's Saturday, but could one of you babysit Fiona for a few hours? I have a meeting."

She didn't share the details of Peter's upcoming interview with the MSP. She knew plans to help him would be hatched later in Avril's kitchen, and she wished she could be there, too, conspiring with her friends over cups of tea and a bag of Oreos.

Right now, her client needed help from all quarters, even one with a zombie pantry.

CHAPTER TWENTY-TWO

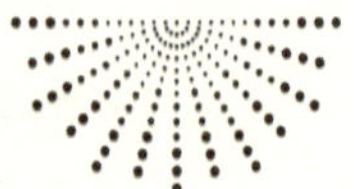

After a construction meeting with Benny, Mac stopped for barbecue chicken and fries on his way back to the station. Desi Marbury had said she was stopping by the department after her shift, and he intended to buy her goodwill with dinner. His hands were full of food bags when he walked into his small corner office to find Aidan Banks with his hands full of the detective sergeant. If the barbecue hadn't been from Three Pig's Deli, it might have been dropped on the floor.

As it was, the three of them just stared at one another until Desi cracked up laughing at the men's expressions. She rubbed a smear of lip gloss off Aidan's bottom lip, and said, "Breathe, hon. He had to find out sometime." Looking back at the still-stunned chief of police, she added, "I'm technically off the clock, sir. Didn't expect to find my guy here, but it was a nice surprise."

"Yes, it was," Aidan agreed, then realized he was still holding her around the waist and snatched his hands back. "You two need to talk, so I think I'll go find us some dinner. Meet you back at my house?" he asked Desi. With a sideways look at Mac's food, he added, "I'll bring barbecue."

"Congratulations?" Mac said tentatively when Aidan was gone. He didn't mean it, and he knew Desi could hear the disapproval in his voice. It wasn't any of his concern, he reminded himself as he set the bags down and checked for messages on the department's call monitor. He had practically raised both Aidan and Desi, professionally speaking, and he couldn't imagine a worse combination of personalities. He also knew it was ridiculous that he felt betrayed.

Desi's throat clearing made him look up. "You and Grace are actually to blame for me ending up with him, you know."

Now he felt betrayed and insulted. "You decided you'd look sedate next to our scandal?"

"No, I decided to try to be as brave as Grace is."

He wasn't sure he heard her correctly until she continued.

"You're a great guy, sir. And I think you know how much I look up to you." The normally sarcastic detective seemed to search for her next words. "But it's not easy being in a relationship with a cop. Only other cops understand us, and those matches fall apart more often than not. Grace took a chance on you. You're in a dangerous job and you're older, and you were both with other people. But anybody can see how much she loves you. I decided if she could go after what she wanted, even when she was pregnant with another guy's baby, I could get up my nerve and see if Aidan was interested. So, I did. And he was."

She didn't end with "so there," but she may as well have.

Mac shook his head. He'd thought he was the only person besides David Farquar who appreciated what Grace had given up to be with him. Her dreams of travel and freedom only started the list. She had taken a lot of criticism from the community, partly because she was an outsider, but mostly because Ashley was very popular. He'd heard that the die-hard romantics still felt cheated out of a wedding starring their favorite vet and the chief of police.

"I'll get used to this. You and Aidan are special to me, and you both deserve to be happy. Now, give me a quick rundown on the investigation and get on home." He hoped she recognized his carefully worded response for the peace offering it was.

She smiled and said, "Thank you. We argue a lot, but it's fun. We—"

"Stop," he interrupted. "You can ask Aidan, I don't talk personal lives, Desi."

"Sure you do." She looked confused. "You're always giving advice, and . . ."

"Not about personal stuff, so knock it off."

"Oh, you mean—"

"I mean, knock it off."

"Okay." Her smile faded. "I have to tell you a couple of things that aren't funny in the least." She checked her watch and picked up a file folder, holding it out to him. "The medical examiner's office says the preliminary cause of the Cutter woman's death is traumatic brain injury from a direct blow to the left side of the head."

"What's the call?"

"Manslaughter. Possibly murder. Whichever, it wasn't an accident. The head wound was determined to be the primary cause of death, but how it came about is interesting. There are two injuries to the same area of the victim's skull." Marbury tapped the red top knot on her own head. "Only one occurred at the time of death, but that one might have been the result of a fall on the steps. The medical examiner is being pretty closemouthed, though. Says something's off, and he's waiting on test results."

"Something's off, like, what?"

"He's your friend. Sir."

Mac smiled and said, "And you want me to pull in a favor and get details?"

"Sure! A blow to the head may—or may not—have resulted in an aneurysm, which could have ruptured, causing the fall on the steps. Or, maybe a brain bleed that had the same outcome, or any one of a number of things, apparently. Or, maybe she got whacked a good one up to twenty-four hours earlier, then later struggled with someone on the steps to Grace's office and exacerbated the wound to her skull."

Desi's eyes shone with her enthusiasm for her work. Mac knew she'd been right earlier when she said normal people would think their conversation was horrifying.

"The tox screens aren't finished," she continued, "and they'll tell us more. If Cutter was under the influence, she could have tripped or passed out on the steps."

"But it's a murder because of the head injuries?"

"At the moment, yes. Lab's still running tests to determine the age of the original injury, but we know she could have been dizzy enough to fall on the steps, and there are the bruises on her arms. Someone grabbed her hard enough to leave print-sized marks. There aren't full sets, of course, so it's hard to tell how big her killer's hands are, but somebody manhandled her."

Mac thought about the death scene on the steps in Grace's office. "So, we can't rule any of the suspects out at this point, right? Even a short person could have been standing on a step or two above the victim and hit her on top of the head."

Desi nodded. "And jerked her around. The injuries to her face don't seem to be from a fall on the steps, either, but the test results haven't been finalized."

"Come on, Desi," he said when she stopped. "What else?"

"It could have been Ashley Greenburgh, or a taller woman like Simone Lancer, but the best bet is still Henry Cutter. It would have been easy for him to stand on the landing next to her, or above her, attack her, and throw her down the stairs."

"And Peter Carlton?" he asked, urging her to get to the point she didn't want to bring up.

"Still interesting," Desi said slowly, "but less so after the statement he gave us this afternoon. His account of seeing the body, thinking it was Grace, and then running fits all the eyewitness reports, and most of it's on the surveillance tapes Cyrus Mosley provided."

Mac kept his expression neutral, but it was hard. This must have been what Grace had tried to tell him. Well, he now knew everything, and he still thought she shouldn't be representing David's son. And she should have told him what she was going to do. It hurt. They weren't on the same side in this case, and there would be other issues they couldn't share in the coming days. He was glad he'd moved back to the cottage yesterday. Glad, and miserable, too.

All he said was, "If Carlton is out of the picture, then we're down to three serious suspects?"

Marbury nodded. "Three in the lead, as of now."

He wondered whom Grace would end up defending if Peter were exonerated. The only thing he was sure of was that she would stay right in the middle of the investigation.

"Uhm, sir?"

He refocused on Marbury, who looked uncomfortable, and he could guess why. "You'd like me to step away from the investigation completely, right?"

"Well, not me, personally, but yes. Thanks for making that easier. You know how it is, the brass thinks you're too close, what with the murder happening in Grace's office and friends of yours involved."

"I've already told Commander Potter I agree. Did you bring the papers with you?"

"Sir, you're still the chief of police," Desi said as she handed him a folder. "You'll never really be out, you know."

When he'd officially signed off the investigation with the proviso that he would be briefed daily, he said goodbye to Desi, then hello to Tremaine, whose enthusiasm for the food Mac had brought was a nice touch in an otherwise unsettling evening. Mac handed the bags over to the young officer. He'd lost his own appetite.

He was the chief of police in the little tourist town where he'd been born and raised, but he wouldn't be handling the biggest issue facing his community. All his skills and experience would be put toward everyday conflicts, while his former staff at the state police solved Mona Cutter's murder. He told himself it wouldn't bother him nearly as much if Grace wasn't going to be in the middle of the action while he sat on the sidelines.

This would not go well. Not well at all.

CHAPTER TWENTY-THREE

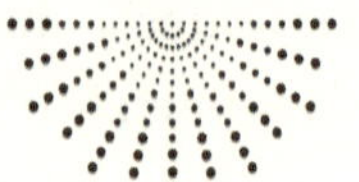

On Saturday morning, Grace loaded Fiona and her diaper bag into the stroller and walked the short blocks to her office. Soft breezes off the harbor and the April sunshine felt like good omens, but they didn't ease her mind. Mac was foremost in her thoughts. Every time she'd closed her eyes the night before, she'd heard Avril saying, "You never put him first," and the image of his hurt expression when she'd last seen him would make her cry. But as much as she wanted it all to go away, she didn't see how anything could change until the charges against Peter were resolved, and by then it might be too late. It might already be too late.

She adjusted the bonnet shielding Fiona's face from the sun and smiled at her energetic wiggling. "Everything will work out," she told her daughter. Everything *had* to work out.

Minutes later, when she caught sight of Peter sitting on the bench behind the office, her spirits lifted. Despite his current situation, she was sure this boy was a good sign, too. He might even be the bridge that brought a fractured family together, but first she had to keep him out of jail. He hadn't sounded happy when she'd asked him to meet her, but he'd shown up. Small victories, she told herself.

A new sister proved to be a temporary cure for a teenage sulk. Peter's anger over learning that David had paid his bail seemed to fade when Fiona grabbed his finger and laughed. Grace swiped warm cinnamon rolls from Cyrus's kitchen and made coffee while the half siblings got acquainted. Their Hallmark movie moment didn't last long but had a calming effect.

"I told you I don't want his money," he said. He was sullen again, but sounded resigned. "I'll never be able to pay him back. I'll owe him for the rest of my life."

"You'll work it out between you. Things will get better, but it's more than the bail." She knew she needed to be transparent with him if she expected him to trust her, but he looked ill as she described the reparation payments David was covering. "If you want to refuse the bail money, I'll lend it to you," she said. "Both David and I trust you not to do anything to cause the court to revoke it. As for the reimbursements of the actual costs to the victims of the accidents, I expect you to repay that to whichever one of us puts up the money."

This idea had come to her last night and felt right immediately. Peter would take responsibility for the damage he'd caused, and when the bail was refunded to David, Peter wouldn't be in debt to his father.

He looked relieved for a moment, then said, "But these compensation payments—won't they be huge? Not that those people don't deserve them, but still."

"I'm sure David will accept a payment schedule you can afford." Actually, she was sure David would refuse to take money from his son. He'd be insulted that Grace had even suggested it, but she understood Peter's need to be responsible for himself.

He didn't respond, then after a time, he nodded, looked up, and said, "How does Farq know for sure that I'm his son?"

Farq came out naturally and without attitude. Grace thought the shorthand had been around a while in Peter's vocabulary.

"I mean, he hasn't asked me for a DNA test, and he isn't on my birth certificate, so how does he know? I look like him, but I could be pulling a scam. He doesn't know who I am. Not for sure."

She hadn't expected him to consider David's feelings. "Do you think he might not be your father?"

"Bethany lied. A lot," he said, his dark eyes earnest but sad. "I never looked for my birth parents because I thought I knew who you were. If you're not my mother, maybe he isn't my father. Maybe she just found a random baby with his coloring and . . ." His voice trailed off. "That's where I get stuck every time. Why would she do that?"

It was going to come up eventually, but did it have to be now? Grace glanced at her watch and saw Peter straighten up. "I'm not minimizing the importance of this conversation," she said, "but we have to prioritize. I'll help you work everything out, I promise, but it's going to take time. Right now, we have to get ready for your interview by the state police. It's in four hours, and I want to go over everything they might bring up. And"—she mentally crossed her fingers—"it will be best for you if David is there with us. The image we want is of a supportive family who's convinced of your innocence."

"But I haven't even met him," he said, looking alarmed.

"He'll come as soon as I call. He's just waiting to hear that you agree."

Peter looked miserable, but he nodded. "You should tell him everything—about the fire and Bethany dying. About her lies. He should know it all. If I'm going to take his help, I want him to know who I am. But when this meeting's over, I want a DNA test. I have to know the truth."

Grace practically had to sit on her hands to keep from hugging him. His words tore at her heart as she watched him patting the foot Fiona was kicking him with.

Fiona, Amalie, and Peter.

There was so much she didn't know about Peter Carlton, but she believed he was Fiona's brother, and that made him part of her family. He was also a volatile teenager, so she chose her words carefully.

"David knows how Bethany died, Peter, and he knows you were charged and that the charges were dropped. He knew within a day of learning that you were here. The district attorney has all the details, and of course, the judge knows. The information isn't exactly hidden, it was all over the news. Your court records are sealed because you were still a juvenile, but the media still got most of the story."

"I suppose Farq will want to talk about it."

"Listen, about that. Can you lose the nickname for now? What the two of you call each other in the future won't be any of my business." The *Farq* tag grated on her, but it would send David into orbit, and they didn't need that today.

"Fair." Peter got to his feet and picked up his backpack. "How long will all of this legal stuff take? How long before I can leave here?"

"I don't know. A while, though. Assuming all goes well and we can get the charges in Chestertown settled, there's still the murder investigation. At the very least, you'll be a material witness in that."

"I'm completely innocent! Why can't I leave now? I'm going into the air force, if they'll have me. I'll get a GED."

Grace stared at him. Every time she thought she'd heard the last of his problems, another one popped out. "You're about to graduate from a prestigious military academy. Why do you need a state certificate?"

Peter reddened, but he looked her in the eye as he told her he was dropping out. "What you said in court yesterday is all over campus. About how I ran when I saw that woman's body. I'm a coward in a military school. Do you know how bad that is?"

"Oh, Peter. You're not—"

"Save it. I mean, I appreciate it and all, but I don't need a pep talk. It's what I do. I run. I ran away from home a lot when I was a kid. I never fit in at the academy, and things are impossible now. I just want to get into the air force and get on with my life."

"Is that even an option if you drop out? Six more weeks and you'll be set."

He shook his head. "I can't do it. I have some money left from my summer job last year. It'll last while I get the GED. I can pass it without finishing my classes, I'm sure."

"Don't throw away the resume you've earned," Grace urged. "Your classes are virtual, so why not finish your degree as planned?"

"It won't work." His voice became strident. "I can't stay on campus. I barely got out of there without fighting. If I hit somebody, I'll be thrown out, anyway, and I could end up in jail for good."

She didn't bother asking if not hitting anyone was an option. Peter may have trouble controlling his temper, but she gave him credit for acknowledging it. "Move off campus, then. Let me make some calls. Where did you plan on staying?"

"I guess a motel until I get a job, and then I'll rent something."

"Pass on that for the moment. This is all short term, so hear me out," she said when he started shaking his head. "I want you in town and close by until we're a little more settled, legally."

"I'm not staying with him. David."

"Then your hotel room will be added to the tab you're running with me. I want you at the Egret Hotel here in town. It's just a couple of blocks over. Don't get used to the luxury, it's only for a few days until we figure something else out."

To her surprise, he agreed and promised to keep up with his classes for the time being. She made the most of this bit of cooperation and quickly ran through her list of questions. Next, in a conference call, she and Peter talked to the dean of cadets at Howard Military Academy.

The conversation was stilted, but in addition to smoothing things over with the dean, they received emailed copies of sign-out sheets and activity reports from Peter's dorm security system for Monday through Thursday. Grace wasn't sure they'd ever need the records, but when the dean said the state police had subpoenaed copies, too, she was glad she'd asked for them.

When everything on her checklist was done, she called Peter's father.

CHAPTER TWENTY-FOUR

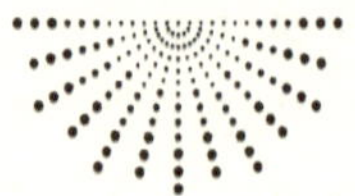

David answered her call on the first ring, and for once, he listened without interrupting. A few minutes later, she was giving Peter directions to The Egret.

"I'll call and arrange for your room, but right now, just concentrate on meeting David. He'll be waiting for you in the lobby. You don't have to discuss the big stuff between you or get all the issues out now. Just meet him as a human being. There will be time to work the rest out later."

"The rest, like who my mother is?"

She so badly wanted to orchestrate this part. To pull the strings that would make David say and do the right things to help Peter understand what must be incomprehensible to him. She said only, "Meet him and see what happens. Give him a few minutes, and you'll know what to do."

The tight timing was a risk, but so was everything else about the situation. Going into the interview without David weakened her argument that Peter had family support. But giving the impression that he knew his father well contradicted his explanation for running away when he saw Mona's body. She was walking a tightrope with her strategy and praying it would pay off.

After a quick run home to deliver Fiona to Hallie and change clothes, she spent a distracted hour reviewing her data for the interview. If it went well, she might be able to petition the court to drop the charges in the Chestertown incident, or at least charge Peter as a juvenile. But she also had to keep him off Desi Marbury's list of suspects in Mona's death.

At one thirty, she packed up and went to the Egret Hotel. At the front desk, she was given directions to a private conference room that David had engaged. She found him with Peter in the midst of an intense conversation that stopped when she stepped into the room.

"Everything okay?" she asked, knowing the question was beyond lame, but suddenly she was at a loss for words. David and Peter had turned to look at her with movements and expressions so alike it was hard not to smile.

"That close, huh?" David said, correctly interpreting her expression.

"The resemblance is remarkable," she admitted.

"Creepy is more like it," Peter countered.

"We have an hour," Grace said, pulling them back to the matter at hand and directing her comments to Peter, alone. "First things first. I'm going to ask David to step out now while we discuss strategy."

"No. Uh—" Peter glanced at David, then said, "We've agreed on some things. He's going to pay your fees and my expenses. I'll reimburse him for all of it." David got a version of his own glare with that statement. "And I've decided I want him here. I want him to know everything. I came to find my parents, and this is as close as I get, for now, anyway."

David said, "I explained to Peter that if Bethany isn't his mother, I don't know who is." His face flushed, but he looked steadily at Grace as he spoke. "I deeply regret the way he's been treated, and my team's at work right now to get answers for him."

The idea of David baring such personal information to his staff seemed unlikely to Grace, but this wasn't the time to discuss it. She paused, regrouped, and tried again. "I still recommend—"

"He stays," Peter said. "Please, Grace."

Out of the corner of her eye, she saw David smile and just as quickly resume his neutral expression.

"Just what I needed," she muttered. "Two of you." But the argument was wasting time, so she moved on to describe her plan to petition the court in Kent County to treat Peter as a juvenile. "But first, I want to try to get the charges dropped."

"How? I did it," Peter said. "I didn't mean to, but I hit the officer, and I caused the wrecks. How can you get the charges dropped?"

David had no reaction except to continue watching Grace.

She took a paper out of her briefcase. "This is the statement you gave me regarding your actions and what you saw at my office on Tuesday afternoon, April ninth. Read it carefully and let me know if you want any changes." Peter reached for it, and she covered his hand with her own. "Take it out into the hall to read. Make any changes you need to. This has to be accurate. I'm going to give it to the police, so no mistakes or exaggerations, understand? It should say only exactly what you know to be true because you saw it, said it, or did it."

Peter stood and took the paper, but hesitated. "You won't say anything while I'm gone, will you?"

David got up, saying, "I need to call my office, anyway, so I'll step out." To Peter, he added, "Just let me know when you're ready."

Peter read every word, then read it all again. When he returned the paper to Grace, the only change was his signature across the bottom of the page.

When David rejoined them, she said, "Do you want to tell him, or do you want me to?"

Peter took his statement from her and handed it to David, saying, "When I looked through the downstairs window at Grace's office, I saw a body on the stairs. I thought it was her. Grace, I mean." His voice was harsh. "I heard the way you'd talked to her on the phone earlier, how mad you were. I knew she was going to tell you that I was your son. I thought you'd argued about me and that you'd killed her."

David looked horrified. "What? That's crazy!"

"No, it isn't," Peter said, his voice flat. "Bethany told me everything you did to her."

When Desi Marbury and Wes Everly arrived, they found a united, if shaky, group. Although the conference room seemed to shrink with the new arrivals, things went well for Peter at first. Both state police detectives seemed subdued, even pleasant. If Grace hadn't dealt with both officers on previous occasions, she might have been fooled, but they were still the police, and she and David were attorneys. All the professional walls stayed in place, and Everly quickly moved into the legal cautions.

Peter said he understood his rights. David was stone faced. Grace waited for the gloves to come off.

Everly took Peter through the timeline and asked what he saw when he looked through the window in the door to Grace's office. Peter described the bright sunlight hitting the glass, allowing him to see only his own reflection until he stepped up to the window and cupped his hands around his eyes. He got all the important details in, the empty foyer, his frustration, then the shock as he looked up to the landing at the halfway point on the stairs and saw a woman's head and arm.

Grace mentally checked one concern off her list. He'd followed instructions and laid the base for his defense and the explanation for why no one else passing by the office had seen Mona's body through the window.

"It's all in here," Peter said and handed his now slightly crumpled statement to Everly.

"When did you first meet Ms. Reagan, face-to-face?" Everly asked.

"It's all in the statement," Grace said.

The sergeant skimmed the paper, then set it aside and reached for a photograph of a smiling blonde woman. Holding it up to Peter, he asked, "Do you know who this person is?"

"You told me it was Mona Cutter the last time we talked." A bit of teenage attitude crept into Peter's voice, earning him sharp looks from Grace and David.

Everly ignored everyone but Peter. "When did you first meet her?"

"I never have, uh, never did. I don't know what you mean." Peter looked at Grace, who knew exactly what Wes Everly meant and lightly touched Peter's arm, their signal for him to be quiet.

Everly nodded and said, "You say you thought you'd seen your attorney, Ms. Reagan, dead on the steps?"

"She wasn't my attorney then, but yes."

"And your statement is you'd previously met Ms. Reagan, face-to-face, before this?"

"Yes."

Everly looked back and forth between the photograph of the blonde murder victim and Grace.

"We get the implication, officer," David snapped.

Everly smiled and said, "Please hold your comments, sir." Without waiting for a response, he turned back to Peter. "Your statement is that the victim's face was covered by her hair. As you can see, Ms. Cutter had blonde hair and Ms. Reagan's is dark. How could you confuse them?"

"It was all crazy. The sunlight was bright, but there were shadows, too, and only part of her was showing, mostly her arm. I don't know." The last part was hushed.

"Why did you go to see Grace the day before?" Marbury asked.

Peter was rattled, but didn't hesitate. "I thought she, I thought Grace was my mother."

David and Grace got odd looks from the officers, then Everly was back at Peter. "Did you get help for her, for the blonde woman you thought was your mother?"

Peter shook his head. "I thought she was dead."

"You thought she was dead, and you didn't do anything?" Marbury asked, sarcasm dripping in her words.

Peter looked as if he'd been kicked. "I thought it was my fault. I thought they'd fought," his voice rose.

"Peter, stop," Grace said sternly when her arm taps were ignored.

But he ignored her words, too, and said, "I thought he'd killed her and I could have prevented all of it if I'd been strong enough to confront him first. I ran away, okay?"

Over Grace and David's objections, Peter told the police everything he knew and everything Bethany had said about David. His unguarded recital would make the state's attorney happy. When the interview was finished, he moved from Desi Marbury's suspect list to the prosecution's witness list. The state could pinpoint the time of death to be within the ten minutes between Marjorie's locking the hall door behind Mona and Peter's arrival at Grace's front door. Peter's time-stamped signature on the academy's sign-out sheet gave him the alibi Grace had hoped for, but it was the only good thing to come from the meeting. What they gained for Peter's defense crushed the earlier progress father and son had made.

Grace followed Marbury and Everly out into the hallway as they left. "How does this affect the Chestertown charges?" she asked as they waited for the elevator.

Marbury shook her head, but Everly said, "You drew Judge Alten, right?" At Grace's nod, the frown he'd been wearing eased. "Ask for consideration as a juvenile, do the usual good-behavior song and dance and make sure Daddy Big Bucks will still fork over the voluntary compensation he offered the victims. Cite mental trauma for Junior and push the Air Force ROTC and college. College is a big plus, and so is the service. Judge Alten has a daughter on active duty." The elevator dinged, and its doors opened. Before he stepped in, Everly added, "I'll talk to the officer Carlton hit. She's good people and word is, she wasn't injured. Might not move the judge an inch, but you never know."

"Thank you," Grace said.

Everly put out a hand to stop the doors from closing and looked back at her. "Don't thank me for doing what's right. That kid is traumatized, and somebody better get him some help. If it'll inspire his cooperation, tell him if he screws up again, I'll walk him into a cell myself and you won't be getting him out."

Peter seemed to be in shock when she went back to the conference room. If he understood anything she said, it wasn't apparent. At some point, he'd realized that everything he'd told the police would be soon be public, and the effect of that hit him hard. There was no longer any option of keeping the questions surrounding his parentage quiet, and his newfound father was furious. David's career would be damaged, the only question was how badly. Peter refused to apologize, saying he was only being honest. It went downhill from there.

Grace wrote *Monday, 1:00, my office* on the back of a business card and made Peter look at it when he took it from her. He apologized again for telling the police too much, but didn't wait for the door to close behind her before rejoining the argument he was having with David.

She didn't think they noticed when she was gone.

CHAPTER TWENTY-FIVE

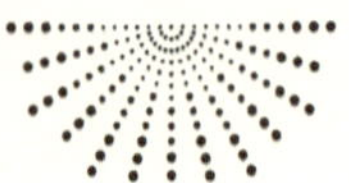

Turning the murder investigation over to the state police didn't mean Mac wouldn't be paying attention when the suspects were right under his nose.

He watched David and Peter Carlton walk out of The Egret, then crossed the street to meet them. Father and son wore identical sour expressions, and Mac had to admit that if Peter wasn't David's child, he was probably in the Farquar family tree. He held out his hand to Peter and said, "I'm Lee McNamara, but everyone calls me Mac."

"Everyone calls him *sir*," David said, interrupting. "Peter, meet the chief of police." Handshake and awkward introduction done, he hustled the boy away, leaving Mac to finish foot patrol thinking of all the reasons Peter might be here in Mallard Bay with a father he just met and supposedly hated.

All the answers he came up with revolved around Grace, because once again she was in the middle of a situation of David's making. Directly or indirectly, their lives continued to be affected by that egomaniac, and Mac was sick of it. The advice he'd given Grace a few short days before seemed laughable now.

There was no way he could ignore David's antics or get along with him.

As he made his way down crowded narrow streets that had been laid centuries ago for horses and wagons, he wondered what life would be like with a woman whose past was uncomplicated. Whose daily life didn't include dead bodies on her doorsteps. Someone without volatile exes and unexpected children popping up around every corner?

Ashley came to mind, effectively ending his mental griping. There wasn't a woman alive who didn't come with baggage of some kind, he told himself as he finished patrol and headed back to the station.

Dogs. Dogs and fishing and baseball. That's where a smart man put his energy.

The Spring Fest parade had wrapped up with no problems, but the farmers market was still running, and the first of the season's outdoor concerts in Memorial Park was at sunset. Tomorrow's antique show and crafts fair at the VFW would keep many of the tourists in town until midafternoon at least, adding to the regular weekend boat tours and Saint Mary's Chapel's annual homecoming services. The little town was packed to overflowing. Not even an unsolved murder stopped the opening of tourist season on the Eastern Shore.

Tonight, he would have his dog, a beer, and a Nationals doubleheader. It was a fine set of distractions, but he was still miserable.

***

Tremaine Harper was on his way out to a neighbor-versus-neighbor dispute when Mac arrived back at the station. "Need backup?" he asked, pushing his long list of administrative issues to the side.

With a chuckle, Harper, who topped out at just under six five and had played football at the University of Maryland, said he thought he could handle it. "Birthday party for a two-year-old has gone rogue, Chief, but I've got it covered."

Mac reminded him to be careful, anyway, although it wasn't necessary. In a lighter tone, he said, "Go and God bless. I'll try to get some playpens set up before you get back with the miscreants."

They both knew that a baby's party could turn just as deadly as any other type of situation, but in a two-man department, most situations got a single officer. At least the better person for the job was handling it, Mac thought. He had yet to see a situation that Tremaine Harper hadn't improved just with his steady, and often charming, presence, and besides, he had some of his own fractious public interaction to handle.

Emails and texts were coming in from citizens and business owners who, for some reason, thought expressing their concerns about Mona Cutter's death would make the chief of police more vigilant. He felt neither steady nor charming as he flipped through the messages.

I saw that Lancer woman on a TV ad, offering to fight for people who want a divorce. Better check her out, Mac.

. . . and my niece, who works at Baldy's Market, says that dog doc was yelling at someone on the phone, right in the middle of the dairy aisle. Have you looked at her? I mean THAT way? She's a come-here, you know.

Henry's a local boy, but he's got one of them vans with the dark windows. Be careful if you pull him over, Mac.

If you can't stop tourists from driving over our hydrants while they're spreading drugs around, what good are you?

I'm standing ready to be deputized, Chief. You know I'm here to help.

He sighed as he read the last text with its rifle-toting avatar and typed out the standard "Maryland State Police have it covered" message.

The public dissection of Mona Cutter's death was getting out of hand as Mallard Bay tried to make sense of a murder happening right in the middle of town, in daylight, during tourist season. He shouldn't have been surprised to see that all four main suspects were named and discussed in at least one message. He made himself read every one, even those giving him a heads-up about political plots and sketchy in-laws. When he was finished, he didn't know anything new, except the writers' opinions.

Ashley, who was a well-regarded member of the community, was still a Come Here. This alone was enough for many to put her at the top of their list of suspects.

Simone Lancer was an unknown, so it wasn't nearly as entertaining to cast her in the killer's role, but as the victim's mother and someone who advertised her law firm on late-night television, she got her share of gossip.

Peter Carlton was also an unknown, but he was a kid, and had already been tagged in the community as Grace's stepson. Mac was tired of correcting people on the nonfamilial status of the two, especially since she was going mama bear on David's son. She wasn't a local, either, but she'd made a good name for herself, and her staunch defense of the boy was enough to deter all but the nosiest of gossips. At least the truth, that Peter had thought she was his mother, wasn't making the rounds. Yet.

Henry was a better bet. And, as Desi had said, if it wasn't Henry, the MSP would be looking at Simone and Ashley. Their statements were identical with respect to timing. Each claimed to be on the phone with the other between four fifteen and four forty-five, but could neither could provide anything in the way of proof.

Mac had been on the phone with Ashley while she cried nonstop for twenty minutes during the first half hour that the murder could have occurred. If Edith Pratt hadn't come in with another of her suspicious-activity complaints, he may have been on the call much longer. At the time, he'd been grateful for the excuse hang up, but Edith's fear of her neighbor's new gardener may have cost Ashley an airtight alibi.

Mac reluctantly closed his notes and opened the schedule he and Tremaine would follow for the next two days. Life went on, and nothing stopped a sunny spring weekend for tourists and winter-tired locals.

It was time to retrieve Rocky from puppy day care—also known as Avril's house. "It takes a village" had been part of Avril's proposal when he was trying to think of every reason to avoid a puppy and adopt an adult dog. So, because Avril wanted a puppy and Benny had a cute one no one wanted, Mac had acquired a teething spaniel and holes in his socks. Today he was glad for the diversion, and that bit of mental wandering made him smile as he locked up the station and went out to his truck.

Planning his next training session for his dog was better than worrying about things he couldn't control. Until Grace was untangled from this murder investigation, he couldn't fix anything that had gone wrong with his life.

CHAPTER TWENTY-SIX

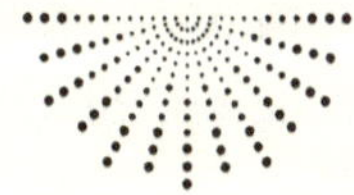

The flashing light on the phone console greeted Grace as she unlocked the door to her office. Her first official week in her new practice didn't start for another day and a half, and already she was working weekends. This depressing realization was forgotten as she heard the outside door on the floor below open and close. Too late, she remembered it wasn't enough to activate the security cameras, you actually had to check them. Locking the door was a good idea, too.

Krissy Farquar appeared on the steps a moment later.

"Sugar! You look exhausted, bless your heart. David told me what happened. Lock this place up. Let's go celebrate your big wins."

Grace wondered how David had described the postponement in Kent County and the chaotic interview with the MSP. "Win" wasn't the word she would have chosen. "I can't," she said. "I mean, I wish I could, but it's already four, and I've got work to finish. Another time, okay?"

Krissy's strained expression said it most definitely was not okay. "Well, I'm sincere about wanting girlfriend time, but I also need advice, and I can do the condensed version. Five minutes?"

Grace tried not to look as irritated as she felt and asked what was wrong.

"What isn't?" Krissy sat on the bench, wiggled around a bit, then stuffed one of the pillows behind her back.

Grace decided the old church pew might have its uses after all. Sometimes it was good not to make people too comfortable. Like now, with this non-conversation. She looked at her watch and said, "Can I call you later?"

"I don't want Peter around Amalie."

"Well, all righty, then. Why not?" She was in no mood to handle another angry person, but she knew Peter was going to need his stepmother, and despite what the local gossip said, that woman was Krissy, and if she had issues, it meant trouble for all of them.

"Do you know where David is?"

"Yes. I left him at The Egret with Peter. We had an interview with the state police this afternoon."

Krissy picked up a needlepoint pillow and held it like a security blanket. "Well, as usual, you know more than I do. David just left before lunch without an explanation except to say you and Peter needed him. Then he told me to get one of the guest rooms ready. What the hell? He's my husband, and I don't have a clue what's going on."

Grace wanted to tell her to get used to it, but Krissy was smart. She'd get the lay of the land, eventually. "I don't know how to help you," she said.

"I knew there could be more junior Farquars showing up in the wake of David's inventory of his past lovers, but this Peter. I don't know, he scares me. The stories about his mama scare me even more. How do we know what kind of damage that boy's suffered? How he might feel about finding his daddy after a whole lifetime of hating him and here're these cute little girl babies in line ahead of him? The boy could be violent, and for all we know, he might have killed a woman right outside your door. Don't get mad at me, but I have to think about these things."

"I respect your feelings," Grace said, assuring her. "But we're meeting Peter at what has to be one of the worst times in his life. His mother just died a couple of months ago. Did you know?"

Krissy sighed and shook her head. "My husband guards information like I'm the enemy. Did he treat you that way?"

"Sounds familiar," Grace admitted. "I hated it. Especially when he'd talk about something as if I knew it because he forgot he hadn't told me."

"Exactly!" Krissy's worried expression softened, and Grace knew she'd been right to explain at least some of the extenuating circumstances. "Peter is under a court order to stay within a fifty-mile radius of Chestertown, so he's stuck here for a while, but believe me, he's itching to leave. He wants to go into the air force as soon as he graduates. Which reminds me, I need to make some calls about that."

If the hint registered with Krissy, it didn't move her. "Well, that explains a lot. I feel sure David intends to move the boy in with us. Look, I said five minutes, and that's gone, but after I scouted around some on the internet, I decided to have a background check done on Peter. I didn't want you to find out later and be mad."

"No worries," Grace said. At least down the road, she, David, and Krissy shouldn't be blindsided by anything in his past. "Can you copy me? It's always good to know what's out there before it gets tossed at me in court."

"You got it. My parents are off-the-chart paranoid about security, and when you grow up that way, it sticks with you. I'll use my best manners with this boy, but my baby comes first, and no one gets close to us unless I know they're clean."

Clearly, there were things Grace still had to learn about Kristen. "Did you check me, too?"

"Yes. And your hunky police chief."

"How'd we do?"

"Honey, either you had a good scrubber work on your personal history or you didn't start living until you drove over that horrible bay bridge. According to what Daddy's people found, you were a model citizen until people started trying to kill you. You should be more careful, Auntie Grace. The girls don't need to see Wonder Woman in action until they're older."

Grace laughed, but noticed Krissy didn't. "Did you check David before you married him?"

"Oh, please. I checked him before I let him touch me. He's not nearly as scandalous as I am. Your Mac is an interesting guy, though. The awards and commendations that man has probably cover a wall in his house. Am I right?"

"No," Grace said slowly, wondering why she didn't know this. Mac had talked about his long career, of course, but it sounded like he'd left a lot out, too. Only two shadow boxes hung in his den, one from the state police and one from his first tenure as chief in Mallard Bay. Each held his shield and rank insignia and a small brass plaque with his dates of service.

"A modest man," Krissy said. "I like that." She stood up, replaced the pillows, and picked up her handbag. "I may decide to take Ammie away for a while. If I do, I'll let you know." As they walked out into the hallway, Krissy pointed to the landing at the turn in the staircase. "That's where it happened, right? Is that why the carpet looks new?" She winced when Grace nodded. "Are you sure Peter's not involved?"

Grace wanted to assure her he wasn't, but said only, "I can't discuss him, you know, but I'm comfortable having him around Fiona and me."

Krissy didn't look any happier.

By the time she had returned calls to clients who had loyally waited for her return to work, and handled a half-dozen tasks for the upcoming week, she was reminded yet again that working alone would not be an option. At the very least, she needed an answering service and a part-time paralegal. She couldn't charge clients her regular hourly rate to do the work Marjorie handled for Cyrus. She needed her very own Bat.

She had Hallie. But Hallie came with Fiona, and Fiona came with baby paraphernalia and noise. And . . . she glanced at her watch and saw she needed to hurry if she was going to be home in time to feed Fiona and rock her to sleep.

Ten minutes later, she walked into a spotless house and dinner in a slow cooker. She was so overwhelmed with gratitude she couldn't even crack a joke at the sight of Aidan playing with the baby while Hallie made a salad.

"We have a proposal," Hallie said when Grace returned from the nursery.

"Does it involve me being able to come home to this every night?"

"Yes, but—"

"Done," Grace said, and took a water glass—a clean glass—out of the dishwasher. "How much? I'm in a weak state, so don't take advantage." She lifted the foil covering a large plate, found half a carrot cake, and said, "Never mind. Name your price."

"Don't you want to know why I'm here?" Aidan asked.

"I'm assuming you vacuumed while she cooked," Grace said, still eyeing the cake. "Thank you."

"I cooked while she vacuumed, actually," Aidan said. "But before that, we ran into each other at the market."

"Fiona was low on diapers," Hallie broke in. "I set you up for auto delivery, so it shouldn't happen again. Anyway, Aidan and I talked about how well things went when the two of us were helping you out earlier this week." Her too-innocent tone glossed over her substitution of "earlier" for "before the murder."

"I'm kind of at loose ends at the moment," Aidan said. "My mornings are free until I get more clients, and I could run the office for you. Just a few hours a day. Just for a few weeks."

"Just for a few dollars?" Grace teased, but she liked the idea.

"We'll work it out," he said. "But there's one thing you should know."

Hallie looked surprised, but before she could say anything, Aidan said, "I'm in a new relationship."

Grace stopped picking at the cake icing and gave him her full attention. "Who?" She held her breath. Hallie was a minor for a few more months, and Aidan was at least fifteen years older, and . . .

"Desi Marbury."

"Ewww!" Hallie squealed.

Grace grinned with relief, then tried to wrap her mind around the unthinkable combination. Aidan and Desi? They hated each other. "I'm so happy for both of you," she said when she could talk and keep a straight face.

"Yeah, yeah," Aidan said, grousing. "Get it out. You're no more shocked than we were. But she's great. I, uhm. She's great."

"Yes," Grace said, solemnly. "Desi is great. Everyone says so."

"*I* don't," Hallie broke in. "She tried to shoot me!"

"Well, she didn't succeed," Aidan said to his would-be partner. "And are you sure you want to revisit your role in that little scene, or do you want a job?"

"I'm afraid it would be too awkward, Aidan," Grace said, ending the argument and her own brief hopes of an organized life. "You could overhear things in the office and—"

"You don't trust me to keep my mouth shut, right?" They both knew she had good reasons for feeling that way.

"Do you see Mac here?" Grace asked as she took out plates for dinner.

"Seriously?" he said. "You and Mac split over you representing that kid?"

"No. Mac and I are being mature and professional. He's just not staying here while the investigation is ongoing. It's too tempting to talk shop when your guard's down."

"But he's not working the investigation," Aidan said. "He and Desi settled that officially yesterday evening. Don't you think it's a little overboard to kick him out of the house?"

Grace didn't bother to correct his assumption that Mac's leaving was her idea. She busied herself with silverware and tried to look unconcerned, but inside, she was a mess. Yes, it was overboard for Mac to stay away when he wasn't in the investigation anymore, so where was he? She'd made it clear she wanted him here, regardless of the circumstances. How were they supposed to have any kind of permanent relationship if he left every time she had a criminal case?

". . . and I could handle things here in the morning and then bring Fiona over at lunchtime when Aidan leaves. Are you listening to me?" Hallie demanded.

No, I'm trying to convince myself I haven't been dumped, Grace thought, as she looked at the ruby on her left hand. If he'd proposed when he gave it to her, she would have said yes. But maybe the ring hadn't been an opening to a marriage proposal, but a thanks-for-the-memories gift. That was certainly what it felt like now.

CHAPTER TWENTY-SEVEN

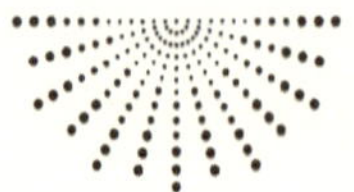

Mac usually didn't mind Sunday morning foot patrol, but he still hadn't had any decent sleep, and unhappiness was sapping his enthusiasm for even his favorite parts of his job. Overnight storms had moved out over the Atlantic, and the streets were crowded with tourists grabbing a last meal of fresh seafood or a final round of shopping before starting the long, traffic-clogged drive back to the western shore. It was a happy, if chaotic, scene, and every bit of it irritated him. He wanted the morning to be over.

Working his way up and down the crowded sidewalks, he stopped often to give directions and chat and, in one instance, help a couple with more kids and packages than they could handle get everything packed up in a too-small-for-them rental car. As he worked, a corner of his mind remained occupied by the conversation he would soon have with Henry Cutter and his lawyer.

His old friend's call had been a surprise, and the request for a meeting was puzzling, but Mac had agreed without asking for details. He might not be on the investigative team, but that didn't mean he had to bypass an opportunity for information. Besides, the kind, soft-spoken contractor had been a friend for years, and as far as Mac was concerned, he still was. He thought most of the town shared his feelings about Henry.

Small-town karma, he thought, remembering his musings about David suffering the consequences of getting the children he wanted. If cosmic retribution had a birthplace, Mac was sure it was a small town. A place where everyone knows you and remembers what you've done—the good and the bad.

He stopped at the station for Rocky and took her along on the last few blocks of his patrol. After that, she was happy to settle in her crate at the station with lunch and a new chew toy. He had an hour and a half to kill before he met Henry in Cyrus's office, and he was too antsy to spend it doing paperwork. Telling his practical mind to shut up, he grabbed his keys, forwarded the department's calls to dispatch, and took his lunch break.

Ten minutes later, he hesitated on the front porch of Grace's house, suddenly unsure if he should knock or use his key. The uncertainty made him mad. She probably wasn't even home, he told himself, imagining her out and about, inserting herself in a new drama that would blow back on him. When he finally stepped inside the quiet house, he felt humbled and foolish. His girls were sleeping, curled together on the sofa, brown curls and blonde ones, Grace's soft blue robe wrapped around both of them. He stood for a long time soaking in the beauty of that sight.

She woke as he was leaving her a note and his bubble burst when her first words were, "Did I know you were coming?" It sounded like something she would say to David.

"I was driving by and stopped in to say hi. I'll call next time." He hated that the words came out harshly, but there was no taking them back, only making it worse. The 'just driving by' line was stupid.

"No. Don't do that." She scraped her hair back and twisted it up, then gave up, letting it fall back into its curly mass. "If you call, it'll really be like you don't live here."

"I don't, Grace." What the hell did she want from him?

"You could." With those words, she picked up the baby and disappeared into the bedroom.

Before he could decide if it was safe to follow her, he heard water running in the shower. He didn't know what to do, but he didn't think leaving now would be a good idea. He also didn't have any better ones, so he made coffee and waited.

When she rejoined him, damp and fragrant and baby free, reality and hard decisions faded away. They were at peace, if only for a little while.

"I wanted you to hear this from me before we go to Detective Marbury," Henry said, once he, Mac, and Cyrus were settled in the conference room.

"One more time," Cyrus said in a tired voice. "This is not a good idea, Henry, and I'd like you to reconsider. This is not in your best interest."

His client didn't agree. "I didn't speak up two years ago when I thought something was wrong with Bryce. Look what happened then. Everyone told me it wasn't my fault, but Grace might not have been attacked if I'd followed what my gut"—he paused and looked at Mac—"my gut and Grace told me. The truth is going to come out, Cy, and it should come from me."

"It will come from you," Cyrus said. "But not like this. He's a sworn officer of the court. He'll have to repeat everything you say."

"That's right," Henry said. "And who better to tell my story than a friend? Whatever happens, happens."

Mac waited, not joining either side of the argument.

Henry said, "Two weeks ago, Mona tried to kill herself."

Cyrus shook his head and jotted notes on a legal pad as his client continued describing how his wife had taken the news that he was divorcing her two years after she'd left him.

"I couldn't understand why she cared. The Mona I knew was a reasonable person. She didn't want me, so why would she object to a divorce? I'm not sure you knew this, Mac, but it'll come out. Bryce and Mona had an affair that was still going when he was arrested."

Mac had known, but since it was immaterial to Bryce Cutter's crimes and his ultimate conviction, it wasn't part of the public record. He'd never told Grace.

"I found out right before his trial. Mona and I had a huge argument when she told me, and the next day I came home from work to find her gone and most of our accounts cleaned out. I guess Simone was savvy enough to recognize that Mona was an addict, or maybe Mona just stopped bothering to hide her habit once she left me. That was always a problem for us. If she had a problem, she'd go to Simone before she came to me. If it was bad, they'd cut me out until I found out by accident. It wasn't a good way to live."

"Henry, none of this is germane to Mona's death," Cyrus said. "When the investigation is over and you're cleared of any suspicion, then talk to your friends all you want. Let's adjourn until then."

"No, sir. I understand what you're saying, but it'll sound even worse if I wait." Turning back to Mac, he said, "So. Nearly two years ago, Mona left me and moved in with Simone, who eventually forced her into rehab—although I didn't know that for a long time. I didn't know about the addiction, either. Both Simone and

Ashley told me Mona wanted to get away from Mallard Bay and from me. Too many bad memories here, they said. They acted like I'd caused the nightmares they claimed she was having. Anyway, I had my hands full with the fallout from what Bryce had done to our business and, frankly, I was relieved not to have to handle Mona in crisis mode. Simone and Ashley told me to stay out of it, and I did."

"For how long?" Mac asked, although he saw where Henry was going.

"It was over the day Mona left me. Remember, I thought she was working, starting a new life that didn't include me and her bad memories. She stayed with Simone, and Ashley appointed herself a go-between for us. She'd try to keep my spirits up and give me bits of news that made it sound like my wife still loved me and would be home soon. I believed that at first, and I called Mona, thinking she wanted to see me. But Simone answered her phone and said Mona didn't want to talk to me. After a while, I was okay with that. Better than okay, because every time I thought of Mona and Bryce and the money she took, I—"

"Stop," Cyrus said firmly. "This isn't a confessional, and he isn't your priest. Every word out of your mouth will be repeated to a jury, son."

But there was no stopping Henry, so Mac began to take notes.

CHAPTER TWENTY-EIGHT

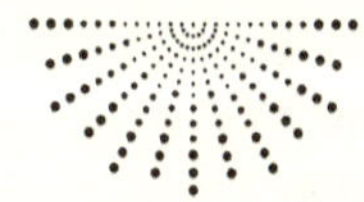

He had been in this position many times, usually with good people who had bad things they wanted to unload. With a little encouragement, everything would spill out, the truths, the guesses, and the if-only scenarios that kept them awake at night. And, after a moment of heady relief, reality would set in. Deserved or not, once guilt was given life, it never died.

Henry said, "Last summer, I told Ashley I didn't want to talk about Mona any more. It was too painful. Then I asked Mr. Mosley to start the divorce process, but I kinda left things on hold."

"Did you tell anyone you were ending the marriage?" Mac asked.

Cyrus's expression didn't change, but Mac thought if there'd been a roll of duct tape handy, he'd have slapped a strip over his client's mouth.

"Only Sierra Nance," Henry said. "Life goes on, you know? We were just friends for a long time, and I was up front with her about my marriage. Eventually, I told her everything. When we fell in love, I promised to end it with Mona. And I tried. But once again, I didn't try hard enough. When Simone said it was a bad time and that Mona didn't want to talk to me, God forgive me, but all I felt was relieved. I decided I was through, and they could figure out for themselves that I had moved on. I told Mr. Mosley to schedule the divorce proceedings and serve Mona. "

"When was this?" Mac asked.

"A month ago. Sierra and I had just found out we're having a baby."

"Congratulations," Mac said, and meant it. Sierra had a calm personality, much the same as Henry's. They'd be a good match—if he didn't end up in prison.

"Thanks. I'm really happy about it." Henry broke into a huge smile that quickly faded as he picked up his story. "Mona called when she got the papers, and I told her about Sierra. I don't know what I expected, but she congratulated me and got a little weepy about the baby, but in a good way. Then, as she was hanging up, she said she was sorry for everything she'd put me through. It kinda broke my heart, but it was a good end, too. I thought everything was going to be okay. The next morning, Ashley showed up at my house, begging me not to go through with the divorce."

"Ashley? Not Mona?"

"Yeah. Eight o'clock and she's banging on my front door. She said Mona had taken a lot of pills after she talked to me, and Simone had found her just in time. That's when she told me that Mona had just come out of rehab for the third time, and if I divorced her, she wouldn't have health insurance. I was furious. She admitted that the three of them had been lying to me all that time. The argument Ashley and I had was bad. Real bad." Henry looked on the verge of tears. "She'd known all along about the drug use and hadn't told me. When I'd ask about Mona, she'd lie and say things were better and Mona was working hard. I thought she meant at a job."

Cyrus interrupted, saying, "He gets the picture."

But Henry wasn't finished. "I didn't speak to Ashley again until last Monday morning in Mr. Mosley's office. Mona and Simone were both no-shows at the meeting, and that enabling liar Ashley said I had to cover Mona's expenses or stay married to her so she'd have my health insurance. That was the scene Grace walked in on. Ashley was out of control, and she threw the divorce papers in my face."

"Move it along, son," Cyrus said. "If you're going to tell it, keep it short."

"I was too upset to work after the meeting, so I went home. A few minutes before noon, Mona showed up. We'd talked on the phone from time to time, but I hadn't seen her in a year and a half, and she didn't look like my wife. She was high. She walked around the house picking things up, putting them down, but she never stopped moving. She said I could have the divorce and that she'd come here to see Mr. Mosley and sign the papers. Then she said she was sorry and started crying. I didn't know what to do with her, so I asked if I could take her to Simone. And just like that, she snapped and threw a lamp at me. Mona. I couldn't believe she escalated so quickly. Then she left. I didn't try to stop her, but I called Simone and left a message, telling her what happened, and I called Mr. Mosley. I never saw Mona or talked to her again. She died the next day, and on Friday, I got a letter."

Cyrus opened a folder and pushed it across the table to Mac. A small piece of paper was the only thing inside.

Everything is your fault and I will never forgive you.

"Who do you think wrote this?" Mac asked.

"Mona," Henry said in a choked voice. "It's her handwriting."

Mac checked the postmark on the envelope. Wednesday, Mallard Bay. One day after the murder. "Then who do you think mailed it?"

Henry's eyes were red. It took a moment before he could say, "Only two people could have found it. Simone or Ashley."

"And that's where the police need to look, Mac," Cyrus said. "You can see another party is involved. Sending that note to Henry after Mona's death is not only cruel, it's intended to make him act rashly. He's a victim here, and he needs your help. He's lost nearly everything except his new family, and now that you can see the whole picture, I'm hoping you'll help him."

"I didn't touch Mona, Mac, I swear!" Henry said, apparently unable to keep it in any longer. "She robbed me, and I don't just mean money. She took years that I could have spent with someone who loved me. She took money we both had earned and saved for IVF treatments for a baby. She bought drugs with the baby money! How could she do that? I hated her for it. I still do, but I didn't kill her."

Mosley shook his head and said, "This is all off the record, Mac."

But Henry had said it, and Mac had heard it, and now everything had changed. "I'll need to call Detective Marbury," he said.

As he pulled out his phone, tears rolled down Henry's face.

Krissy's voice was strident, and a half octave higher than usual when she pulled Grace from what would have been her second long nap of the day if she'd remembered to shut off the phone.

"Is this too much? Calling after I barged in on you yesterday? I'd say I'm not stalking you, except I kinda sorta am."

Grace yawned, slipped out of the nursery, and went into the kitchen for a cup of coffee. It was too late in the day for caffeine, but with any luck, Mac would come back, and she wanted to be alert if he did.

"Oh, Lord," Krissy said. "Did you hang up? Double Lord! Did I wake you up?"

"It's fine," Grace lied.

"So, can I come over?"

At least she asked this time, Grace thought. Besides, Mac was unlikely to come right back, and if he did, she'd throw her new best friend out on her ear. He'd never said why he'd stopped by, but to be fair, she hadn't given him much time to talk. She didn't care why he'd shown up, and he'd only grinned when she asked him.

"It'll keep," he'd said as he kissed her goodbye. "We covered the important stuff just fine."

She decided if he was happy, that was enough.

Krissy was harder to please. "This situation is a nightmare," she announced as she swept into the house and handed an adorable little girl with wispy brown hair to Grace. "Hold Ammie for a sec, will you?"

Amalie had other plans and immediately wiggled to get down. Fortunately, she was easily entertained in Fiona's playpen, because Krissy had brought croissants, and Grace was suddenly starved. "Does David know you're here?" she asked as she set out plates and a pitcher of orange juice.

"No. Does he need to?"

"Just trying to keep straight what he's in on and what he isn't."

"Sugar, the big guy and I are never gonna have one of those tell-all, in-each-other's-pockets kind of marriage. I'm just aiming for negotiated peace once in a while." Krissy pulled the top off a croissant, then dropped both pieces on the plate and sighed. "Peter's moving into the carriage house today. I gotta tell you, that boy is just odd." She scrambled around in her purse, which to Grace's untrained eye looked like a genuine Gucci, despite the apple-juice stains. Producing her phone, she tapped a few screens and said, "There. Daddy's people came through. Peter's background report should be in your email. Nothing that we didn't know, but interesting. Poor kid."

Grace avoided that opening and said, "How did that come about? The moving in, I mean. That was fast."

"You're not kidding! When I got home from seeing you, I found them in the sunroom yelling at each other. It was a lovely introduction to my new son. Neither he nor my darling husband even acknowledged my presence, so I left them to it and took Ammie outside. When it got quiet, I went back in, and David had that stressed look he gets when he demands something and is ready to do battle, then he gets yes instead of no and isn't sure if he should shut up and take it, or demand more."

Grace not only followed Krissy's colorful and circular way of talking, but also knew exactly what she meant. "So, what'd he do? Take the win and quit, or go for the extra point?"

"The boy's moving in this morning, so he won regardless of the score. I came over here. I'm letting them settle things between them. It's David's house, David's son, and David's problem, as far as I'm concerned. He certainly isn't taking my feelings into account in any of the decisions he's making, so I'm staying out of the way."

Fiona woke, and the babies shared their first playtime. As Grace watched them, she tried to feel hopeful. A week ago, she'd never heard of Krissy, Amalie, or Peter, and Mona Cutter was alive. The special dinner and the proposal were still a go, and her plans for the future were all possible.

Bells can't be unrung, she thought, but maybe she could get a do-over.

CHAPTER TWENTY-NINE

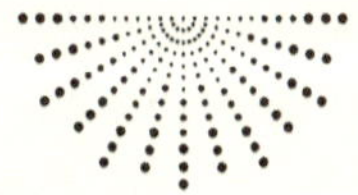

The hives were bad, and Grace knew they would get worse. A little woozy from antihistamines, she nonetheless raced to get dinner ready. She'd fiddled away the afternoon, lost in thought after Krissy and Amalie left, and now she had only an hour before Mac was due for The Dinner.

She should call him and tell him not to come. What had she been thinking? Just because he stopped by that morning with no notice and apparently only one purpose in mind didn't mean they were okay. But she'd believed him when he said they were, and impulsively resurrected her grand plans from a week ago.

It was a simple meal to prepare, but each step seemed difficult and time-consuming. She grumbled to herself that Krissy only had to hand a menu to her chef when she wanted a last-minute special dinner. "Cattiness does not become you," she told the wild-haired woman who looked back at her from the mirror over the kitchen table. Besides, she lectured herself, it was better to cook for Mac every night for the rest of her life than to be with David for one chef-created dinner.

She was immediately disgusted with herself for letting him

into her thoughts at a time like this. As soon as the thought formed, she looked toward the baby's room and smiled. She couldn't call her relationship with David a mistake, but she certainly didn't want him around tonight.

Sick of making herself crazy, she declared the dinner prep done and got busy making herself presentable. Work—major work—was needed if she had any hope of enticing Mac into more than a roll in the hay, and right now, he'd need a blindfold for that. She looked awful. At least Fiona was down for a long nap. Small mercies, she thought, as she turned on the water for her second shower of the day.

At one of their girls' nights, Niki had opined that if women had historically been responsible for marriage proposals, there'd be a better way to get engaged by now. A face-saving way for the smitten party to maintain his or her dignity if the proposal went horribly wrong. Ideas had flown back and forth, but the conversation was fueled by Chardonnay and took a turn to the ridiculous as the cousins tried to top each other with horror stories of grand gestures gone horribly wrong. They polished off the last bottle of wine with a pinky swear that such a calamity would never happen to them.

"But did I learn?" Grace muttered as she tamed her hair into a chignon. "Noooo."

A new cluster of hives bloomed, and she tried to decide if she should move dinner to the old picnic table in the back yard. Proposing outside at night was as close to saving herself as she could get, short of forgetting the whole nerve-racking idea. Even if he said yes, and one thing led to another, when she took off her long-sleeved dress, he'd see the hives. He called them her body's lie detector.

She could propose by email, she thought as she scrubbed the potatoes and preheated the oven. No, text. Text was better—she'd know right away if he said yes. And she could stop taking medication if he said no.

She thought about their lives since Fiona. Those months had given her the courage to do what she'd wanted ever since the day she'd realized she loved Mac. Watching him hold her baby, seeing the love in his eyes when he looked at them, had eased her fears. It had taken weeks to decide the perfect setting, the perfect meal, the perfect words.

She'd planned and shopped for the surprise dinner without the first tingle of hives. But then he'd chosen his job over her, and she'd done the same to him. If she waited any longer for the perfect time, who knew what could happen?

No, for better or worse, tonight was the night.

Mac's first reaction to the dinner-invitation text was to beg off, citing the long day. But instead, he'd typed "C U @ 6" and hit the arrow. Staying away from her was never the long-term plan, but it wasn't working in the short run, either. He tried to feel guilty about his earlier unannounced visit, but that didn't happen, either. He wanted to do it again, minus the opening argument. When he arrived that evening, he caught her rubbing cortisone cream onto the underside of her wrists. Her throat already shone from its lathering. Clearly, he wasn't the only one suffering from their joint stupidity.

"What's up?" he asked, taking in the silky dress and the glamour-shot hair and makeup.

"I'm so glad you came." She moved into his arms, effectively ending the conversation.

During dinner, she plied him with enough wine to ensure he

wouldn't drive home. When the steak, shrimp, and potatoes topped with sour cream and crisp onion rings were gone, she brought out the cheesecake.

"Is your goal to kill me or just have me too full to say no to whatever it is you want?" he asked, afraid she'd bring out cigars next. Then he remembered the cortisone cream. "What *do* you want?"

"I want to get married, and I don't know how to ask you. Damn." She pinked up and added, "I had a better speech. Want to hear it?"

He couldn't think of anything to say that wouldn't hurt her, but he didn't think he'd ever known anyone less ready for marriage than the woman he loved. Eventually he spoke, only to break the silence and keep her from passing out. She hadn't taken a breath. "Let me see your arms," he said, gently.

"No."

"Then no, I won't marry you."

"They aren't looking their best right now. But it means nothing, Mac. I love you."

"That's not what your neck says. You look like you're spiking a fever, too. If you can't even talk about forever without being medicated, what chance would we have?"

She looked so hurt, he almost took it all back, but she didn't trust him, and he didn't know how to fix that. There was no arguing, not even a debate. She stayed in the nursery, and he spent the night alone in her bed.

Neither of them slept a wink.

CHAPTER THIRTY

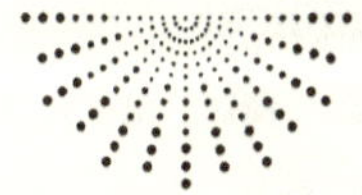

He braced himself to face Grace on Monday morning, but when he walked out of her bedroom at ten past six, the house was silent and the door to the baby's room was shut. He told himself it wasn't cowardly to leave without seeing her, but it still felt like the walk of shame as he let himself out of the house, easing the door shut behind him.

After a quick stop at home, where he checked in with Benny and grabbed a shower and change of clothes, he drove north to MD 301 and turned west. He'd started his day running away from a problem that needed solving, and now he might be about to create a new one. Doing the right thing had seldom caused him such misery.

First up on the list of irritating things to handle was the William Preston Lane Jr. Memorial Bridge. Four-plus miles of soaring, twisting stretches of concrete, asphalt, and rusting steel connects Maryland's western and eastern shores over the Chesapeake Bay. Sweaty-handed drivers negotiate the so-called World's Scariest Bridge with eyes averted from the open metal grates beneath their cars, not that the view out over the railings is any more comforting. Most locals just get on with it, but "Is it over the bridge?" is a deciding factor in decisions large and small.

Even after decades of twice-daily crossings, Mac still offered a quick prayer as he left land to face two-way traffic on the aging westbound bridge. This morning had seemed like a good time to get out of Mallard Bay and let his mind settle. Ironically, picking up the dishwasher for Grace's dream kitchen provided the perfect excuse. He was an uncomplicated man who had screwed up his life to an unrecognizable state, and he hoped three hours of driving and two trips across the bay would give him some perspective. If he didn't figure out a way to make things right, he'd have a state-of-the-art kitchen and only a dog to appreciate it.

He'd already decided the first step.

Zara Wingate looked more relaxed than the last time Mac had seen her. Today they were in the lawyer's Annapolis office and she wasn't defending a cop killer, and yet he was nearly as uncomfortable as he'd been at the trial in which she'd grilled him on the witness stand.

Because he hadn't had any better sense than to offer Ashley his condolences on Mona's death, he'd inadvertently encouraged her to ask him for help. In a weak moment, he'd agreed to help her find legal counsel. After his meeting with Henry, he knew it wasn't in her best interest to have the same representation as her sister. The pool of murder suspects was shrinking, and while it was hard to think of Ashley as a killer, someone was, and she wasn't acting like an innocent bystander. He'd made the appointment for her with Zara, but wanted to have a chat with the attorney before she met her new client.

He was in luck. Zara was available and seemed glad to see him. Shutting the door on the Monday morning office noise, she said, "What's so urgent that you had to see me in person before I meet with your Dr. Greenburgh?"

Mac thought he'd give a lot if all the women in his life were like this straightforward lawyer. "I had to come over to pick up a dishwasher, of all things, and I decided to see if you were free. What I need to say is awkward, and will hopefully come out better if we talk face-to-face."

Zara's only response was a raised eyebrow. She sipped her coffee and waited.

"When I made the appointment for Ashley, I wasn't clear with you about our relationship, and that was a mistake. Ashley and I don't agree on the boundaries." He'd struggled with the wording and now decided he sounded like an ass.

"I wondered why you wanted me to represent her," Zara said. "You gave me the basics of the case when we talked, but it's unusual for the chief of police to scout out attorneys for potential suspects. There are always extenuating circumstances, though."

"You're being kind," he said. "She used to be a friend of mine. And for a few months before Grace and I got together, Ashley was more than a friend."

"Ah. And Grace?"

"Wouldn't represent her in traffic court," he admitted with a sigh. "Besides, Cyrus and Grace are representing two of the other parties of interest." He hoped she'd leave it at that, but knew she wouldn't. He was here because Zara was good, not because she was polite.

"I read the news reports and talked to a few people," Zara said. "There are four suspects."

Mac nodded. "The victim's mother is Simone Lancer. She's representing herself and wants to represent Ashley, who's her sister. I didn't think that was a good idea."

"I'm aware of Ms. Lancer's work. She's good, and much too smart to represent either herself or another family member."

"Good sense sometimes goes out the window when family members are involved." He was thinking of Grace and Peter, then realized how the comment sounded. Ashley wasn't his family and yet, here he was.

Again, Zara skipped the niceties. "Does your Dr. Greenburgh need me because she killed her niece or because she didn't?"

"I'd tell you if I knew. I cared for her once, and now she's in trouble. That's the extent of what I know for sure. I can't help her, but I won't leave her in need, either. She needs representation."

"And now she has it, thanks to you. What else did you come to tell me?"

Suddenly, his idea to get things straight with Zara didn't have much appeal. He'd planned to be diplomatic in his wording, but when he spoke, he was as blunt as she had been. "I don't know what happened to Mona Cutter. I also don't know if Ashley is innocent. I hope she is, but if she isn't, she won't get any breaks from me, and I'm not asking for any on her behalf."

"I never thought you were. Someone killed a woman literally on Grace's doorstep. They may even have been after Grace." Zara stood and held out her hand. "You've helped someone in need, but that's where your involvement ends. You're a good person, Mac."

He doubted very much that Ashley would agree. "A final favor, if I may?" he said as they walked to the door.

She gave him a sideways smile and said, "Don't do anything to give Ashley the impression there's hope for the two of you?"

"Thank you," he said, relieved.

"Well, then, you'd better get moving. She'll be here soon."

He went on to collect the dishwasher, then reversed course and drove home. The whole time, his mind was on Grace. They needed to talk.

CHAPTER THIRTY-ONE

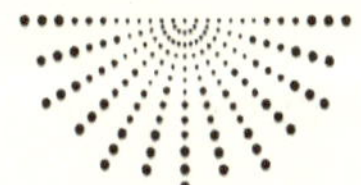

According to the paperwork that had been set up weeks before, Monday was the first day of operations for Mosley and Reagan, LLC, but the new partners hadn't spoken since the meeting in which they had agreed to a postponement of their actual collaboration. Grace checked her emails over breakfast and found two new client referrals from Cyrus. She decided he was operating on a "do as I say" basis, which was half their usual game plan. The other half was she did what she thought best. In short, they were operating as usual, except her staff consisted of a part-time ex-cop and a babysitter with illusions of grandeur. She decided things could be worse, but didn't let herself dwell on what such a situation might look like.

Other than the hollow feeling she got whenever she thought about Mac, the morning started off well enough. Hallie arrived at eight, and Grace made it to her office at nine to find a neatly dressed man sitting at the secretary's desk. The scent of fresh coffee wafted in from the kitchenette.

Aidan said, "There are warm bacon croissants for breakfast,

but don't get used to the food. Tomorrow, bring whatever you want to eat, but no sugar crap allowed in the morning."

"Where's your stash?" she asked. "You forget I knew you when you stocked the police station with Little Debbies."

"I forget nothing, madam. But I have changed my ways. No sugar." He didn't look up from the computer screen, but his wicked grin made her laugh.

"Just in the morning?"

"I'm working on it. I think I can fake it until I leave here. Which means—"

"No sugar. Got it."

As she passed his desk, he hit a key with a flourish and said, "You also have a new website, if you'd care to review the draft before it goes live. I just sent it to you."

Why hadn't she thought of this? She ate her breakfast slowly and clicked through screens that described the work of a firm of experienced and accomplished attorneys and their staff. Everyone looked professional, happy, and ready to slay evil on behalf of their clients. She didn't know where he'd found the photos and strongly suspected most of his time had been spent doctoring the best of the lot. Mosley's unshiny and age-spot-free scalp and her clear, bag-free eyes were a testament to his artistry. The description of the firm and its services was excellent. She'd hire herself in a second after reading her bio. Mosley sounded like a candidate for the Supreme Court—or God. Even Marjorie looked like someone who would hold back the fires of hell until Mosley or Reagan could take your call.

"Who are these people?" she called out to the outer office.

"Your avatars. Try not to embarrass them."

"I'm not worthy." She walked out and handed him a short list. "It's excellent, Aidan. Thank you so much for thinking of this. The old site had to change, but I don't know when we would have gotten to it. Just these few corrections and you can run it past

Cyrus, but he'll probably ask you to hold off for a while. We're not quite ready to start up yet."

He looked at the list and handed it back to her. "Unless he's changed his mind in the last thirty minutes, Mr. Mosley's good. The whole project was his idea. He told me to tell you to check your shared files on IDrive and to"—he checked a notepad—"set up a firewall. He said you'd know what he meant."

Grace looked at her list as if it might suddenly hold the explanation she didn't really need. On one hand, she'd lost another round to the old lawyer downstairs. All of Aidan's "mistakes" had been in the firm's name on each page. A month ago, after much arguing and revising of paperwork, Mosley had given in and listed his name first as the senior partner. But, according to the website, and, no doubt, the version of their contract she would find in their shared file, the firm was named Reagan and Mosley, Attorneys at Law. It was, she thought, a name fit for their avatars, not a sleep-deprived new mother and a would-be full-time golfer about to enter his ninth decade of winning arguments.

Still, she wasn't operating totally alone, after all—it only felt like she was. The firewall meant they would just maintain a strict divide between them in all matters concerning Mona Cutter's murder. She thanked Aidan again and went downstairs to see her partner.

Who, of course, wasn't there. Instead, she found Marjorie admiring her page on the website.

"When did he change the firm's name?" Grace asked without preamble. She knew The Bat was just waiting for her to ask.

"As soon as he threw up his hands and told you to call us whatever you wanted. I knew then you'd lost. I hope you're pleased with yourself." Marjorie looked up from her own glamour shot long enough to give Grace a warning glare. "Don't get any ideas about ordering me around. I work for Mr. Mosley. No one else."

"Don't worry. I'll get enough pleasure just hearing you answer the phone, 'Reagan and Mosley.'"

"As if," Marjorie muttered, then perked up. "You have a client going up to your office." She pointed to a small monitor on the corner of her desk. "One of your baby daddy's other children."

That answered the question of whether the interior security cameras were working. Grace didn't bother sniping back, but left to see why Peter had arrived early for their one o'clock appointment.

So far, her new partnership was just as irritating as her old one had been.

Peter didn't look happy—or cooperative. Grace took him into her office and made small talk while she got bottles of water for both of them and opened a new package of cheese crackers, pushing it toward the boy.

"Eat," she said in her best motherly voice. "I don't share my emergency stash with just anyone, you know. It's these or carrot sticks and apples." She wasn't sure, but she thought she saw a fleeting smile as he took a handful of the life-affirming fat, salt, and imitation cheese. When his mouth was full, she said, "I talked with Krissy yesterday. She said you'd met and you're moving in."

"Yep," he mumbled. "The garage apartment over top of the other trophies."

He sounded so much like David, she wondered if he was doing it on purpose. The look he gave her also belonged to David. It was long and appraising and said she didn't fool him with her clumsy prying. He finished off the crackers and said, "It's better that I'm out of the house and they can pretend we're a normal family."

"Let's have it," Grace said. "What's happened now?"

"Krissy keeps looking at me when she thinks I don't see her. And he keeps asking me to talk about my feelings. That's when he isn't trying to get me to throw a football or talk about cars."

"And that upsets you?"

"Yes! All I want is for him to find my mother. I don't want to live with them, and I hate football."

Grace laughed. "So does David. He's just trying to be a dad, and he doesn't know how."

Peter mumbled something that sounded like "whatever."

"Would I be too nosy if I asked if you're at least comfortable in your apartment there?"

"Would it stop you if I said yes?"

She laughed again, and this time got a real smile.

He said, "The only good thing is I get to drive the Land Rover. Other than that, the answer is no. School may suck, but their place is out in the middle of the woods. It's so quiet, it's creepy. I hate all of this. Do you think you could get permission for me to join the air force now? I was serious. I can take the GED test today. I found a sample online, and I knew practically everything."

Grace tried to look as if she were giving his proposal some consideration. "What do you have left to complete in order to graduate with your class next month?"

He looked embarrassed and picked up another handful of crackers instead of answering.

"It can't be much at this point," Grace said, prompting him.

The rest of the bottle of water disappeared, then he looked her in the eye. "I. Hate. School. In person, virtually, whatever. The kids are like I would have been if my parents had stuck around when I was born. But they didn't and now—"

"Now you're going to show David how screwed up you are so he'll feel bad? Listen to me," she said, all humor and gentleness gone. "You can always get into a GED program, but you've earned those grades, and you're going to get them. You say you're an adult? Act like it. This is your last tantrum, understand? You have work to do."

The words weren't magic, and it was a while before he gave in, but eventually Peter agreed to tune into his afternoon classes and finish his outstanding school assignments. The next argument concerned how and where he was going to accomplish this feat. He insisted on working from the corner coffee shop instead of the office kitchen, as Grace suggested.

"Your apartment is quiet," Grace reminded him.

"Maybe I would be better off back at Farq's house. At least his wife is chill."

With a not now look at Aidan, who'd come to stand in the doorway, she said, "Do what you please. But I'm telling you it's in your best interest to graduate from Howard Military Academy. You're going to owe me a lot of money, and a good job will be easier to find if your resume shows you had the ability to finish a rigorous educational program."

Peter looked stunned. "But Farq is paying—"

"I'm not taking a penny from him," she said. "David has nothing to do with our agreement. Daddy doesn't buy you out of your adult contracts, not the ones with me, anyway."

Aidan went back to his desk with a smile on his face, but Grace felt sick. There went her safety net. Her only answer from Peter was a jerky nod before he took his backpack into the kitchen and shut the door.

She tried to count it as a win, but she felt like a failure. A soon-to-be-broke failure.

CHAPTER THIRTY-TWO

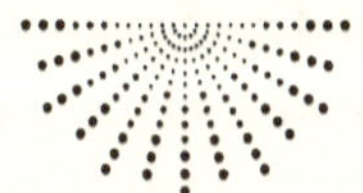

The mood in the office lightened when Hallie arrived at noon with Fiona. After being introduced to Peter, she unceremoniously dumped the baby in his lap and said, "I'm Grace's assistant and part-time secretary. Mind your sister a minute while I fix her bottle."

With a comical expression, Peter quickly stood, moving the squirming baby away from his laptop and holding her like a ticking bomb. When Hallie retrieved her charge, she glanced down at the screen and said, "Whoa! What are you working on? That looks like Chinese."

"Mandarin."

In the next room, Grace and Aidan looked at each other. "Don't think that's on the GED," he whispered.

True to her deal with Hallie, Grace bought lunch for everyone. They were cleaning up the remains when Zara Wingate walked in.

"What a nice surprise," Grace said, after making introductions. "I'm so glad you finally made it over here."

Zara looked embarrassed, but held out a gift bag to Hallie,

who had Fiona in her arms. For once, the baby was awake, full, and clean all at the same time.

"She's a beauty!" Zara said as Fiona played with the tissue paper from the gift bag that held a teddy bear in a bright green sweater.

"She's smart," Hallie corrected, frowning.

"That's a given," Zara agreed. "And while I would love nothing better than to spend some time with her, I was hoping to confer with Grace. If she's free, of course."

The request was made to Hallie, who checked her calendar with a swipe of a finger and announced that Grace could spare twenty minutes. The two lawyers made their escape before she changed her mind.

"That's one of the daughters from your polygamist case, right?" Zara asked as they walked down to Memorial Park, taking advantage of the warm April sunshine. "Is that how small-town practices work? They hire you, and you return the favor?"

Grace laughed and said, "Sometimes. But her parents were polyamorists, not polygamists. Their family union wasn't illegal. And I should be so lucky to keep Hallie, but she'll be off to college in a few months. For right now, she's keeping my life straight, and she's amazing."

"Your newest client is also going to stay in your life after his legal troubles are settled, isn't he?"

"You weren't just driving through, were you?" Grace pointed to a bench near the water. The park was nearly empty as the last of the weekend visitors' boats were being readied for departure. It was a good place to talk, but it wouldn't be a conversation between girlfriends. She said, "Whom are you representing?"

"Let's say my visit is a happy coincidence. I've been meaning to get in touch, but you know how it is. Tomorrow is always busier than you think it will be. Anyway, after talking with my client this morning, I decided to make my baby visit do double duty and get some background from you, if you're okay with that. I'm representing Ashley Greenburgh."

Ashley. Grace shook her head. "How do you know her?" she asked, unable to stop the question from popping out. She hoped she didn't look as upset as she felt.

"Mac recommended me to her." Zara delivered the news while studying a sleek black yacht that was inching slowly out of its rental slip.

Grace read the signals. Zara didn't want to pry and didn't want to be involved in any personal issues. The last time she and Grace had discussed a murder investigation, Zara had congratulated her on being with Mac, but hadn't asked many questions then, either.

"I'm glad to help if I can," Grace said, relieved that her voice was steadier than she was.

"A good, qualified answer," Zara said with a smile. "So, who do you think killed Mona Cutter?"

Grace kept her answer equally short. "Not Peter Carlton."

"Touché. But if you can't make things easy for me, will you tell me what you know about my client and her sister? I'm assuming you're aware of Simone Lancer's reputation. She isn't happy about Ashley having separate counsel."

Grace described Simone's visit to her office the day before the murder.

"You made a smart call," Zara said. "Lancer practices cutthroat law, and she's not known for her scruples. Her daughter was okay with the divorce, but Simone and Ashley weren't. They'd been hemorrhaging money for the victim's upkeep and therapy, and Simone wanted the husband to take over."

"Ashley was paying, too?"

"According to my client, the reason she moved to Mallard

Bay was to be a support for Mona, who was having problems with depression. They've always been close."

An answer clicked into place for Grace. She'd assumed that jealousy over Mac was at the root of Ashley's animosity toward her. But if Ashley associated her with Henry and his cousin Bryce, it could be another reason for her behavior. "So, who do you think is the killer?" she asked, turning the question back to Zara. "You may as well tell me. If we can agree that our clients are in the clear, we might wrap all this up faster."

Zara wouldn't be rushed, but after a moment, she said, "From everything I've learned so far, I believe Dr. Greenburgh and Ms. Lancer only wanted what was best for Mona Cutter and did what they could to help her. They both spent significant sums of money on her welfare. Mr. Cutter's divorce plea states his wife took more than fifty percent of the assets out of the marriage when she left him two years ago. He petitioned the court to award no further financial settlement upon issuing the divorce decree, which means her mother and aunt would have been stuck paying most of her expenses. Mona hasn't been able to keep a job since she left here. Her alimony award would have been small, if she had gotten anything at all. It was an unusual divorce action."

Grace said, "Sounds like three highly motivated individuals. Henry, Simone, and Ashley would all be better off, financially, if Mona died."

"If any of them had wanted her dead, all they had to do was hand her a few bucks and drop her off in downtown Baltimore." She stopped and looked around the park. "Or anywhere else, for that matter. An addict can always find a fix, and when Mona had money in her pocket, she got trashed. Lately, those events were ending in overdoses. Her mother and aunt had known that for months—why kill her now?"

"Passion," Grace said. "Anything could have happened

between any or all of them. And as for Henry, the day she died, Mona told him he could have the divorce on the terms he wanted. Maybe he followed her to the office to make sure she went through with it."

"Which she did."

"He still had plenty of reasons to be angry with her. She'd put him through hell for two years."

Zara shook her head. "You're stretching. None of the family had a reason to wait around while she was in Mr. Mosley's office, then chase her up the stairs to your office and kill her."

Grace knew she'd just heard Zara's opening statement for Ashley's defense. It was good as far as it went, but she still thought Mona's family looked better than a random stranger. Or Peter.

Zara interrupted her thoughts by asking, "Did any of the four suspects have a reason to want you dead?"

Desi Marbury had asked her the same thing, but had dropped that line of investigation when nothing panned out.

Grace said, "I didn't know Mona Cutter. Although I'd heard of her, I didn't know Simone Lancer until she walked into my office. As for Henry, until last week, we hadn't spoken in two years. And while Ashley might climb over me to get to Mac, I doubt she'd kill me. And don't even try to pretend you don't know what I mean."

"TMI, Counselor," Zara said, and chuckled. "Now, what about your client? He's already testified that he saw Mona's body on the stairs, thought it was you, and yet ran off without getting help."

"He's a traumatized kid, not a killer. He didn't do it."

Zara stood and looked down at Grace. "I don't like us being on opposite sides. I'm beginning to wish I hadn't taken this case, but I won't back out because I've discovered I don't like all the players." She held out a hand, clasped Grace's. "Take care of yourself and your sweet baby. Be careful. I'm going to worry about you."

After a long, and clearly conflicted, moment, she sat back down and told Grace why.

CHAPTER THIRTY-THREE

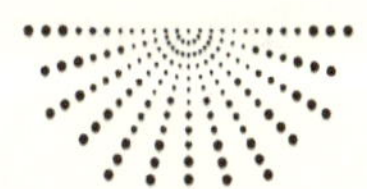

"I don't like that woman," Hallie announced when Grace walked back into her office. "Why didn't you make her get an appointment? You have to stay on the schedule if we're going to have you home at a reasonable time."

Grace ignored her. The conversation with Zara was still running through her head. She'd remind Hallie later that "assistant" didn't mean "overlord."

After checking on the baby, who was napping in the conference room, she shut the door to her office. For the next half hour, she updated Peter's file with Zara's information, adding it to the report she'd gotten from the private investigator and the background check Krissy had sent her. Those few pages detailed a childhood marred by neglect, accidents, police reports, and foster homes. His adolescence was more of the same, but his role shifted from full-time victim to occasional perpetrator.

David's son had his temper as well as his looks.

Zara's second revelation had been the news of a reduction in the suspect pool. A red-light camera on Route 50, twenty miles away from Mallard Bay, caught a clear shot of Simone's Tesla racing through an intersection just minutes before Mona arrived at Cyrus's office.

That left Henry and Ashley in the MSP's spotlight. Zara was building a case to replace both of them with Peter. In her narrative, he was a hotheaded, emotionally scarred young man with a quick temper and firsthand knowledge of how far addicts such as Bethany Carlton and Mona Cutter would go for their drugs of choice. He'd gone hungry often enough when his mother bought alcohol instead of food.

It was impossible for Grace to believe that the boy who sat in the next room working on his Mandarin translations while stealing peeks at Hallie could be a dealer, but she knew a prosecutor could make him look like one. Her laptop registered an incoming email from Zara.

"Wow," Grace whispered as she read the attachment. "When you go out on a limb, you climb all the way to the end, don't you?" She hoped her friend never had to explain why she'd shared a copy of a juvenile arrest record.

Her heart sank as she read about the felony assault charges that had been dismissed against a thirteen-year-old Peter. As she closed the file with its damning information, she remembered Zara's parting words and knew why she'd sent the email.

"Do you remember Betsy Forester?" she'd asked Grace as they stood on the sidewalk in front of the office.

Grace said it would be hard to forget the mother of the psychopath who'd tried to kill her. "Did she ever come to terms with what Tyler did?" she asked and regretted her words when Zara's eyes filled with tears. Too late, she remembered Zara had been Betsy's best friend for more than thirty years.

Zara said, "I defended him from the time he was a teenager because she begged me to. I made the same poor choice over and over again of arguing that he was innocent. I usually got him released, and look what happened. Betsy died two weeks ago.

Heart failure was the diagnosis, but I know who caused it. Tyler killed her as surely as if he'd shot her."

Grace deleted Zara's email as thoroughly as she could, but she couldn't erase the memory of what she'd read.

She had only two hours before her office closed and Peter went back to David's house. There was no time to weigh options. She had to level with Peter.

Hallie, of course, objected to being sent home early.

"I don't understand why you changed your mind," she complained as she packed up. There's plenty for me to do here, and Fiona is happy in the playpen."

"Hallie." It came out sharper than Grace had intended. She took a breath. "What I need is for you to mail these letters before the post office closes. Then you can get Fiona home and see if she'll eat a little of the cream of rice mixed with apple juice." Then she thought of five things Hallie should know about feeding the baby. It didn't feel right that they should mesh with the questions she needed to ask Peter about his juvenile record.

One thing at a time.

"Post office, apple juice and cereal, three teaspoons max. A walk in the park, and make a salad for dinner, if you have time. Please."

It might have been the "please," or Hallie may have sensed she was pushing the edges of their tenuous working agreement, but she got Fiona gathered up and out the door without further complaint. Grace hoped the next conversation she had went as well.

"You want me to leave, too?" Peter asked.

"No. We need to talk."

Peter looked wary as he took a seat on the bench. She sat next to him, hoping to put him at ease. She thought he'd had a lot of uncomfortable conversations with adults on the far side of tables and desks.

"Who's the woman you went out with?" he asked abruptly. "Hallie didn't know her. We thought she might be a social worker."

It made sense, of course. Both Peter and Hallie would know about Children's Services, and if that was what Hallie had been worried about, they'd have to talk.

"No," she said. "Zara Wingate is an attorney and a friend of mine. She came to see me to tell me she was representing Ashley Greenburgh. Do you know who that is?"

"Well, yeah."

She summarized each of the four suspects in the murder, ending the list with Peter.

He looked stunned. "But I thought the police understood I never got near that woman. What's changed to make them suspect me?"

"They never completely ruled you out, Peter. I think they believe the others have better motives, but you had the opportunity. You also have a tragic history, and there are similarities between Mona Cutter's death and Bethany's."

He wouldn't meet her gaze.

"Why didn't you tell me she had a head injury when she died?"

The private investigator's report on Bethany Carlton's death had been basic and short on details. While smoke inhalation was undoubtedly accurate, it wasn't the only factor. Niki's old boyfriend left a lot to be desired in the professional arena, too.

Peter still didn't look at her, but he mumbled, "It was an old injury. Bethany was driving drunk and had a wreck. She had some permanent damage, but when she got out of the hospital, she pretty much seemed the same to me. Nurses came to the house a couple of times, and I heard them telling her she couldn't drink the way she used to, but she didn't stop. I don't know if she was drinking more or if I was seeing her as she really was for the first time. I tried to watch her and hide the booze, because as bad as it was living with her, I could take care of both of us and no one bothered me."

"Bothered you?" Grace asked gently.

"Yeah. Over the years, I was in five foster homes. Five that I remember. One was real good, but I was little then. Three of them were okay, but Bethany always got me out."

"And the fifth one?"

"It doesn't matter."

When a minute went by in silence, she said, "How old were you when she had the auto accident?"

"Thirteen."

Five years. It was hard to absorb, but he was finally looking at her, so she tried not to let the shock show.

"Not all of it was as bad as it sounds," he said. "We both knew if I was removed one more time, I wouldn't be coming back, so we made a deal. She'd try to not get caught drinking, and I'd cover for her until I turned eighteen and could live on my own. She had disability payments, and I got a job after school in a grocery store that let me take home out-of-date stuff that was still good. We made it work most of the time, but then she got bad again, and the police were at our house a couple of times on noise complaints from the neighbors. My lawyer said that was actually a good thing for me, because it made my story believable when I said she fell asleep smoking and caused the first fire. It took the cops some time to figure it all out, though, 'cause she blamed me."

Grace had read the brief news reports.

"Then when I was seventeen, she got her third DUI in two years and went to jail. That turned out okay for me, too," he said. "I always did okay in school, and a guidance counselor who'd always been nice to me was already working on a scholarship for me at Howard. She knew somebody there and pulled some strings, and they let me in midsemester of my junior year. At first it was great, then it wasn't."

She had his school transcripts in her files. He'd ranked at the top of his classes in both schools, maintaining near-perfect scores. What could he have accomplished academically if he hadn't had a perpetually drunken mother and a night job? She was so glad she'd bullied him into getting his certificate.

But Peter's story wasn't finished. He talked on, and the longer he went, the closer she came to tears. When he was finished, he said, "What are you going to do?"

She didn't weigh the pros and cons or think about the rules of law. She didn't say anything, only opened her arms and let him hold on tight.

CHAPTER THIRTY-FOUR

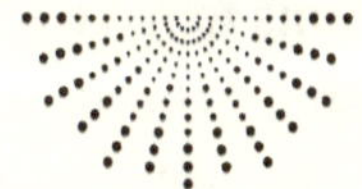

"Have you lost your mind?"

Zara had called Mac, and now he stood in Grace's living room, in no mood to hear that she couldn't discuss her client. As he lectured her, the thrill of seeing him evaporated. She wanted to explain herself, but couldn't—and he knew it.

When he slowed down, she said, "Thank you for stopping by this evening to inquire about my mental health, but no, I haven't lost anything, except, apparently, your trust." She stopped abruptly before her voice broke. She would not humiliate herself again.

Mac stepped back, the heat ebbing from his face. He looked tired, and despite her anger, she ached to hold him. But when he spoke again, that all changed.

"Your client isn't a helpless kid. He's a grown man who had an abusive background. I don't care how smart he is, he's volatile. He attacked a police officer, Grace! Zara has the report from his juvenile hearing two years ago. She was astonished to find him in your office holding Fiona. And you left him alone with the baby and Hallie!"

"Wonder whom else she called? Remind me to thank her for her unethical behavior."

"We are all worried about you."

"Well, all of you need to take a step back," she said. "Two years ago, Peter was barely sixteen—a child—and yes, he lost his temper and took a swing at an officer who was trying to arrest his mother. Now, remind me again how confidential sealed juvenile records work. Zara sure seems to have a lot of them."

He ignored the sarcasm. "The charges against Carlton may have been dropped in the case of his mother's death, but it wasn't the first time their house had burned, and the investigators aren't convinced he didn't set both fires."

"I am. And in this house, his name is Peter."

He didn't let her get away with it. "Don't change the subject. He's in David's home right now with Krissy and their baby! How can you let—"

"He didn't do it." She knew she sounded like a broken record. Why did she keep putting herself through this? Mac would never stop questioning the motives of suspects and their attorneys, not even when it meant he was doubting her. Then he turned the tables on her.

"Say whatever you want, but I won't leave you and Sweet Pea alone with him."

His use of Fiona's nickname said he wasn't gone from her yet. She tried one more time to reason with him. "Peter didn't set any fires, and he didn't kill Mona Cutter. He's not violent, just wounded. He's had a rotten life, and I won't abandon him."

He gave her nothing but that steady, disappointed gaze.

"Even if you don't trust me, I still have to do my job, Mac. We won't have a future with this between us."

He shook his head. "Either you tell David everything, or I will."

It tipped the scales. She was done.

"You do think I'm incompetent, don't you? Incompetent and so overrun with my maternal emotions that I'm blind to what's right in front of me."

"No, I don't."

She threw her hands up in exasperation. "Either you think I'm hormone riddled and stupid, or you think I'm lying to you." Her voice faded on her last words as the truth hit her, hard. "Oh, Mac, that's it, isn't it?"

In a moment that seemed suspended between them, her heart shattered, and all the fears their love had held at bay rushed in at once. She saw her broken dreams and the long years ahead without him.

He believed she was Peter's mother.

In the time it took her to walk to the front door and open it, she made her decision. Turning back to face him, she spoke quietly. "David already knows everything. The good, the bad, and the pitiful, which is where most of his son's life lands. But you are right about one thing. I have been blind. Until now, I have had blind faith in you." She opened the door wider. "When you go over to make sure David and his family are safe, ask him to show you the DNA tests that prove his son's parentage. I'm not his mother, but I would have considered it to be an honor."

The unfairness of it all was too much. When he passed her and stepped onto the porch, she said, "You and Zara are a few reports short of a full file."

He turned back to face her, and she knew she had to trust him one more time. Trust that he wouldn't twist her words when he repeated what she said to Desi Marbury.

"Peter didn't set the fire that killed Bethany Carlton. Despite the life he had with her, despite every lie she told him, she was the only mother he ever knew. The night of the fire, she was drunk, and they argued over his decision to join the air force. Things escalated, and she said she wished they were both dead. She started the fire, Mac, but she screwed it up, just like everything else she touched in that miserable, sick life of hers."

"Was she his mother?"

"Ask David," she repeated stubbornly. "Look at his proof. There was no adoption. Bethany gave birth to Peter and couldn't live with a child who looked like the man who'd rejected her. Just my take on things, though. Go talk to David and get an answer you can trust."

"Grace—"

She shut the door gently and turned the lock.

CHAPTER THIRTY-FIVE

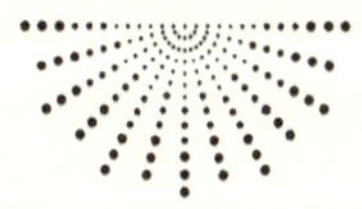

Tuesday morning arrived in a gentle lightening of the bedroom that increased until sunlight cut through the morning fog in Mac's sleep-deprived brain. Benny's painters had taken down his blackout curtains, and he'd stumbled into bed too late the night before to notice. He'd taken to falling asleep in front of the only television that was still connected downstairs. Last night, the nap he got during the end of Monday Night Football was the only rest he'd had until he'd fallen into a deep sleep just before dawn. He felt hungover and wished he had a reason to be. A few drinks the night before might have eased his thoughts of Grace. Or not.

He had a decision to make, and nothing in his life was going to improve until he made it once and for all. He was a calm, cautious, and organized man. If he was going to upend his life, he'd do it with a plan.

This last thought made him smile. He could hear Grace saying, ". . . and if that doesn't work, I'll . . ." She always had a plan, and a backup plan, and at least a couple of contingencies. It was one thing they had in common if you didn't count the fact that his plans were sensible and hers often fell somewhere between impossible and crazy.

That thought yanked him back to the night before and he winced, remembering how he'd spoken to her. It was becoming a habit, feeling bad about Grace. It all needed fixing, but he'd definitely limited his options. Far from having the moral high ground in their argument, he was in a deep pit he might never get out of.

After checking in with Tremaine and taking the morning off, he inspected the downstairs of his home. The cottage was finally looking like a construction site instead of a demolition project, and he was impressed with the progress that had been made in the past week. The roof was finished, the exterior walls were in place, and as long as he kept his shoes on and watched where he stepped, he could sleep in his own bedroom.

He hated it.

The solitude he'd enjoyed for so many years now felt like a punishment. He didn't have Grace and Fiona. He didn't even have his dog. Benny was boarding Rocky at his house for the next few weeks. Mac could have left her with Avril and let Louise and Leo teach her some manners, but he thought the little spaniel was going to need more training than Avril's dogs could give her. He made coffee and refocused his thoughts. Rocky was fine with Benny's pack. It was the rest of his life that needed to be straightened out.

He started with the easy issues.

He wanted to share the transformation of the cottage with Grace. His plan to surprise her was one of the worst ideas he'd ever had. She should be here to watch the changes and make the thousand and one decisions that would determine the final look and use of the new open-concept space.

Back at Christmas, she and Avril had been looking at old plans for the renovation of Avril's family's homestead out near Wye Mills. The conversation had drifted to Grace's definition of a dream house. As soon as he could, he'd written down everything she'd mentioned, from the farm sink to a gigantic three-door, stainless-steel refrigerator in a kitchen/family room combination, to four bedrooms that he thought was overkill, but whatever. He'd measured and sketched and paced around his house until he could see how it might all fit. By opening the kitchen into his den and the formal living room, she could have her main floor plan, and enclosing part of the patio gave her a sunroom similar to the one she loved at Avril's. Adding another bedroom wing gave them the extra space she thought they needed, and a wraparound porch to the front and right side of the cottage turned it into a modern farmhouse.

He'd engaged an architect, booked Benny, and arranged a mortgage, all on the premise that if Grace liked the new version of his home, she might live in it. If she didn't, he'd sell it. Waterfront property went fast, so he wouldn't lose money, only the land that had been in his family for generations. He'd never once thought it would come to that, but now he wasn't so sure.

He refilled his cup and did another walk through, imagining the place put back together and telling himself the newly abbreviated renovation plan was a sensible decision. If Grace's front door was permanently locked, he could still live here, and the exterior of his family home would retain its original look.

It was a good pep talk, but as he looked at the view of the river from his new sunporch, he knew he'd never be happy here alone again. Every time he came downstairs into the big kitchen and great room, he'd be reminded of what he'd lost. Whom he'd lost.

He got his canoe from the boat shed and loaded it into the back of the truck. It was a short ride to Morning Rise Point, and he was on the water by eight. Late for fishing, early for pleasure boaters. It was the perfect time to talk to his wife.

His trips out to this particular bend of the Wye River had

grown further apart in the last few years. The need to be here eased a bit, not because of Grace, but because he had gradually accepted that he had a life he wanted to share with someone who wasn't Meri.

He still came occasionally to talk to her, though, and he never left without an answer, or at least a sense of peace. This was where he'd proposed to Meri and where, twenty years later, he'd scattered her ashes. He'd told her about Grace out here, and now he told her what he'd done, and how things stood between them.

He thought if anyone would understand his point of view, it would be Meri. She'd worried as he spent his uniformed years in patrol cars and on search teams. She'd held him when he grieved for the people he couldn't save and applauded when the medals were pinned on his chest for the ones he did. She sacrificed her own peace of mind for him, and it was only when he lost her that he knew the anguish she'd endured. He'd almost lost Grace, too. She'd nearly died after Fiona's birth, and he hadn't been with her.

He explained it all to Meri, the danger Grace welcomed with open arms and her refusal to compromise despite his concerns. He also admitted that he'd failed her. He'd been sure she didn't trust him enough to tell him the truth, to give him a chance to understand what she'd done all those years ago. Not that he would have accepted Peter with open arms—he knew himself better than that —but they could have worked it all out together.

He waited to get something in return for his confession. A lightening of his heavy spirit, perhaps, but this morning the river and Meri were quiet. He was alone.

The little canoe rocked and drifted, the gentle motion eventually soothing him as he tried to sort his thoughts. After a time, he had to acknowledge that the misery he felt was shame. And it had nothing to do with Grace. She'd behaved exactly as she always did. She saw someone in trouble and she jumped in to help, while he had tried to stop her every way he could think of, and as guilty as he felt about that, he was still furious that she would risk her safety and Fiona's.

But had she?

The uncomfortable question bothered him. He'd been a cop too long not to suspect someone such as Peter Carlton, but Grace still asked him to trust her read of the kid. He hadn't even tried.

Why?

Because Peter Carlton looked, walked, and talked like David Farquar.

Was that why he was angry with Grace? Because she believed what David's son told her instead of what he'd said? Meri would have taken his side.

"Good Lord," he said out loud. "I'm jealous." For some reason, this realization astounded him, although he'd been eaten up with jealousy when he'd thought Grace was going to marry the jackass.

Wasn't that why he was remodeling the house? To give Grace what David hadn't—a home exactly like the one she'd said she wanted. That had been the plan, anyway. Then he'd gotten cold feet and didn't trust her to accept his gift if it came with a lifetime commitment. Now he had a place that was too big for him and not big enough for her. Not that she was ever going to speak to him again.

Is it better this way?

He knew they would spend the rest of their lives arguing with each other. He would end up out here on a regular basis, sitting in a canoe and wondering how she could have done whatever it was she was bound to do that would infuriate him. Why had that ever seemed like a good idea?

He poured coffee from the thermos and thought about that. He'd had ten years of a quiet life in his little cottage. When he'd let his heart open up again, there was only one woman he'd wanted. He knew they weren't a good match, so he'd tried all the logical alternatives. He was sure Ashley would be appalled to know that was how he thought of her. An alternative and a lightweight one at that. When all else had failed, he'd let himself love Grace.

And?

Well, there it was. He waited for a different answer, a hint, a sign of any kind that would direct him to a peaceful life. The current slowed as the minutes passed, and even nature seemed to abandon him. It was time to stop drifting. He knew how he wanted to live his life, but it meant getting Grace to trust him one more time.

As the canoe slid onto the sandy edge of the river, a gaggle of geese flew overhead and, in their calls, he heard Meri's laugh.

CHAPTER THIRTY-SIX

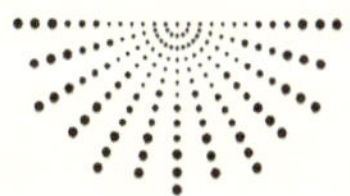

Operating on autopilot, Grace made it through the morning handoff to Hallie and arrived at her office to find a note taped to her inner door. *Errands. Back by noon. A.*

Wondering which of the long list of chores Aidan had taken on first, she hurried inside and answered the ringing phone. She tried to sound chipper, but stumbled over the firm's new name. "Mo—, Reagan and Mosley, how may I—"

"There you are!" Marjorie's shrill voice cut her off.

Grace jerked the handset away from her ear, but could still clearly hear The Bat's complaints. "I'm not your receptionist, you know, and you can't tell people to wait for you down here."

People? She checked her calendar, which was clear, but she realized she hadn't turned her cell phone on. There were three voicemail messages. Aidan, Peter, and David.

"Well? Are you coming down here to get them?"

The small bit of patience she had in her evaporated. "Marjorie, you're being rude. More so than usual, I mean. My clients are our firm's clients, and the downstairs is not your sanctuary." The silence that met this statement told her the enemy was regrouping.

"Please tell me who's there and what the problem is. Quietly, so no one is embarrassed. Embarrassed *again*."

More silence. Why hadn't she tried this before? She wouldn't have thought it possible to shame the woman.

"Your stepson and Ashley Greenburgh." Marjorie's whisper came across as a hiss that Grace was sure could be heard out on the sidewalk. "Of course, I've had to keep them separated."

"Please ask Mr. Carlton, who is not my stepson, but who is my client, to come up."

"But what about poor Ashley?"

Grace tightened her grip on the handset to keep from bashing it on the desk. *Poor Ashley*. "I wasn't expecting her, and I'll call her when I'm free. And Marjorie? I'm sorry you were inconvenienced. I didn't mean for that to happen. My office manager is out on an errand, but I'll try not to cause you any more trouble before he returns."

It was mean, and as soon as she disconnected, she laughed out loud at the thought of the tizzy The Bat would be in now. The only thing worse than handling work for Grace was sharing her power with an interloper. With Aidan, of all people.

The day was looking a little brighter until Peter arrived.

"Farq and I had a fight," he said, dropping his overloaded backpack on the floor and sinking down on the bench.

"Good morning, Peter. How are you?" She wasn't sure what he mumbled as he put his head in his hands and decided that was for the best. "Hungry?"

No response.

She went into the kitchen, made coffee, and put the ham biscuit she'd picked up for her own breakfast on a plate, all the while listening for sounds of life from the other room. When she carried the loaded tray out and set it beside him, he finally looked at her.

"Eat," she said. "Then talk." She pulled a chair up to sit across from him. It was a compromise between the intimacy of their last meeting in which she'd treated him like a grieving child and the professionalism she needed this morning. Once they got past whatever was upsetting him, they had to discuss his defense.

He finished the sandwich in three bites.

"What did you and David argue about?" she asked.

"We didn't argue. We had a fight." Peter held up his hands. The right one looked swollen and painful. "A real one. I can't stay there anymore. I have my things in the car."

Grace was appalled. "Are you saying you two actually hit each other? Are you hurt?"

"No, I can handle myself," he said, grousing. "Farq's gonna remember me for a while, though. Don't worry, I'm not crashing in on you. I can get a room somewhere. The Egret's out of my budget, but I can swing a cheaper place."

She was having a hard time moving on from the visual of David and his son in a fistfight. She knew their relationship wasn't any of her business, but Peter's residency was. There had been a measure of protection in having David and Krissy to vouch for his actions if the need arose.

"I don't think that's a good idea."

"Well, Farq's place is out. He was mad, but Krissy was atomically piss . . . uh, madder."

She pushed aside the question of housing and asked what started the fight. Peter looked down at his skinned knuckles. She could imagine the conversation she would have with David. And Mac. Scratch that. One fewer argument on her agenda. "Start talking," she said.

"I was kinda wiped out after I left you. I mean, I felt better, but just kinda empty, you know?"

She nodded.

"And Farq was waiting for me when I got to his house. He started right in asking questions, like he was trying to trip me up.

You know, coming at me from different directions, but asking the same thing. He's like the shark in that old movie, circling me in the water, sizing me up, then coming at me without any warning."

Grace was dismayed, but impressed that Peter had nailed David so perfectly.

"Hey, sorry. Did I say something wrong?"

"It's just sad. What happened next?"

"I was over everything, and I didn't want to play his stupid games. I told him I was tired and was going to skip dinner. He said we had to talk, and he pulled out my court records. The juvie ones I thought no one could see. He asked how long Bethany abused me. I couldn't go through all of that again. I just couldn't. I did what I always do, I left, or tried to, anyway. He stopped me, then Krissy came in and wanted to know what was going on, and he yelled at her. I told him to leave her alone and if he wanted to help me, he could tell me who my mother was, because it sure didn't look to me like his team was doing anything."

Grace held her breath as she watched Peter's face crumple.

"He said they weren't looking for her anymore, because Bethany was my mother. Then he said he'd never known she was pregnant, and that she was a sick person who'd lied to me my whole life. That's when I hit him." The heat seeped out of his last words.

Grace let him have a moment while she checked the message David had left her.

Call me. Urgent!

Since she was already dealing with his urgent matter, she closed the phone again, even as another call was coming in.

Mac.

He could just forget it.

CHAPTER THIRTY-SEVEN

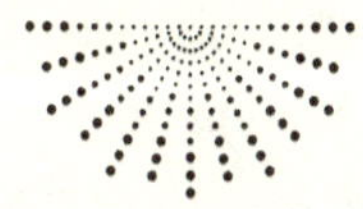

"So," Peter mumbled without looking up. "Are you gonna keep me as a client, or do you think it's dangerous to have me around, too?"

"Is that what David said?"

He shook his head. "Krissy. I can't go back, Grace. I spent last night in my car at the end of their road—you know that little turn around area that's out of sight of the house? I was afraid to leave his property without checking with you first. I didn't want to violate the terms of my bail."

"Don't worry about it. We'll figure something out, and you and David will get things straight, eventually. Whatever happened between your parents, whoever your mother was, is in the past, and none of it is your responsibility. Let's get your future on the right track, and then I'll help you get all the answers, okay?" She spoke without thinking about the consequences of what she was promising. About the damage she might do to her relationship with David and whatever she had left with Mac. This felt right.

They heard the outer door open, and a moment later Aidan appeared. "Sorry. Am I interrupting?"

He obviously was, but Grace thought he looked sympathetically at Peter. It was hard to tell with Aidan, but he wasn't hostile anymore.

"We'll be finished before long," she said.

Aidan nodded. "Okay if I make a little noise out here? I'm going to assemble those bookcases you want in the conference room." Peter sat up and rubbed his face, but Aidan went on as if he hadn't seen a thing. "Hallie says you were a carpenter's apprentice last summer. Wanna give me a hand when you're done? I'm operating on basic skills and a YouTube video."

"Not sure that's a good idea," Peter mumbled.

"Yeah, me, either. But I figure if I ruin it, I'll tell her she should have paid more and hired someone with skills. Plus, we can make noise and bother the lady downstairs. I just got an earful from her, and I heard you two met earlier."

"Yeah," Peter grinned, slowly. "She's probably still cleaning the chair I sat on. But sure, I can help you, if you want."

Grace was happy to turn Peter over to Aidan, even if it meant that in less than thirty minutes, the contents of Aidan's toolbox covered the office, and one wall of the conference room had a chip in the plaster. But as the two would-be handymen worked, Grace heard them talking and smiled to herself as she eavesdropped. Peter said he needed to find a cheap place to live, and with only a brief hesitation, Aidan said he was looking for a roommate.

Grace decided not to look too closely at the unlikely coincidence. She shut her office door and went back to work, grinning every time she thought of Desi Marbury's face as she realized who'd be subleasing a spare room from her boyfriend.

She hadn't made much progress on her list of projects when the intercom line rang. "Incoming. Get ready," Aidan said when she picked up the phone. A minute later, the phone buzzed again, and he announced, "Dr. Greenburgh to see you."

Ashley was still here? Grace glanced at her watch and realized it had been nearly two hours since Marjorie had said she was waiting. There was no time to worry about what Ashley was up to before she was in the office.

"I see you're finally making headway with your cleanup," Ashley said as she stood in the doorway and surveyed the room. Today's outfit was a red knit suit with a peplum waist and simple pearl buttons on the cuffs. A black alligator clutch purse tucked under one arm and three-inch black patent heels completed her look. She struck a model's pose as she gave Grace a stern look. "We need to get some things straight."

Grace pointed to her paper-covered desk. "Sorry. Not today. Marjorie should have made an appointment for you. I'm busy."

"Oh, don't worry, I didn't wait down there all this time. I'm a busy woman, too. I wouldn't have come in the first place if it wasn't important."

Grace wondered how a veterinarian could work in that getup, but then she took a closer look as Ashley sat down. Not large to begin with, she'd dropped a good bit of weight, and the results weren't pretty. She looked her age and then some, but Grace couldn't take any pleasure in the transformation. A wicked little voice in her head said no matter how this meeting turned out, Mac would give Poor Ashley a shoulder to cry on. After all, Grace was worried about the woman and she couldn't stand her. "All right. What's wrong?"

"You have to ask? What's wrong is you. There's a killer standing right outside that door. You know that boy murdered Mona, and the only reason you're defending him is to make me look bad."

As the rest of her lecture unfolded, Grace learned Zara had shared her concerns with her client. There was nothing to be gained by arguing with Ashley, so Grace waited her out.

"Nothing to say for yourself?" Ashley demanded. Her face flushed when Grace still didn't respond. "You should know how worried Lee is. You two may not be getting along these days, but I swear it isn't my fault. Don't do this just to get even with me. You know Henry. He isn't my favorite person anymore, but he couldn't kill anyone. Simone can prove she was nowhere near here, and she and I were talking on the phone while Mona was . . ." She stopped, choking on tears that ran down her cheeks.

Grace handed over a box of tissues and tried to look unconcerned about what she'd just heard. Had Mac discussed his concerns with Ashley? A week ago, it would have been a ridiculous suggestion.

Ashley blotted her face, then looked around, frowning. "You need a waste can in here. You probably make people cry all the time, don't you? Where can I put this?" She held out the wad of damp tissues.

Stifling the answer she wanted to give, Grace kept her mouth shut as she held out a cardboard box from the pile next to her desk.

"That's better," Ashley said, as if her dignity had been restored. "Now. Whatever you think of me, I could never kill my niece. That boy of yours did it. Mona must have had his name as someone who could get her drugs. He's already done awful things, and you know it because my attorney told you. He could hurt you."

Grace sat up a little straighter. She had expected Zara to discuss the other suspects with her client, but this felt like a threat. She wished the security cameras picked up this room.

"Didn't you hear me?" Poor Ashley, the kind and patient veterinarian, looked ready to jump out of her skin. "Lee got me a very good lawyer, you know. You should pay attention to what she says."

Grace didn't answer. She wanted to see what else would come out of that treacherous mouth.

"If you won't think about the loss Simone and I have suffered, at least consider Lee's feelings. He's worried sick about you and your baby being around a killer." Ashley stopped and leaned in closer. "You've made that face twice now. You and Lee are fighting, aren't you? It was only a matter of time, you know. We're a perfect match, and he'll come back to me."

"Is that all?" Grace snapped. This witch needed to leave before there was another murder.

Ashley sighed and got up. "Did you give him my box?"

The damned box.

Grace crossed to a filing cabinet and yanked open the bottom drawer. There it was, right where she'd put it and forgotten it. She handed it over, then crossed her arms and made herself say, "Sorry. Like I said, I'm busy."

Ashley frowned. "It isn't as heavy as it was. Did you take something out?"

"Of course not. I didn't even open it. Now, I have work to do, and I want you to leave."

Ignoring her, Ashley set the box down, opened it, and poked through the contents. "Where's his hammer?"

"What?"

"Lee's hammer. He fixed some things around the farm for me, and he left his hammer. It was in the bottom of the box under the beach towel. What did you do with it?"

The intercom interrupted the argument. Grace snatched up the handset and snapped, "What?"

"Chief's here to see you," Aidan said.

"By all means," she replied, and smiled at Ashley. "Send *Lee* in."

CHAPTER THIRTY-EIGHT

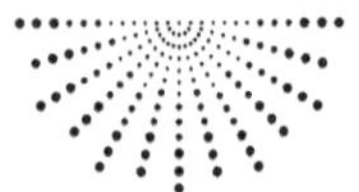

Ashley blinked, but didn't miss a beat. As soon as Mac cleared the doorway, she burst into tears and grabbed his arm. Over her head he looked at Grace with a what-the-hell expression, which, before today, would have signaled that whatever was going on, they were in it together. Now, it just made the distance between them wider. He was mad because she'd made Ashley cry.

"Did you leave a hammer and all this other stuff at Ashley's?" she demanded, pointing at the box.

He stiffened, then peeled Ashley off his arm and eased her onto the chair before saying, "What's this about?"

"She's got that criminal working here, Lee!" Ashley popped back up and began to repack the box. "The boy who killed Mona is right outside."

"So, why are you still here, Ashley?" Grace asked through clenched teeth. "You burst in, have a meltdown, and eat through a half hour of my billable time, even though I've asked you twice" —she paused to glare at Mac—"*nicely* to leave."

Being a wise man, he didn't respond, which was good, because it was his turn in the line of fire.

"As for what's going on, why don't you tell me, Mac? Ashley says we've broken up and the two of you are getting back together. She's also accused me of stealing your hammer from this box, which she says contains things you've left at her house when you slept over. She brought it to me last week and asked me to give it to you. I forgot it, okay? But now you can take it and her and go. I'll buy you another damned hammer." She stopped only because she couldn't believe what she was seeing. He was trying not to laugh.

For a moment, both women wore identical outraged expressions.

Mac cleared his throat and said, "Ashley, we've talked about this. I don't want to repeat that conversation and embarrass you. Grace has asked you to leave. Don't make things worse by waiting for me."

"Fine." Apparently reenergized, Ashley stood and stalked to the door. "Just so you know, I wasn't going to say anything, but there were also three twenty-dollar bills and some change in the box, and that's gone, too. The last night we were together, you emptied your pockets on my dresser. You must have missed the money when you got dressed in the dark, trying to sneak out on me. I could never think of a way to get everything back to you without looking like a fool, but I guess I am one, because I asked her to help me out. I won't make that mistake again."

When she was gone, an awkward silence filled the room until Grace said, "Well, what's in there?"

Mac opened the box and looked inside. "This is embarrassing."

"And the last ten minutes weren't?"

He pulled out a pair of lime-green socks and held them up.

"Are those really yours?"

"Technically. She said I needed to jazz up my wardrobe and gave these to me for Saint Patrick's Day. They came with a tartan tie. She'll probably find that somewhere one of these days. I gave it to the cat to play with."

She didn't want the rush of feelings that almost made her smile. They were through. He thought she was a liar and she would always disappoint him. A few minutes of camaraderie wouldn't bridge the gulf between them. "Sorry about your hammer. Believe me or don't, but I didn't open that box, and I forgot about it after I put it in the file drawer. She's such a pain, I try not to think about her."

"You look tired." He held up a hand and said, "Correction. You look beautiful, but tired."

"Correction noted."

He hesitated, then said, "Do you still have the cash from the box? We could go out for a late lunch."

"If it's not in there, then it never was. She's crazy, Mac."

"Yeah, I know," he said, then came around the desk and pulled her into his arms. "This is ridiculous. She's ridiculous, and I'm worse. I hurt you and saying I'm sorry won't make it right, but I am. I want you and Sweet Pea back. Can we be mad later? I can't take much more of this."

"No." She pulled away and picked up the box. "Take this with you, please."

"Grace—"

"I love you, Mac, and I always will, but I need stability, no matter how unrealistic that might sound, especially given what you think of me. I can't constantly be worrying about doing and saying the right thing to keep you happy. I've lived like that, and I won't do it again. If you could think I would lie about Peter, you don't know me at all."

"I thought you didn't know how to tell me. I asked if you were his mother, and your answer was that you didn't meet David until four years after Peter was born. Then when you got so irrational about protecting him at all costs, it just made sense. I knew you'd tell me when you were ready, but in the meantime, you were in danger."

"Oh. You mean you also thought I lied about when I met David? Just tell me one thing, then take your box and go. What exactly do you want from me? Tell me what it takes to make you happy, because I sure don't have a clue." Not so long ago, it wouldn't have mattered what she had to change, or give up. She'd have lived on antihistamines for the rest of her life with a case of hives always coming or going. Now, she was heartbroken but itch-free. Maybe it was time to listen to her body and give her emotions a rest.

Mac was so still, she thought he'd never answer her.

"I don't want you to change," he finally said. "I don't want you to give up anything for me, or make allowances for me. I want us to fit together without either of us having to change."

She almost asked what color the sky was in his dream world. Instead, on impulse, she said, "Why did you give me this ring for my birthday?"

This time, he didn't let her push him away. He kissed her neck and said, "To see if you'd get hives."

"It was a test? Well, for God's sake! Did I pass or fail? Oh, wait. There was no proposal, so I guess I failed."

She tried to wiggle free, but he didn't let her go. "Nothing," he whispered in her ear. "Absolutely nothing could change the way I feel about you." He gently eased the elastic from her braid and loosened her hair before he kissed her again.

"I can't." This time when she pushed him away, he stepped back. "You refused to marry me because you thought I lied to you. I can't get past it, Mac."

He sighed. "I turned down your eloquent proposal because

you were covered in hives and I won't do that to you. We can love each other without being married, can't we?"

"So, you didn't think I lied?"

"Will you stop it? Yes, I thought you lied, and I didn't care. Not about that, but I cared plenty that you thought I wouldn't understand what you'd done. But we don't have to understand everything, Grace. We just have to love each other."

Those few seconds were all she needed to pull her emotions together enough to ask, "Do the hives bother you that much?"

"Only when I cause them."

"Sorry, but I don't always have the luxury of hiding my true feelings."

"I get it," he said. "But I was trying to protect you. I'd promise not to behave that way again, but you know I will. I love you, and I'll always want to keep you safe."

"I don't need you to take care of me. I need you to trust me." Her words held no heat. It was hard to be stoic when her heart had a higher tolerance for his shortcomings than her brain did. "I thought you'd know why Peter was special to me, but I guess I didn't explain it well, did I?"

"Later." He took her left hand and held it up. "This ring has a matching wedding band."

When she could trust her voice, she said, "Do you think the jeweler still has it?"

"No. It's in my sock drawer, with all my boring, regulation black—"

Her kiss cut off the sock discussion and sealed the deal.

Before they stopped talking altogether, he said, "I have a confession."

"Does it involve that box?"

"Sort of. I have something to give you. It's a bribe, and it's not finished, so you may have to buy me that hammer."

"Why?" she tried to look stern, but couldn't keep the laughter out of her voice.

"Because it's short two bedrooms and a master bath."

Every once in a while, unsolvable problems resolve themselves, warriors step back, and the cautious step up, all of their own accord. In those times, a wise person knows when to be still and when to give a helping hand.

Avril Oxley had been biding her time, letting her projects percolate. She'd meddled in Hallie and Peter's relationship, but only enough to plant the seed in Hallie's mind that the boy needed a friend. Aidan Banks thought he'd decided all on his own that young Peter needed rational adult male guidance and a better place to stay than David Farquar's garage apartment.

Lee and Grace were her masterpiece.

With those two, Avril's role was more of a devil's advocate, since neither one was ever going to leave the other, despite what anyone, including Avril herself, might think was best. She listened, suggested, soothed, and landed a few sorely needed thumps on the skulls of those two stubborn, lovesick people, and it had all paid off.

She was well pleased to see all her recent successes gathered in one spot when she, Hallie, and Fiona arrived at Grace's office late Tuesday afternoon. She met Peter Carlton for the first time and gave him high marks for being polite when he didn't know who she was.

"Grace and the chief are in a meeting," Aidan said when they'd made the introductions.

Collectively, they all turned toward the closed door to Grace's office.

"How long have they been in there?" Avril asked, her innocent tone fooling no one.

"Since Dr. Greenburgh left," Aidan answered, and was rewarded with a shocked look from Hallie and a wide smile from Avril.

"Are you sure they're okay?" Hallie asked.

Aidan nodded. "Dr. G came in mad and all wired up. Wanted to know if I had her hammer." He and Peter rolled their eyes. "Then she walked right in on Grace. That didn't go well, then the chief showed up." This time he and Peter high-fived each other. "There was heavy-duty yelling, and the doc looked rough when she came out. Spent forever in the bathroom before she got herself together and left."

"I was asking about Grace and Chief Mac," Hallie said impatiently.

"I think they're fine," Aidan said. "Either that or she's killed him, but I'm voting for fine. No screams, no noise, and no blood seeping under the door."

Peter looked confused at first, then correctly interpreted the grins that spread over everyone else's face. They all went back to watching the door.

"I could make some popcorn," Hallie offered, but didn't move.

"Okay," Avril said with a bark, making the other three jump. "I'll be going now. Tell Grace I stopped by to say hello, and I'll catch her later. Hallie, you're going to take Fiona down to the park, aren't you? I'll walk down with you. Peter, would you be so kind as to give us a hand with the stroller?" A pointed look at Aidan sent him back to the unfinished bookcase.

Once she'd disbanded the little group of voyeurs, she kept Peter talking until they reached the sidewalk, where she offered him a handyman gig paying twenty dollars an hour. Having done what she could for those who needed her, she went home to a well-deserved gin and tonic.

"Who is that?" Peter asked as the big Mercury Marquis pulled away from the curb.

Hallie looked thoughtful, then said, "Sometimes, it's hard to tell, but mostly I think of her as an elfin godmother. You're lucky she likes you."

"I just met her."

"Doesn't matter."

Back upstairs, Mac eventually let Grace fix her hair, and then took her to see her new kitchen. It was a very strange afternoon, but at least two people thought it was magic.

CHAPTER THIRTY-NINE

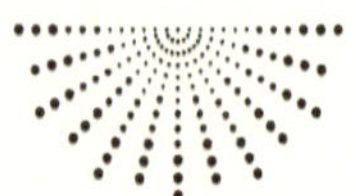

After months of ups and downs, maybes and maybe nots, secrets that shouldn't have been and surprises that weren't, the world fell into harmony for a little while. Just long enough to give Grace and Mac a taste of what life could be like when the current crises were settled and Mallard Bay returned to normal.

He laughed when she said this out loud, and he didn't stop even when she hit him with a pillow. She said he was a cynic, he said she was beautiful, and the subject was forgotten during a lovely, undisturbed evening with Fiona. Not a single call or text marred their dinner or playtime with the baby or the long, blissful night that followed.

When they turned on their phones and checked their emails Wednesday morning, the same problems awaited them, and yet, everything had changed. They had decided on a quiet elopement over the Fourth of July weekend. Both doubted they could pull off such a nonevent, but that was the plan.

"I want you all to myself, but you deserve a parade and fireworks," he told her.

It seemed the universe agreed with him about the fireworks,

anyway. They didn't make it through breakfast before the text tones on their phones went off a half second apart.

"This can't be good," Grace said.

Mac checked his messages and saw that she was right. For a moment, the kitchen was silent, then they were both on the move.

"I never called David back yesterday," Grace said as she got up. "And Peter didn't tell him he was staying at Aidan's. This will be a fun conversation."

"Desi wants to meet. I'm also talking to Rotary at lunch about the police cadet program, and Tremaine has in-service hours to do at the firearms range. I don't know when I'll be home." He dropped one last kiss on her upturned face and was rewarded with a smile.

"It doesn't matter," she said. "We'll be here."

She had tears in her eyes as he left. He decided it was a woman thing and was nearly a block away before he realized he'd said "home" and meant her rental house.

His home was wherever Grace lived.

David didn't answer, so she left him a text saying Peter was staying with a friend and hoped that would be enough to keep him off her back. Yesterday's glow still warmed her, but the morning was firmly rooted in reality.

It took longer than usual to turn Fiona and the household over to Hallie. The baby was fussy with her sore gums, and Hallie sang the nerve-jangling "Baby Shark" song to distract her. Grace eventually escaped, but was certain the music would pound through her brain for the rest of the day.

Aidan called when she was a block from the office.

"On my way," she said as she answered, her fingers drumming *do, do, do-do-do-do-do* on her steering wheel.

"That's good," he said. "We have a situation."

"I thought you should see it first," Aidan said as she walked through the door. "In here."

She followed him to the doorway of the restroom. "First before what?" she asked, looking down at the newspaper he'd spread on the floor. "Did you spill something toxic?" She didn't smell anything, but this was Aidan. The old linoleum might be dissolving as they talked.

"The paper's just to protect any prints. That's what you need to see, and don't touch it."

She leaned into the narrow room for a better look. "You do realize that's a paper bag lying on the toilet seat? I'm going to need a little more information."

"It's the chief's hammer. His initials are on it."

"Well, that's just lovely. The Crazy Lady was right," she said with disgust. "Where'd you find it?"

He caught her arm as she stepped toward the bag. "I told you not to touch it. Don't touch anything. The head of the hammer and the shank have dried bloodstains."

She backed up. "Explain."

"You need better soundproofing in your office. Peter and I both heard Ashley going on about you stealing the chief's hammer that he left at her house when he—"

"Not that. What do you know that doesn't involve my love life?" If she hadn't been so worried, she'd have enjoyed seeing him squirm. "Where did you find the hammer?"

"Shoved up under the pipes in the sink cabinet. I looked under there because The Bat's still whining about the water stain in the downstairs kitchen. The cabinet's as dry as a bone, but that's when I saw the hammer. Only I didn't know it was a hammer at first. I wasn't sure what it was, it was dark under there, or I'd never have touched it."

Grace weighed the various possibilities and their implications. "Do you think . . ." She stopped, not wanting to put ideas in his head if she was wrong.

But Aidan was ahead of her. "We know when Dr. G says she brought it in, and we know who's been here since then. Any of us could have gotten it out of the box, used it, and hidden it in there."

"It's a dumb place to hide a bloody hammer," Grace said. "Somebody must have been desperate to get rid of it."

"If that somebody killed her niece and had to get rid of the murder weapon, it would be a pretty smart place to leave it. She did a lot of snuffling and flushing in here yesterday. It would have covered any noise she made under the sink. And if we're going to consider only people who also had an opportunity to kill Mona Cutter, Dr. G leads a very short list."

Grace shook her head in resignation. That list included Peter, and she knew who Ashley was going to blame. "Did she bring her purse in here with her?"

"Sort of an envelope-shaped lizard hide bag? Yeah. But she wouldn't have had much room for a hammer."

"She wouldn't have needed much. The only important thing she had to get in here was the hammer." The elegant purse Ashley had carried would have been just long enough.

"Chief or Desi?" Aidan asked.

"Cover the bases. Call both of them."

CHAPTER FORTY

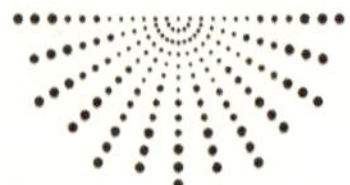

It wasn't the first time Grace had waited out a search team led by Desi Marbury. She voiced the same objections every time and always got the same results. The only difference was that today Mac was the officer who waited with her while her office was turned upside down by the state police.

Aidan took his exile to the police station without complaint, and Grace tried to be as well behaved about her own situation. Mosley stayed in his office, but only because she wouldn't let him come upstairs and take charge.

"The police are doing what they have to do, and I'm watching it all, Cy," she told him when he called for the third time. Then inspiration struck. "It would be helpful if Marjorie could arrange to have a cleaning crew standing by—they're making quite a mess up here. Oh, and they're taking the vanity, so the wall behind the sink will need to be repaired, and since we don't need a tub, the carpenters can take that out and give us some storage. Painters, of course, and new fixtures?"

He agreed immediately and was barking orders at Marjorie as he disconnected.

"Smooth," Mac said. "And a not a little frightening."

"Not as frightening as pink-tiled walls and a tub from the 1950s. Avril loved it, but no way am I missing my chance for an upgrade."

They sat side by side on the bench, and it was hard not to reach for his hand as she watched one tech lift fingerprints while another one bagged bits of who-knew-what kind of potential evidence. Then Desi called out for a utility knife and an extra set of hands. In a rare display of consideration, she even used her mag light to show Grace the back of the cabinet where the hammer had been found. The Luminol spray revealed shimmery blue spots. Blood.

Grace said, "There's a box in my office you'll want to see, too."

Desi looked at Mac, who shrugged and said, "You're going to enjoy this way too much."

"I've had a call from a friend who could use a hand this afternoon. Mind if I take off?" Aidan's tone was nonchalant.

"You're finished giving your statement?" Grace asked, glancing over her shoulder at Desi, who was organizing the removal of the sink cabinet.

"Doesn't take long to say 'I looked, I saw, and I called the boss.'"

She waited, and when he said nothing else, she wondered what they were really discussing. "Have you heard—"

"It's my new roommate. He needs a hand moving in. You know how that goes. I'll make up any work tomorrow, okay?" He was gone before she could say anything, which was just as well, because Desi was bearing down on her in full cop mode.

"We'll be packing up soon, but this office is a crime scene

until we release it. Gather the personal items you need to take, and I'll inventory it."

"Can't you just block off the restroom?" Grace asked, knowing the answer was no.

"No files, no computers," Desi cautioned, then offered a short "Sorry."

Twenty minutes later, Mosley joined Grace on the front porch as she watched Mac leave with the last of the MSP. "I'm sorry, Cy," she said. "At least with my side locked up, no one will see the crime-scene tape upstairs."

"Well, m'dear, you'd better come inside before someone snaps photos for your next headline." He gave her elbow a gentle tug, and she followed him through his front door, past Marjorie's desk, and down the hall to the bright office she'd once occupied.

"I've learned something distressing," he said, and shut the door behind him.

———

"Should I even bother to ask how you found out?" she said when he'd finished giving her the same report Zara Wingate had. Peter's juvenile arrest records weren't nearly as hard to access as they should have been.

"I have colleagues on the lower shore who had heard about the case. How'd you find out? Did he tell you?"

"Not all of it and not until I asked," she admitted with a sigh. "Zara gave me a heads-up. The background check I'd ordered on him indicated a troubled past, but didn't go into juvenile records. The fatal fire was in there, of course, but not the first one. The case was just listed as closed and sealed."

"Do you know why the assault and arson charges were dropped in the first one?"

"Because he wasn't guilty, Cy."

He waved a spotted hand and said, "You know what I mean. His mother testified against him."

"That's the sound bite, but the truth is Peter refused to talk about anything at all, so initially the police believed Bethany Carlton when she said he had a habit of starting little fires when he was drunk. She was trying to explain away the stash of vodka bottles they'd found in the house." Grace felt sick, remembering the boy's voice as he described Bethany's lies. "She overdid it and said he'd been drunk when the fire started. She didn't know the police had tested Peter, and he didn't have a drop in his system. Because she was adamant and he wouldn't talk, he was charged and taken into custody, but eventually released. The fire marshal's office determined that the fire started from a cigarette, and Bethany was a heavy smoker."

"Was either of them charged?"

"She was given probation, and he went to a group home. Once he got out of the hospital, that is." She stopped to gather her patience. Cyrus was saying only what would be all over town before long. "This past January, Peter was home on a school break. He'd come to tell Bethany he was going into the air force after graduation. He'd turned eighteen, and she couldn't stop him. They argued, and when he went to bed, Bethany set the second fire, the one that killed her. I can't get into the details, except to say she was very drunk and fell. The investigation isn't closed, but it cleared him, Cy. She also had a head injury that contributed to her death. It was several years old, and she caused that, too, so please don't perpetuate the rumors that are going to fly around."

He frowned and glanced down at the papers in his hand. "Even so, you have to know how it looks. The odds are against him coming out of that childhood with clean hands. It's easy to believe he might have been meeting up with Mona to buy or sell drugs."

"Maybe. If you didn't know he's vehemently opposed to

illegal drug use. With his arrest for the first fire, stints in group homes, and random school drug tests that always seemed to hit him, he's passed more tox screens than a pro ball team on a winning streak." Cyrus was listening to her, just as she hoped a jury would, but she could tell he hadn't made up his mind. "If you're the glue that holds your family together, you're opposed to anything that tears it apart. From the time he was a small child, Peter took care of Bethany, not the other way around."

"Poor boy," Mosley said softly.

"Everything she did was calculated to hurt Peter, from lying about adopting him, to telling him his parents abandoned him. She told him over and over how much he looked like David, and said she hated him for it. Can you imagine living with that? David said she was always volatile, but wasn't an alcoholic when they were together. I'm not sure he'll ever forgive himself for how things turned out."

Mosley shook his head. "So much misery, Grace. All we can do is pick up the pieces and carry on."

She declined his offer of the use of her old office. Mac wouldn't be free for hours, but there was something constructive she could do while she waited for him. She might not be able to patch up David and Peter's relationship, but then again, maybe she could. She grabbed an apple and cheese crackers from the kitchen, added a go-cup of coffee for good measure and thanked a protesting Marjorie for the stolen food as she went out the door.

It was her turn to drop in on Krissy.

CHAPTER FORTY-ONE

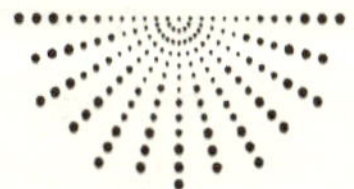

"I was wondering when you'd show up." The friendly, southern charm was missing, and without it, David's wife looked older and, Grace thought, formidable. "The big guy is in Washington."

Grace said, "Okay. I need to talk to both of you, so if you want to wait for him, I can come back."

It was easy to see that Krissy wanted to shut the door, but she said, "I don't need to wait for my husband to handle whatever else it is that you have to dump on us."

Grace had been so used to eager, friendly Krissy that the words stung. Apparently, there was a limit to how much change the new Mrs. Farquar was willing to accept.

"Staff's day off," Krissy said irritably as she stood back for Grace to enter. "And Ammie's asleep, so keep your voice down. She's got an earache, and we were up all night."

Grace looked around as they walked through the house and out onto the patio, which now had seating areas, umbrellas, tables, and a fountain. Everywhere Grace looked, she saw something else to admire and was happy to give her compliments sincerely as she tried to lighten the mood. "Have you changed the DC condo as much as you have this place?"

"No. I don't enjoy being in the city enough to even try, not that he'd let me." Krissy's frown deepened, but she directed Grace toward a set of wicker rockers with bright red cushions.

"Why wouldn't he?" Grace asked, genuinely curious. "You have marvelous taste. This place looks like a magazine shoot."

Krissy looked at her for a moment before answering. "I believe he wants to keep it just the way you left it. There've been a lot of changes in his life, and that place seems to be his safety net."

Grace sat back, surprised. "The last time I changed anything had to have been five, maybe six years ago. And I think it was only slipcovers for the sofa."

"It's getting some age on it, that sounds about right. I just count my blessings that he doesn't talk much about you. If he was all 'Grace would do this' or 'Grace wouldn't do that,' we'd have a problem. A bigger problem."

"I think the three of us have enough of those already, don't we?" Grace said. "I can see you're angry and that's why I'm here. I have only Peter's side—"

If Krissy had been angry before, she was livid now. "Why do you get to have any side at all? He's not your child, and David isn't your husband. I had a chance, maybe a long shot, but a chance of a real family, and now I may be divorced before Ammie learns to say 'Daddy.'"

Grace sighed. What could she say? There was no easy solution to David's instant, unexpected family. Families. Add in a murder investigation and a fistfight with his oldest new child, and they had a big can of worms to work through. So that's what she said.

Krissy leaned her head back against the rocker and closed her eyes, flexing her feet just enough to set a gentle rhythm. Eventually, she stopped and gave Grace a rueful smile. "'Can of worms.' I may be rubbing off on you, girl." The rocker slowed, then stopped. "David told me you were good at settlements. The way he described it, he'd go in, blow up the opposing counsel's case, and you'd come behind him wiping tears and tying up the deal. He said you were a team, the two of you. I know he misses that."

Grace thought one day she'd explain to Krissy that the wiping and tying took more skill than the blowing up. But salvaging her own ego wasn't the point here, saving a family was. "Well, today, I need help wiping tears and tying up some loose ends for Peter."

"And David?" Krissy's eyes were red rimmed and wet, but totally focused on Grace. "Is Peter the only one you want to help?"

Grace knew this conversation wasn't likely to end in one take. She wanted to stay on topic, but she needed Krissy's cooperation. "I want Fiona's father and his family to be happy and stable. But no, David doesn't need my help."

"But you loved him."

"Yes. But love can turn toxic when it's between the wrong people. It took me way too long to learn that. And"—she raised her voice as Krissy tried to interrupt—"you and I are not doing this. Not today. David's your prob—husband. It's Peter we all need to help."

Krissy got up and crossed to the patio bar, returning with two chilled bottles of water. Handing one to Grace, she said, "The boy shouldn't be here. Not until this whole situation is worked out, and now that I'm semi-over my snit fit with you, I think maybe the two of us should decide the best way to handle things. David's actually turning into a dad. Better late than never, I guess, but he's over-the-top emotional about that boy."

Warily, Grace clinked her bottle against the one Krissy held out. "Peter told me he and David came to blows. That must have been awful."

"Yeah, well, my husband certainly could have used some of that charm I married him for," Krissy admitted. "The thing is, he had his reasons, and I think it was my fault that everything went so badly. David and I are still getting used to each other, too, you know? We each keep stuff we don't share, and it causes problems. When I finally heard about the fire and Peter's life with Bethany, I was furious. David already knew and hadn't told me, and neither had my new best friend."

"That's right," Grace said.

"That's all I get? What the hell? I trusted you to tell me if that boy could be a danger to my child and me."

"You can trust me. Peter's damaged, not dangerous. He's overcome enormous odds, but now he's overwhelmed."

"I'm overwhelmed, too. Do any of you care about that? I'm overwhelmed and at the end of this little experiment in modern family life, understand? You and Peter and the whole damned world need to leave us alone, or David and I are done. I can't do this."

"I'm sorry." The words bounced off Krissy without making a dent in her anger. "You've been open and welcoming to my child and me, and I wish I could have been the same with you. I want the relationship you offered me, but I don't have an operational manual for instant families with multiple ex-partners who fly in and out of each other's lives creating problems."

"Is that how you feel about me?" Krissy said. "Because, I—"

"Feel the same way about me?" Grace asked and got what she was coming to think of as a Krissy look, something between a slight smile and a "bite me" glare. "Look. We like each other and we're in the same foxhole, but we're still strangers, and we both have our problems. You and I will work it out, Krissy, but this thing with Peter is right here and now and can't wait. For better or worse, you're his stepmother. Will you help me help him?"

"Sunday night went pretty well, all things considered," Krissy said. "But that didn't last long."

Grace wasn't sure if she'd soothed Krissy's feelings, or just piqued her curiosity, but now wasn't the time to work on that relationship. She listened without interrupting as Krissy described an awkward dinner at which she and David made small talk and Peter picked at his food.

"The next morning, David went for an early run. I went out to the garage to get something from my car, and I saw Peter lifting weights in the gym we have out there. I guess he thought no one would see him." She drained her water, then took a deep breath. "He was facing away from me and was wearing only shorts. I saw his back and the calves of his legs. He's got some bad scars."

"What kind of scars?" With a sick feeling, Grace remembered the kitchen fire and Peter's temporary removal from Bethany's custody.

"Some were red and raised. Burns, I think, but there were others, too."

"And you told David."

She nodded. "Peter left while David was still out. He didn't say anything to me, just went. David was mad when he came home and saw Peter's car gone. He acted like I'd been irresponsible, and like a fool, I didn't wait until he'd calmed down to tell him what I'd seen."

Grace winced.

"Yeah," Krissy said. "I'm learning, but not fast enough. I expected him to get upset, but not like that. He went all pale, and his hands shook. He made me tell him everything again and again, and then he told me about the juvenile records and the fire, then shut down like none of it concerned me. That didn't go well, as you can imagine."

"What happened when Peter came home?" Grace asked, remembering the state Peter had been in when he'd left her after confessing that Bethany had tried to kill him. She couldn't imagine a worse scenario for the emotionally exhausted boy to walk into.

"I tried to keep David from jumping right into it with him, but neither one of them paid any attention to me. David asked where he'd been, Peter said he had something to ask David, and David said not before you answer my questions, and they were off to the races. They ignored me completely, except when I screamed a couple of times there at the end."

"What started the fight?" Grace asked.

"There wasn't one, not really. You have to have two people for that. When David said Bethany was Peter's mother, and that she was a sick liar, Peter walloped him. Caught him right on the jaw. David went down, and I nearly had a heart attack." Krissy's anger seemed to fade as she talked. When she'd wiped her eyes, she said, "Bless that man, he was a father. He was back on his feet in a second. Peter swung at him again, and David threw his arms around the kid in a bear hug and held on. He kept saying, 'I'm sorry,' and 'It will be okay,' over and over while Peter was hitting him on his back and arms—wherever he could land a blow. It was horrible. I grabbed a pitcher of ice tea and dumped it over them, and that ended it. Peter ran out, and David wouldn't speak to me. So, I did what I usually do. I jumped in and took over and may have ended my marriage."

Grace waited while Krissy pulled herself together. She'd never thought Peter would be dangerous, but she hadn't considered David in that equation. It was a sobering realization that his safety had never entered her mind. And Peter had left all of it out of his accounting of the confrontation.

Krissy said, "While David was cleaning up, I told Peter it would be better if he left for a while. I tried to give him some money. He threw it back at me. He was in his car and gone before David was out of the shower."

"Where is David, now?"

"When I told him what I'd done, he was so mad at me, he went to Washington. I haven't heard from him since."

"This was—"

"Yesterday morning."

The timing matched Peter's account. The stomping off and leaving an argument matched David's behavior pattern. But otherwise, Grace felt like she was in uncharted territory. Then she remembered—it wasn't her problem to solve.

"I feel like something worse is coming," Krissy said. "We can't fly with Ammie's ear the way it is, but I'm packing and we're leaving as soon as she wakes up. The staff and I are driving to New Orleans. Larry and April are ready to take a break from this soap opera and go back to work for my folks, so I may as well let them get me back home. When David gets things straight, we'll talk, but this"—she waved her hand at her beautiful home— "doesn't feel like a good place for my baby."

Grace's phone erupted. "It's Peter," she said, looking at Krissy as she answered.

CHAPTER FORTY-TWO

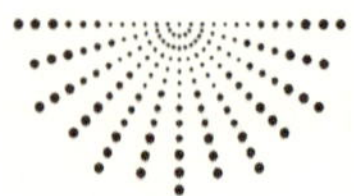

His voice was high pitched and panicky. "I'm sorry, Grace, really sorry. She said she could fix everything, but she wanted to talk to me alone first. She said you would say no, and I shouldn't tell you. I thought I could handle it. I shouldn't have gone, and I've made things so much worse."

Grace looked at Krissy, who was on the edge of her seat and making shooing motions. "I can come to you right now, but who are you talking about?"

"That woman you don't like. That vet, Dr. Greenburgh."

Ashley?

"Where are you?"

"At Aidan's. I went out to her house like she asked me to. At first, she was nice, then she asked me how I'd met Mona. She was smiling when she said it, but it was creepy. I said I was sorry about what happened, but I'd never met her niece. She said she knew about the drugs, and it was okay, it wasn't my fault. She said she knew this Henry guy had killed Mona, and if I knew anything about it, I needed to tell her and the police. I tried to leave, and she got between me and the door. She kept saying I had to tell the truth, no matter what you said. Then she yelled, 'Why did you have to push her? You didn't need to kill her!' I panicked, Grace, I didn't know what she was going to do. I got my phone out and said I'd call you if she didn't let me leave. It was so weird, like she woke up or something. She said she was sorry, and moved, and I got the hell out of there."

"Where'd you go?"

"To your office, but it was closed, and you weren't home, so I called Aidan and came back here. He said I had to call you, but I would have, anyway."

When Peter sounded calmer, she told him not to worry and made him promise to stay where he was until he heard from her. There was a mumbled exchange, and Aidan came on the line. "He's okay, Grace, but it sounds like Dr. G is seriously unhinged. Want me to call the chief?"

"No. I'll take care of it, but Aidan, nice work helping your friend who had to move. Consider yourself on the clock and stick with him. Keep him there if you can."

"No prob. Listen, the conversation I had with the MSP this morning? They're looking seriously at Ashley, and I should have told Peter. Warned him away from her. But here's the thing, they're looking at Peter, too."

She disconnected, trying to decide what to do.

"It isn't good," she said to Krissy. "Peter's got a new problem, but this one's mine."

"What a mess! Go on, then. I'll handle the family end, and you do the legal stuff." She hesitated, then seemed to make a decision, and held out her arms for a hug. "I'll see you again one day, but you have work to do, and Ammie and I are just complicating things here for David and Peter."

Choked with emotion, Grace returned the embrace and told her to be careful.

"I've got my team, we'll be fine." Krissy said with a sad

smile. "David will get with the program or he won't, but you and I will stay connected. Deal?"

"Yes." Grace made herself stop moving and look at her new friend as she added, "I promise. You and Amalie are important to us." As she grabbed her tote and keys, she said, "Okay, look, I'm probably blowing this way out of proportion, but if I am, there's nothing lost. You understand who the other suspects in the murder are?"

"Oh, Lord. Of course. The husband, the mother, and the dead girl's aunt."

"Don't talk to or go near anyone you don't know. Call me later tonight or tomorrow, and I'll explain everything. But two women, Ashley Greenburgh and her sister, Simone Lancer, could be dangerous."

"What about the murdered woman's husband?"

"Henry Cutter. Stay away from all of them. The murder investigation just took a turn for the worse for Peter, I think."

"Maybe I should wake Ammie and go now."

Grace started to agree, but it was Krissy's decision, not hers. "Tell David everything. Don't keep secrets this time, okay? I'll also call him when there's news on Peter's situation. I left him a voice mail earlier and told him where Peter was and that he's safe —well, he was when I left the message, anyway. I'm sorry I didn't call you, too. I won't let it happen again."

Krissy nodded. "I'm sorry to leave you with all of this."

"Hey, same foxhole, remember?" Grace said as she left. "Just be careful."

Peter called again as she was pulling away from David's house. "I didn't tell you the random thing Dr. Greenburgh went off on me about, and Aidan says it's important."

Something in his voice made Grace pull to the side of the driveway and stop the car. "Let's hear it."

"She asked me when I hid the hammer. She sounded strange and it weirded me out."

"She asked you when you hid it?"

"Yeah."

"Not if you hid it."

"When," he insisted.

"What was she talking about?" Grace said, more to herself than Peter.

"How would I know? You guys are the ones going on about hammers!"

Aidan said something in the background, and Peter mumbled an apology.

"I'm going to check into it," Grace said. "But if Mac or the state police, or David—if anyone asks you what happened, you tell them the truth even if I'm not there, understand? You made a bad decision this morning, but you didn't do anything illegal, now don't do anything to make it look like you did." Then she remembered his compulsive oversharing with the MSP when they questioned him the last time, and she added, "Tell the truth, but only exactly what you know happened. No guesses or assumptions. It will only make things worse."

As she pulled away from the house, she called Mac and listened as his voice mail picked up. She left him a detailed message describing Ashley's call to Peter, and his visit to her house. She knew it rambled too much, but left it, anyway. Maybe he'd call back sooner if it confused him.

Avril was next. Grace asked her to get Hallie and Fiona, take them to her house, and keep everyone, including the dogs, inside. When Avril protested, Grace interrupted her midsentence with one word. "Please."

She'd reached a stop sign at a rural intersection two miles

from town. If she turned right, she could be at Ashley's farm in five minutes. Left would take her to town and Mac and the state police—where she'd promptly be shut out of everything. Would they even believe that Ashley threatened Peter? Was Aidan right about them looking at Ashley as the lead suspect? If Ashley claimed Peter came to her house, uninvited, and threatened her, who would sound more sincere—Poor Ashley or a teenager with a troubled history?

"Are you still there? What's wrong?" The indignation in Avril's voice had been replaced with concern.

"I need help," she said, and chose her next words carefully, knowing Avril would never let her down, but could easily go overboard. "I'm fine, but I'm in the middle of something and can't get back there. I'll tell you everything when I can, but for right now, just trust me. Don't talk to Ashley, her sister, or Henry. Don't, under any circumstances, let any of them into the house." She remembered David. What would happen when he got home and found his family gone? "Oh, hell, just keep the doors and windows locked and don't let anyone but Mac or me in. I'll be there as soon as I can."

To her amazement, Avril agreed.

Grace told the phone to redial Mac's number, and she turned right.

CHAPTER FORTY-THREE

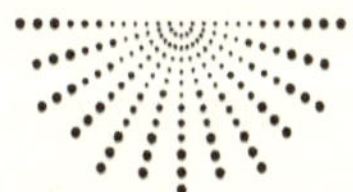

For the second time that day, she paid a surprise visit and almost got a door in her face for her trouble. Not in the mood to placate Ashley, she said, "I heard about what you did this morning." Without waiting for an invitation, she entered the house and looked around an elegantly furnished sitting room.

"This is outrageous, even for you," Ashley said. She closed the door and went to stand behind one of the white club chairs that flanked a sleek leather sofa. "You're scaring me. I should call Lee and ask him to come get you. I'm certainly not strong enough to throw someone of your size out of my house."

Grace could only imagine how this scene would sound when Ashley described it later. There was no point in stopping now; she was going to look bad no matter how this turned out. "Why did you call Peter Carlton and asked him to come here?"

Ashley looked offended. "I didn't. He just showed up and scared me to death. He said something like, 'I'm here, and I want to do the right thing, so what do you want to know?' Well, I didn't know what to think, but he actually seemed confused and not so scary and there's so much I want to know about Mona, so I let him stay and asked my questions."

Grace hesitated, reconsidering. Peter was being set up. She didn't see any other explanation for Ashley's actions, and a direct confrontation could escalate her intentions. "What did he say?"

"He lied right to my face. Said he'd never met Mona, and we all know that's not true. That's why she was there, at your office, to buy drugs from him."

Grace forced herself to keep calm. If she could get Ashley to see reason, the situation could still be salvaged. "I'm sorry for what your family's been through, but your niece went to Cy's office to sign the divorce agreement. There are witnesses to that."

"That was just a cover so she could meet your son! She was so strung out, she called him, and he agreed to meet her there with the drugs."

Reason wasn't working, so Grace tried sympathy. "You have to know that's not true. Please don't do this to Peter. He's a kid, Ashley, and he'd had a hard life."

"Who hasn't? Why shouldn't he have to take the blame for what he did? Our girl died. And it never would have happened if you'd helped us. If you'd just talked Henry out of the divorce, Mona wouldn't have been upset and needed the drugs and gotten herself killed."

Grace shook her head at this fairy tale. "That doesn't make any sense at all and couldn't have happened. There wasn't time for me to see Henry. Your sister asked me only the day before, and—"

"Don't you dare try to make Mona's death sound like our fault!" Ashley's small frame shook as she shouted. "What if she was killed when she came to sign the divorce papers? If you'd talked to Henry, she wouldn't have been there. And she wouldn't have come here and she wouldn't—"

"Shut. Up."

Neither of them had seen Simone come into the room.

"You are such a whiny snot, little sister. You'd give everything up just to get one over on her, wouldn't you?"

"Oh, no, no. What are you doing?" Ashley said with a gasp, and moved quickly to put Grace between herself and Simone.

"And you're a coward," Simone said. She was also laughing, which made the revolver she held shake even harder than it had been. "'Let me handle it,' you said." She thrust a hip sideways and fluffed her hair with her free hand. Pitching her voice closer to her sister's soprano, she did a passable impression of Ashley. "When they find the hammer, they'll realize the kid did it. It's one more dealer off the street, so it's not even wrong, really."

Despite the tense circumstances, the pieces fell into place for Grace. "You called Peter and told him you were Ashley," she said and was rewarded with a nod from Simone. "No wonder she didn't know why he came here." Then, hoping to gain an ally, she added, "What else did you do that poor Ashley doesn't know about?"

But it turned out that Ashley hated that name, too. Giving Grace a shove, she yelled, "Leave us alone!"

Simone steadied the gun in a two-handed grip. "Do you still think your story will fly with your old boyfriend? Or should we see if there's another alternative?" She was talking to her sister, but the gun was pointed at Grace.

"You sure about this, Major?"

"It all fits," Mac said. "But whether it was an accident or deliberate, I don't know."

They sat about a quarter of the way down the single-lane road that led from the highway to Ashley's farmhouse. Hidden from the house and outbuildings by a stand of woods, they were waiting for backup.

His morning had been spent talking with Desi, her supervisor, and the state medical examiner's staff, after which he'd been invited to rejoin the task force investigating Mona Cutter's murder. In the first ten minutes of his morning meeting with Desi, he learned why. Peter Carlton had been cleared. So had Henry Cutter. The MSP needed his help because he was the person with the best chance of getting Ashley Greenburgh to tell the truth. Mac's hammer was going to put the sisters behind bars.

He'd wanted to be a part of the investigation, to use his skills and experience to close this tragedy with truthful answers. He'd just never seriously considered that a woman who'd once said she loved him could be involved. He opened his phone for a last check for messages, filling the time until he walked into Ashley's house to arrest her.

"Five minutes," Desi said as she checked her phone.

"Oh, damn."

"Major?"

Mac reread the transcription of his latest voice mail. "It's Grace," he said and hit redial. A mechanical voice told him the party he wanted was not available. Of course she wasn't. She was busy trying to reason with a killer. He told Desi they had a complication and repeated Grace's message, omitting only the last two words.

Love you.

"But you said you thought Simone Lancer killed her daughter," Desi protested.

"And I haven't changed my mind," Mac said.

The medical examiner had blown Simone's alibi. Although Mona had died while her mother was speeding through a red light twenty miles away, her fatal brain aneurysm had been caused the day before. "She could have been saved if Ashley or her mother had stepped up," he said, anger coursing through him again. The truth didn't improve with the retelling. "She died because they didn't get her to a hospital."

"And Grace figured it out," Desi said as she started the car and alerted the MSP tactical van pulling in behind them.

"No," Mac said. "Nothing that easy. Grace thinks she can talk Ashley into exonerating Peter Carlton by appealing to her better angels. How well do you think that'll play?" He checked his weapon. "Let's move, Desi, or I'm going in alone."

"Slow down, sir. I'm with you." They rolled slowly and almost silently down the macadam driveway to Ashley's farmhouse. "We'll get her out."

<hr>

"You don't have any alternatives," Grace said with a confidence she was totally faking. "Only one of you is facing manslaughter charges right now, am I right? One of you accidentally killed Mona, and you've both been covering it up. Shoot me, and you're both charged with murder."

Behind her, Ashley gasped.

Grace grabbed the opportunity. "Tell her, Simone. She should know what you're getting her into. Everyone knows she hates me, so there won't be any doubt about who wanted me dead. You'd get off, though."

It was such a lie, Simone just shook her head, which made the gun wobble again. Grace froze, but nothing happened. Then Ashley said, "You have to stop this! No one will believe her against me, but if you shoot her—"

"You mean like this?" The gunshot was loud, and a sofa cushion disintegrated into a smoking pile of watered silk. "Just so we all understand I'm serious," Simone said, still looking at Grace.

"What do you want from her?" Ashley screamed. "I'm telling you, we can still get out of this."

"She doesn't want out, do you, Simone?" Grace knew she'd hit the truth when the gun wobbled again. "You're framing Ashley and then, what? Will you be happy with your revenge?"

"Will I be *happy*?" Simone's voice broke on the last syllable.

Another shot took out the matching pillow.

One hand out in a plea to Simone, the other behind her waving Ashley toward the door, Grace moved slowly backward. If they both broke away, they might have a chance. "Tell me why, Simone." She didn't try to hide the quaver in her voice. A hard shove from behind threw her off balance just as the door burst open. As she fell, she yelled, "Gun!" and reached up to pull Ashley down beside her, receiving a hard kick in the ribs for her trouble. Then Mac and Desi were through the door. "Gun!"

Screaming, Ashley launched herself toward Mac just as her sister fired for the last time. The answering volley from the police officers was deafening.

In the chaos that followed, all Grace saw was Mac holding Ashley, and the blood that covered both of them.

CHAPTER FORTY-FOUR

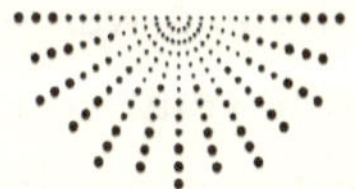

It felt odd. Odd and wrong to be the one sitting beside the bed.

"Not much fun, is it?" Mac said with a crooked smile.

"Nope." At least she could talk now without laughing hysterically. Shock, the doctors had said as they pushed her off to the waiting room.

As if that would calm anyone down. As if she were going to stay there.

"I only have a twisted knee," Mac said, skipping over his bruises, dislocated shoulder, broken nose, and the other injuries that required a frightening array of tubes and machines. "You always manage to get in here with something exotic. Spider bites, smoke inhalation, feloniously induced childbirth." His voice trailed off.

"Is that even a thing?" she asked, but felt his grip on her fingers loosen. She squeezed her own tighter. "I mean, it's seriously ungrammatical. Is that a word, ungrammatical? Or is it like irregardless?" She rambled on about nothing and everything until he was asleep, then slipped out into the hallway.

Avril had dropped off lightweight cotton slacks and a

matching tunic to replace Grace's bloodied clothes. With her hair twisted up and an oversize surgical mask she'd swiped from the cabinet next to Mac's bed, she didn't look out of place as she walked along the hallways looking for a private spot inside the secured area. She found it behind a bank of elevators. Two small benches tucked into an alcove had the look of a well-worn sanctuary.

Her first call was to Peter and was short, but joyous. Even her warning that he would still have to go to court on the hit-and-run in Chestertown didn't dim the news that Mona's killer had been identified.

Krissy took a bit longer. While she was also relieved with the resolution, she was determined to go home to New Orleans. Not my problem or my business, Grace reminded herself as they repeated their goodbyes.

Desi, Avril, and Cyrus were next, and they picked up the task of spreading the word. Mac would be fine, she was fine. It was all over. She had to call one more person, but she leaned her head back against the wall behind her, exhausted and numb.

"Grace?"

The soft voice came with a gentle hand on her shoulder, and she opened her eyes to a welcome sight. Amber Gonzales, the nurse who'd been her stalwart support in the days after Fiona's birth, was sitting beside her, a concerned look on her face.

"I heard what happened." Amber gave her a shoulder hug. "I'm so sorry about Chief Mac, but it sounds like he'll be out of here soon. You, on the other hand, look done in."

"Is that a medical term?" Grace asked with a weary smile. "I'll be okay as soon as I get him home. How much do you know about what happened?"

"Word gets around. The chief and Dr. Greenburgh are well respected around here, as you know, so there's a lot of interest. I'm discounting about ninety percent of what I've heard."

"Which is?"

"You were there, right?" Amber asked, looking uncomfortable.

Grace tried to smile. "I was knocked half unconscious, then all I remember is Mac." She stopped, knowing one more word and she'd be bawling again. Or laughing. It all came from the same place, apparently.

"Now, stop worrying," Amber insisted. "I'm sure it must have been awful for all of you, but the chief's going to be fine, and so is poor Ashley."

It was nearly impossible to be quiet while her well-meaning friend repeated Ashley's description of how she had saved Mac's life.

"By the look on your face, I'm guessing some of what I heard isn't quite right, huh?" Amber asked.

"Try all of it," Grace said bitterly, then regretted her tone. No doubt Ashley had been convincing with her delusional description of the shootings. "Not to worry, it will all come out, eventually." She tried not to let her relief show when Amber said she had to get back to the maternity ward.

After checking on Mac, who was still sleeping, she returned the call that had gone to voice mail while she talked with Amber.

"Are you okay?" she asked, once she'd determined that the thick, croaky voice that shouted *Where are you?* had actually come from David.

After a pause and much throat clearing, he said, "Sorry. I thought you were Krissy. She took Ammie and left me. They've all left me, Peter, too. But you know all that, don't you?"

She waited for the explosion, the threats and ranting, but there was nothing.

"I'm so sorry, David. I thought Krissy was going to call you."

"She did. I tried to get her to come back, but she wouldn't even tell me where she was, just that they were driving through

Virginia. Amalie's sick, and they had to stop at an Urgent Care, but she says everything's fine." His voice gained strength as he talked. "Are you all right? Peter was worried enough to call me. He told me the police had arrested someone, but Mac was hurt in the process."

She gave him the pertinent details and again waited for a reaction that didn't come. She had stashed his son with a bodyguard and advised his wife to take his daughter and leave town, and all without a word to him, but he didn't mention any of it.

After a moment he said, "Thank you for taking care of them when I . . . didn't."

"It will be okay," she said, because she had no other words. If David did the right thing, it might be okay, but it was all up to him and to Krissy.

She hurried back to Mac, her mind on her own family.

CHAPTER FORTY-FIVE

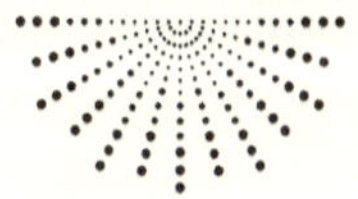

It was a theme that was repeated throughout the following days. Poor Ashley had saved Mac's life when her deranged sister had tried to kill Grace. Since Simone died at the scene and everyone involved in the investigation was cautioned not to discuss what happened, gossip ran unchecked—for a while.

In some versions, Grace was the agitator who started it all. In others, a Baltimore lawyer killed Poor Henry's wife, framed Poor Ashley, and tried to kill Grace for unraveling the whole sordid mess. The truth, which was more shocking than the ever-evolving rumors, wouldn't be told in its entirety until Ashley's trial.

"The more times the good doctor spins that crap, the better for the prosecution," Desi told Grace on the morning after the shootings as they waited in the lobby of the hospital for Mac's release. "Simone Lancer caused the injuries that eventually killed her daughter, and there'll be a statement released today to that effect. Ashley says her sister and niece were alone at the Ashley's house when Simone caught Mona, who was already high, holding a syringe. Simone tried to take the needle away, and Mona stabbed her with it. Mom grabbed a handy hammer and defended herself.

It was that hammer blow that caused the wound that led to the aneurysm that burst when Mona fainted on your steps. That's what the medical examiner thinks, anyway."

"Is there physical evidence?" Grace asked. She preferred her own theory that everything was Poor Ashley's fault.

"Yep," Desi said. "But you know I can't tell you about it." After a moment, she relented. "Doc Greenburgh tried to cover up for her sister. There were bruises and a puncture mark on Simone Lancer's body and you already know there were bloody finger-prints on the hammer."

"Simone's?" Grace asked, and got a nod from Desi. "Any proof Ashley planted the hammer in my office?"

"Nothing that will stick. Only your testimony and Aidan's. And there are statements that your office was left open and unat-tended at least once after Mona was killed."

"Thank you, Marjorie," Grace muttered. Even if it was never proven, she knew the hammer with Simone's fingerprints had been in Ashley's purse the day she delivered the box of Mac's forgotten belongings. No wonder Ashley was losing weight. All that scheming and hiding bloody murder weapons would be nervous work.

Desi said, "Oh, and if I don't get the chance, tell the chief he was right. That note that Henry Cutter got in the mail after his wife died? Mona Cutter did write it, but she sent it to the doc."

"Mona sent a note to Ashley?" Grace asked, momentarily pulled out of her own thoughts.

"Yeah. Just tell him he was right about the note. He'll know what it means."

"It's sad, isn't it?" Grace hadn't meant to say that out loud, but pity was the emotion that was weighing on her.

"Which part?" Desi asked, but she was already checking her phone and tapping out messages. The detective was ready to leave, but she paused to look at Grace. "It's all pretty grim if you let yourself dwell on it."

"Mona Cutter. Marjorie said when she came into the office, she complained of a bad headache and being dizzy, but spoke rationally. It's so hard to believe she walked around for twenty-four hours with a head wound like that and then died all alone. She must have been so scared."

"Not necessarily," Desi said. "Look, Grace. People like you make my job harder. You want concrete answers, and when there aren't any, you what-if every possibility until you hit something you can live with, even if it makes you miserable. Cutter was an addict. Period. She was also somebody's child, somebody's wife, somebody's lover. But most of all, in my opinion, she was an addict who didn't want to be saved."

"But I ran into her, almost literally, as she was coming into the office. She wasn't pleasant, but she knew what was going on. She talked with Marjorie, then came up the stairs looking for me—"

"And fell, hit her head again, and lights out. She was high, you know. I guess maybe you guys don't get too many clients like her, so maybe her condition wasn't obvious. Anyhow, if you want to feel bad about something, how about this. Surgery could have saved her if she'd been taken to the hospital after Mom bopped her on the head, or even later when her loving auntie saw her pupils didn't match. The nice vet is going to take a beating in court for that, and for trying to guilt-trip Henry Cutter into thinking he was responsible for his wife's addiction, but don't expect too much to come of it in court. Ashley will blame everything on her sister and probably walk away with probation and some community service."

The elevator doors opened, and a smiling Mac rolled out. After that, there were crutches, bags, and flowers to deal with and no more time for regrets.

By Friday afternoon, Grace had turned her phone off except for occasional checks for messages from the few people she wanted to talk to. The inner circle fluctuated depending on her mood, which is how she missed the call from Marjorie. She was in the nursery with Fiona when Rocky let loose with a growl worthy of a Doberman.

Mac didn't sound concerned as he reassured the puppy, but Grace still hurried as she scooped up her half-dressed baby and went out to the living room. He could move about easily with his crutches, but getting up and down was painful.

"Good girl, Rocky," she said when she saw The Bat at the door.

"Well, finally!" Marjorie said as she marched inside, her arms full of Tupperware containers and foil-wrapped packages, all of which were unceremoniously dumped on the kitchen counter. She joined Mac on the love seat, saying, "What are you doing out of bed and sitting in here all alone? Let me take you to my house, Lee."

With his left leg bandaged from ankle to knee, his left arm in a sling, and a face covered in bruises that included two black eyes, Mac had looked bad before his sister-in-law arrived. Now he looked scared, too. "I'm fine," he said hastily. "This isn't as bad as you think it is. My nose will go down—"

"Your nose! Is it broken, too? Oh, Lee!"

"Here, Marjorie," Grace said with a sigh as she handed Fiona over. "I need to get his medicine. Can you hold her for just a minute?"

She put the food away in the kitchen, listening to Mac downplay his injuries while Marjorie continued to moan that he needed competent nursing. When their conversation veered into baby talk with Fiona, she set up a tray with a pot of tea and slices of

Marjorie's chocolate cake. Telling herself to be nice, no matter what, she pasted a smile on and went to deliver Mac's Tylenol. Her fake politeness paid off when Marjorie shared her news.

"Ashley is being discharged from the hospital tomorrow, can you believe it?" she asked, shaking her head. "These days you have to be dying to get any medical attention. The poor thing has lost her sister and her niece and has a bullet wound! I don't know how she'll manage. A group of us from Saint Mary's are setting up a care chain to help her with food and to stay with her when her private-duty nurse isn't there."

Mac gave Grace what could have been a wink or a twitch from one of his blackened eyes, then said, "That's very nice, Margie, but are you sure the Detention Center will let you in to see her?"

"You know very well she'll never be in a cell," Marjorie sputtered. "That was just mean, especially when she saved your life."

Mac was still looking at Grace, who gave a quick shake of her head. Marjorie and most of Mallard Bay would never believe the truth, and it was better saved for the courtroom.

He ignored her.

"Margie, I want you to listen to me. I'll be testifying against Ashley at her trial. I'm telling you now because you're family." He took Grace's hand with his unbandaged one. "The family that Grace and Fiona and I have created. You're our family, and I want you to know the truth."

Fiona had fallen asleep on Marjorie's shoulder, and teardrops fell into the baby's curls as Mac explained what Simone and Ashley had done. "They decided to frame Peter Carlton for Mona's murder, but Simone didn't trust her sister to stick with the story they'd concocted. She lured Peter to Ashley's house, so he'd be implicated if she had to kill Ashley later."

Marjorie gasped. "But Ashley—"

Mac went on as if she hadn't interrupted. "Grace ruined

Simone's plan when she showed up after Peter left, so, in a sense, Grace saved Ashley. Kind of funny, isn't it?" Neither woman looked amused, but the stricken look on Marjorie's face said she got his point. "When Desi and I entered Ashley's house, Simone was holding Grace and Ashley at gunpoint. Grace used the distraction to drop to the floor and tried to pull Ashley with her, but Ashley kicked her."

The large, painful bruise on Grace's side ached with his words.

"But why?" Marjorie asked, looking bewildered.

Fiona woke, not at all happy that her bed was making noise. Grace took her and went into the nursery, leaving the door between the two small rooms open. As she rocked her daughter, she listened as Mac walked through the painful story.

"Oh, no!" Marjorie gasped when he got to the last minutes of Mona's life. "You mean I could have saved her . . ."

It was too late now to shut the nursery door and give them privacy, so Grace rocked and waited while Mac's low and steady words eased his sister-in-law's guilt. But when Marjorie was calm again, he made sure she understood the whole truth.

"There are a lot of rumors going around about the shooting at Ashley's," he said. "But the people who were at the scene know the truth. When Desi and I arrived, Ashley ran toward me, screaming for help. Simone shot her deliberately, firing just as Ashley reached me. She wasn't a hero, Margie. She was trying to save herself."

CHAPTER FORTY-SIX

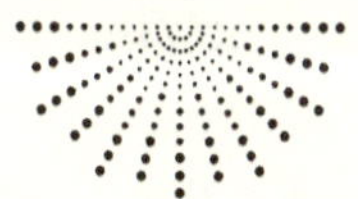

Official statements were released concerning the death of
Mona Cutter, and a fresh line of gossip made its way
around town. Most of it was true, give or take the inevitable
adjectives and side stories added by each teller.

The state police determined that Simone Lancer had assaulted
her daughter, delivering head wounds that eventually caused her
death. Ashley Greenburgh was charged with assisting her sister in
covering up the assault, failing to seek adequate medical help for
her niece, tampering with physical evidence, and several lesser
charges.

Most townspeople believed everything they heard about
Simone, but had their doubts about the rest. Poor Ashley's tale of
sacrificing for her self-destructive, drug-addicted niece and her
heroic attempt to save Mac's life played well in the community.
Bail was waived, and her support group had no trouble replacing
its founding member when Marjorie resigned.

On Ashley's instructions, the funeral home handling Simone's
body placed her ashes next to their parents in the family plot in

Baltimore. The graveside service was arranged by Simone's firm, and its employees were the only attendees.

Mona's Celebration of Life was held three weeks later in Mallard Bay. After much debate, Grace and Mac decided to attend, but by the morning of the service, Grace was having second thoughts.

"Maybe it's not a good idea," she said as she tugged at the sleeves of her new jacket. The simple cut fit her well, and the navy blue linen made her looked rested and calm. She was neither, and it wasn't the jacket that worried her.

"It looks great on you," Hallie protested.

"What?" Momentarily yanked back from her multiple internal arguments, Grace realized they weren't talking about the same thing. "No, the suit's beautiful. I'm very happy with it." With a quick look over her shoulder to make sure they were alone, she added, "No more shopping for a little while, though, okay? Let's just work with what I have."

"I can mix and match only so much," Hallie said. "I told you not to get rid of all of your old things."

Grace gave her a stern look. "Let's just wait a little while, please. This suit was a great buy, though. I'll definitely be sending you shopping again."

"What are you waiting for?" Hallie's question sounded more like a challenge. "You can trust me, you know. I don't tell Avril everything. Especially not secrets."

As usual, the girl's earnestness touched a chord with Grace. Impulsively, she said, "I can't decide if I should go to Mona Cutter's funeral. Ashley won't like it, but I think it will send the wrong message to Henry if I don't go."

"You said Henry was your friend."

"Did you get the whole story from Avril?" It was a rhetorical question, and Grace didn't wait for an answer. "He used to be my friend, but I don't know if he'll want me there, either."

"Miss Avril seemed to think he did, and she said she's sitting with you."

"Well, that's that, then. It's a command performance."

"At least you have this afternoon to look forward to," Hallie said with a smile. "Niki said I should make sure you don't lift a finger for the preparations. She's got everything under control for the party and I'll take care of Fiona. You and Chief Mac can relax."

When her cousin had first proposed a family picnic at Mac's not-quite-finished house, it hadn't felt right to hold it on the day of Mona's funeral, especially when "family" meant everyone close to them. But Mac had agreed that they would all be at loose ends after the service and could use something to lift their spirits.

"Thank you for helping Niki and for everything you do. I'm not sure how I've made it so long without an assistant."

And, as usual, Hallie ran with the compliment. "That's great, because I have a lot of ideas, such as, maybe you and Chief Mac could make today super special by making a big announcement."

"Oh, for heaven's sake." Grace laughed as she slipped on her shoes. "Will you at least let me break the news?"

"Of course," the assistant answered demurely, then threw her arms around her boss.

Saint Mary's Chapel on Mallard Bay gleamed from two hundred years of loving care and countless applications of beeswax to every inch of its ornate woodwork. Sunlight filtered by the simple squares of stained glass covered the flagstone floor with puddles of color.

Mona and Henry had been married here a decade before, taking their vows near the spot where her ashes now sat on a pedestal. Her portrait on the memorial booklet showed a beaming young woman in her wedding gown. Grace found it hard to connect the beautiful bride with the corpse on her office steps.

Ashley made the most of her appearance in the role of grieving aunt and was propped up, petted, and protected by a cadre of best friends who also enjoyed their share of the limelight. The women took the center front-row seats. Henry arrived just before the service started and sat with Cyrus and Marjorie in the pew in front of Grace, Mac, and Avril. Without stopping to think how it might be received, Grace reached out to pat Henry's shoulder and was answered with a squeeze from his calloused hand.

It wasn't a long service. Grace thought later it was almost as if the priest had a celestial heads-up that the drama after the benediction would be the real show.

A collective gasp from the front of the church was the first sign that anything unusual was happening. Henry and Mac were shaking hands when a voice rang out, cutting through all the conversations and bringing an expectant silence to the sanctuary.

"May I have your attention!" Everyone who'd been about to leave sat back down. Everyone but Ashley, who faced the crowd, arms flung wide and her face wet with tears. "I have something to say."

Mac's hand found Grace's, and on her other side, Avril took her arm. She tried not to smile as her bodyguards closed in.

"I have something to say," Ashley repeated.

Someone behind Grace muttered, "Well, get on with it." That sentiment was followed by a smattering of other protests. It seemed at least some of the shine had been knocked off Poor Ashley's crown.

Apparently unconcerned about how she was being perceived, Ashley hung on to her bully pulpit. "Some of you think I shouldn't be here today. That I should be in jail for trying to save my sister, who in a split second of anger made a terrible mistake. And I've admitted to being overly protective of my sweet Mona." She placed a hand possessively on the silver urn. "I tried to help my sister deal with what she'd done, because I knew going to jail would kill Simone and I couldn't bear to lose both of them."

She had everyone's full attention now, and she dabbed her eyes.

"I was right to be afraid, because that's exactly what happened to me. I've thought long and hard about this, and after talking to my son and daughter"—she gave a young couple in the second row a sad smile—"I have one more admission to make." Then, stretching herself as high as her tiny frame and three-inch heels could take her, Ashley announced she was Mona's mother.

Reactions ranged from Henry's explosive "Liar!" to Father Kemp's suggestion that he and Ashley talk privately, but she didn't give up her stage.

"I was fifteen!" she cried, holding on to the priest, but not budging. "Simone adopted her, but Mona was always mine, and I tried to do what was best for her."

This time, whatever Father Kemp whispered in her ear got her attention. With her entourage and her children, she allowed herself to be led out through the choir door.

"Wow," Avril said, winking at Grace. "That girl can put on a show, can't she? Now, aren't you glad you came?"

Mac snorted with laughter, then caught himself and moved to Henry. "Come with us," he offered. "Pick up Sierra and bring her, too. We're having a small group of family and friends over for lunch, and we want you there, too."

So, on the day that Mona Cutter was placed in the columbarium behind Saint Mary's and Ashley faced an uncertain social and legal future, when David and Krissy and their baby were flying home from a long vacation in New Orleans, and Peter was interviewing for the air force, Grace and Mac held their impromptu party at their soon-to-be home on the river.

Mac made a toast to Grace that included the poorly kept secret of their engagement. He said she and Fiona made his life complete.

Not yet, she thought. *But soon.*

CHAPTER FORTY-SEVEN

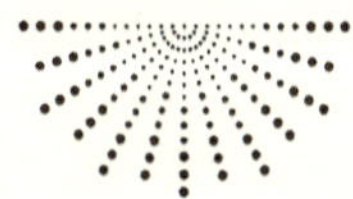

After the last toast was lifted and the final hug dispensed, Mac and Grace were finally alone in the house he'd reconstructed for her. They were both exhausted.

"We're going to need some new furniture out here," Mac said as he returned from the kitchen. He'd insisted on putting the last of the food away while Grace admired the sunset in the new sunroom. The view was so arresting, it took him a second to realize he was talking to himself.

He found her in the new foyer. It was the only area he'd furnished, mainly to have a safe place to stash the tall mirror that had been in his family so long, no one knew who'd first acquired it. He watched her turning this way and that, studying her reflection in the wavy glass. He thought she looked pleased with herself.

"Come on over here," she said when she saw him. "I love this piece, and I never really noticed it before."

He wrapped his arms around her waist and pulled her back against him. "Let's get married now, Grace. I don't want to wait."

He watched her face in the mirror, relieved when her smile grew wider.

"You heard all the talk," she said with a laugh. Avril's planning a wedding that will include the whole town."

"I hope she'll be happy with whomever she marries in that ceremony." He was rewarded with a kiss. "I'm serious, let's do it this week. No more waiting, no wedding, no people. We'll get the license tomorrow, take Sweet Pea to the beach next weekend, and come back married."

She seemed to consider the idea, but then said, "We'll need a photographer at least. I want wedding pictures to show the children later."

"We'll ask the officiant to get a shot of the three of us."

Grace pulled his arms tighter around her. "I said *children.*"

"Oh." He didn't want to spoil the moment, but couldn't think of anything to say except the truth. "I don't know if that's a good idea. I don't want you to go through that again. Last time—"

She shook her head. "I'll be fine."

He kissed her shoulder, not wanting her to see his face. To see how much he wanted to believe her. "We can discuss it later," he whispered. "Let's get married, and then—"

She turned to face him and patted his cheek. "You know, for such a smart man, you are being incredibly dense. I'm pregnant, Mac. We're having a Christmas baby."

Later, when he could think of anything besides the gift he'd been given that day, he realized she was one step ahead of him again.

And he was okay with that.

Thank you so much for reading *Twisted Karma!*

I'd love to give you a free Eastern Shore short story. Check out my website for details:
www.CherilThomas.com

I hope you enjoyed your visit to the Eastern Shore and Mallard Bay. If you did, and would like to help other readers discover the series, please leave a review on Amazon, Goodreads, or any social platform. I'll be very grateful!

Thank you!

ACKNOWLEDGMENTS

The errors within these pages are my own and they exist mainly because I'm incorrigible. I always have to change just one more thing in the final, final, completely finished, ready for print manuscript.

That being said, the hard work of the following talented people is sincerely appreciated:
First readers Vicki Ellingson, Cindy Haddaway, Judith Hohman, and Roxanne Tury provided excellent feedback, as always. Their help and encouragement are invaluable to me. Thank you, ladies.

The wonderful author Helen Chappell continues to inspire and encourage me, and I am so grateful for her support.

Elaine Hyatt of Clarity Editing Services saved me from clunky passages and dropped story lines.

Due to my relentless nitpicking and rearranging, final proof-reading services are essential. These were provided by Leighton Wingate. Thank you, Leighton! (I only meddled a little bit after you signed off. Don't worry, that whole thing where I accidentally erased all of the formatting was easy to fix, so I didn't bother you with it.)

As always, thank you to my family: Ron, Patrick, Kate, James, and Jack. As Mac says in the last chapter, you make my life complete.

Finally, to Miss Ellie Grace, the Wonder Spaniel—I hope you approve of Rocky.

June 2022
Easton, Maryland

One more thank you . . .

I have the most wonderful readers any author could ask for. If you've ever wondered if your reviews or social-media comments matter to a book's author, please know that they are sincerely appreciated by this one.

For years, I wrote into the void: no sales, no notice, no attention. Turns out, you have to actually let people read your work for that to happen, and like so many writers, I just couldn't take that last step. Then, when I finally sent send my books out to fend for themselves, I found out about a pesky little thing called marketing. There's more to this writing business than just telling stories, but eventually, it all seems to come together.

The last four years have been life changing for me, and it is all because of readers like you. I am so grateful.

Until next time, happy reading!
Cheril

ALSO BY CHERIL THOMAS

The Eastern Shore Mysteries:

Squatter's Rights

A Commission on Murder

Bad Intent

Death and Consequences

Twisted Karma

The Eastern Shore Mysteries Box Set, Books 1-3

A Little Christmas War (A Grace Reagan short story)

The Nineteenth Gift (An Ellender York short story)

Readers' reviews for the Eastern Shore Mysteries

☆☆☆☆☆

For *Squatter's Rights*:

". . . Cheril Thomas is a masterful storyteller and had me guessing the whole time."

". . . The characters are fun and clever . . . an engaging page-turner . . ."

". . . I got up in the middle of the night to finish reading because I couldn't get the story out of my mind!"

". . . I read it straight through to the end without putting it down."

☆☆☆☆☆

For *A Commission on Murder*:

". . . A witty thriller and great summer read . . ."

". . . Another great read . . . Storytelling at its finest. I strongly recommend adding this selection to your summer reading list. . . ."

". . . A witty thriller and great summer read, the plot is twisty and turn-y with a lot of small town charm and genuinely laugh-out-loud situations . . . All thumbs up!

☆☆☆☆☆

For Bad Intent:

". . . Suspenseful, funny, and tragic, and filled with more mysteries than Grace wants or needs, Bad Intent is Cheril Thomas's best offering yet."

". . . Enjoyable page-turner with equal parts humor and suspense."

". . . an entertaining, fast moving mystery . . . Follow Grace

Reagan as she navigates the complex world of polygamy, crime and murder.

☆☆☆☆☆

For *Death and Consequences*:

". . . Every time I thought I had it figured out—I didn't! Great ending . . . loved revisiting my favorite characters . . ."

". . . I loved this book. I have read all of the Eastern Shore Mysteries and look forward to the continuation of the series."

"Secrets, plots, and mysteries . . . The most complex and diabolical of the Grace Reagan series yet, this is sure to please readers.

☆☆☆☆☆

Advance praise for *Twisted Karma*:

"Number 5 is a winner! So many changes for the main characters and I love the ending!"

". . . Really enjoyed the read, getting to visit with old friends, twists, and turns to keep things moving, and a murder that kept me guessing!"

"If you're a fan of this series, you're gonna love this latest installment. The title says it all: Twisted Karma, indeed!"

ABOUT THE AUTHOR

Cheril Thomas is the author of the Eastern Shore Mysteries series, numerous short stories, and articles. When she's not writing at home in Easton, Maryland, she's traveling with her long-suffering husband, an otherwise brilliant soul who for some reason doesn't mind being married to a woman who researches methods of murder. Their lives are directed by a sassy little spaniel named Ellie Grace.

Connect with Cheril on her website:
www.cherilthomas.com